A Tourist's New England

Hardscrabble Books—Fiction of New England

Laurie Alberts, *Lost Daughters*

Laurie Alberts, *The Price of Land in Shelby*

Thomas Bailey Aldrich, *The Story of a Bad Boy*

Anne Bernays, *Professor Romeo*

Chris Bohjalian, *Water Witches*

Dona Brown, *A Tourist's New England: Travel Fiction, 1820–1920*

Joseph Bruchac, *The Waters Between: A Novel of the Dawn Land*

Josph A. Citro, *Shadow Child*

Sean Connolly, *A Great Place to Die*

Dorothy Canfield Fisher (Mark J. Madigan, ed.), *Seasoned Timber*

Dorothy Canfield Fisher, *Understood Betsy*

Joseph Freda, *Suburban Guerrillas*

Castle Freeman, Jr., *Judgment Hill*

Frank Gaspar, *Leaving Pico*

Ernest Hebert, *The Dogs of March*

Ernest Hebert, *Live Free or Die*

Sarah Orne Jewett (Sarah Way Sherman, ed.), *The Country of the Pointed Firs and Other Stories*

Lisa MacFarlane, ed., *This World Is Not Conclusion: Faith in Nineteenth-Century New England Fiction*

Kit Reed, *J. Eden*

Rowland E. Robinson (David Budbill, ed.), *Danvis Tales: Selected Stories*

Roxana Robinson, *Summer Light*

Rebecca Rule, *The Best Revenge: Short Stories*

Theodore Weesner, *Novemberfest*

W. D. Wetherell, *The Wisest Man in America*

Edith Wharton (Barbara A. White, ed.), *Wharton's New England: Seven Stories* and *Ethan Frome*

Thomas Williams, *The Hair of Harold Roux*

Other Books by Dona Brown

Inventing New England: Regional Tourism in the Nineteenth Century
(Smithsonian Institution Press, 1995)

A TOURIST'S NEW ENGLAND

Travel Fiction, 1820–1920

Dona Brown, editor

University Press of New England/Hanover and London

University Press of New England
publishes books under its own imprint and is the publisher for Brandeis University Press, Dartmouth College, Middlebury College Press, University of New Hampshire, Tufts University, and Wesleyan University Press.

Published by University Press of New England, Hanover, NH 03755
Introduction, chapter introductions, and this collection

Printed in the United States of America 5 4 3 2 1

Library of Congress Cataloging-in-Publication Data

A tourist's New England : travel fiction, 1820–1920 / Dona Brown, editor.

p. cm. — (Hardscrabble books)

Includes bibliographical references.

ISBN 0-87451-900-4 (alk. paper)

1. New England—Description and travel—Fiction. 2. Travelers' writings, American—New England. 3. Travelers—New England—Fiction. 4. American fiction—19th century. 5. American fiction—20th century. 6. American fiction—New England. I. Brown, Dona. II. Series.

PS648.N38T68 1999

813.008'03274—dc21 98-48769

Contents

Introduction 1

I. The Uses of Scenery

1. Nathaniel Hawthorne, from "Sketches from Memory" (1835) 21
2. Nathaniel Hawthorne, "The Ambitious Guest" (1835) 30
3. Sarah Josepha Hale, "The Romance of Travelling" from *Traits of American Life* (1835) 40
4. Susan Warner, from *Nobody* (1882) 54
5. Charles Dudley Warner, from *Their Pilgrimage* (1886) 76

II. Pleasure and Danger at New England Resorts

6. Emma Dunham Kelley, from *Megda* (1891) 91
7. Susan and Anna Warner, from *The Gold of Chickaree* (1876) 105
8. Harriet Beecher Stowe, from *Pink and White Tyranny: A Society Novel* (1871) 119
9. Edith Wharton, from *Summer* (1917) 134

III. A Visit to Old New England

10. Edward Bellamy, from *Six to One: A Nantucket Idyl* (1878) 155

11. Sarah Orne Jewett, from *Deephaven* (1877) 162
12. Thomas Nelson Page, "Miss Godwin's Inheritance," *Scribner's Magazine* (1904) 173
13. William Dean Howells, from *The Vacation of the Kelwyns* (1920) 192
14. Sinclair Lewis, from *Babbitt* (1922) 207

A Tourist's New England

Introduction

No matter where we live, New England beckons. Calendars, magazine covers, travel brochures—even the pictures in the history books we read as children—all lure us to visit this rural landscape of tree-lined town commons and white churches; wooded hills decked out in blazing autumn foliage; coastal villages with lobster pots stacked against aging docks. Most of us envision New England this way even if what we see from our car windows when we tour the region is mostly parking lots, video rental stores, and strip malls.

At first glance, the subject of vacationing may not seem to require much discussion. It is what we do when we are trying to get away from whatever really matters in our lives. Nevertheless, how and where we travel reveals some crucial information about who we are. It makes a difference whether we choose to visit rural Vermont or bustling Martha's Vineyard, the rocky coast of Maine or the dunes of Cape Cod. It even makes a difference what town we select on Cape Cod: the student-filled night spots of Hyannis, Barnstable with its quaint and carefully preserved architecture, or Provincetown, vacation mecca for lesbian and gay tourists.

This collection explores tourists' responses to New England in an earlier era, during the century between 1820 and 1920. More precisely, it explores the experiences of one particular set of tourists, those who wrote—and published—fictional accounts of their experience. We do not need to go far in reading these selections to see that they concern themselves mostly with the preoccupations of wealthy, or at least prosperous, Northeastern city dwellers. That is no coincidence. In the first half of the nineteenth century, vacationing was largely confined to the professional and upper classes. Leisured travel was a very "conspicuous" kind of "consumption," accessible only to those with extra time, extra money, and the training to tell them what to do with it. If only for that reason, tourism was vitally interesting to wealthy and cultivated Americans: it announced their purchasing power. But it did much more. It revealed their sense of style, their talents, their hidden longings. On tour, daughters chose husbands from the right—or wrong—social backgrounds. On tour, parents took children to see the rural world they had left behind. Men went primitive, women found important work outside the drawing room. No wonder, then, that the experience of travel plays such an important role in nineteenth-century fiction.

By the end of the nineteenth century, people farther down the social scale—shopkeepers, bank clerks, schoolteachers—found themselves able to take short vacations. Even factory workers took an occasional Sunday afternoon trip to the beach resorts that catered to them. But such people did not publish fictional accounts of their experiences. The writers included in this collection shared the native-born, white Northeastern urban backgrounds of their characters. Emma Dunham Kelley, an African-American author whose novel *Megda* is excerpted here, is a partial exception. Nevertheless, like the other writers here, she situated her story in the world of respectable men and women who could afford at least a short vacation.

In other ways, the writers assembled here are not so similar to one another. Some of them bear the names most often seen in American Literature courses; others are now almost unknown. Women and men are almost equally represented. Many of the selections are from the minor or overlooked works of well-known authors, like Edward Bellamy's 1886 novel about his Nantucket experiences, *Six to One*, or Harriet Beecher Stowe's *Pink and White Tyranny*. But the greatest differences among these selections are the result, not of race or gender or class, but of changes over time. Between 1820 and 1920, a great transformation took place in the ways people traveled, and in the ways people wrote about traveling.

Tourism is actually one of the oldest industries in New England—as old as the industrial revolution. As early as the building of the mills of Lowell, as early as the workshops of the Blackstone River valley, the business of tourism began to take shape in the northeastern United States. But those first tourists of New England had interests that might sometimes seem bizarre to contemporary travelers. Basil and Margaret Hall, for example, came over from England in 1827. Their tour of Boston included one place that is still a tourist attraction—the Bunker Hill monument—but they also visited the cluster of new charitable institutions in Charlestown—an orphanage, an asylum, and a prison—and they took a day's side trip to the new industrial community in Lowell, where they looked at all the factory workings and toured a workers' boarding house.

Tourists like the Halls were engaged in social and political analysis. Following the pattern of European travelers making the "grand tour" in the eighteenth century, they sought information about foreign institutions that would shed light on the great philosophical and political debates at home. In the United States, such early travelers typically took on big political questions like the functioning of democracy, the future of slavery, or the relationship between culture and social class.

Such travelers wrote voluminously about their experiences, but they wrote little fiction. Their writing took the conventional eighteenth-century form of "travels"—letters or journals whose truthfulness and accuracy were insured by the scrupulous daily note-taking of the authors. Timothy Dwight's *Travels in New-England and New-York* (1821), for example, became a travel classic. Dwight, who was president of Yale College, used the time when school was not in session to make several horseback tours of New England. He collected and published his remarks as letters. Each one recorded his responses to a specific place, but also addressed such topics as the effects of frontier life, the importance of education, or New England piety. The purpose of his book was didactic, even argumentative: it was intended to counter the accusations of English tourists that America's republican experiment could not work.

This collection does not deal with such weighty matters. It begins instead with works of far less gravity—with tourists in search of beautiful scenery. In the United States, the search for scenery first took shape in the 1820s with the development of the "northern" or "fashionable tour," a trip from New York City up the Hudson River and west to Niagara Falls. Travel writing—and touring itself—took a sudden turn away from those earnest travel accounts as the English craze for "picturesque" and "sublime" scenery finally hit the American scene. Writers struggled to find new forms of description that would feed the new appetite for scenery, and as they did so, travel writing became more subjective, more descriptive, and more emotional. It also took on new forms. Instead of journals and letters, scenic writers wrote poems, vignettes, and "sketches," a term intended to suggest that writing could create a mental picture of scenery as vivid as an artist's pencil "sketch."

Two pieces by Nathaniel Hawthorne open this collection, in part to illustrate the close relationship between scenic touring and literary work. In 1832, the twenty-nine-year-old writer made a "northern tour" from Boston to Niagara Falls, returning by way of the White Mountains of New Hampshire. Part of Hawthorne's itinerary was chosen to escape the cholera that raged that summer, but he also had a more important goal in mind. As he only half-jokingly put it in a letter to his friend Franklin Pierce, he was traveling "on account of a book by which I intend to acquire an (undoubtedly) immense literary reputation."[1]

It would not be entirely far-fetched to claim that Hawthorne's "immense literary reputation" *did* grow in part from the tour he made in the summer of 1832. In addition to the pair of selections here, he also wrote at least two other stories based on his White Mountain experiences: "The Great Carbuncle" and "The Great Stone Face." The stories included here exemplify the mixture of fiction and nonfiction that was typical of scenic writing. "Sketches from Memory" follows Hawthorne's White Mountain travel itinerary more or less directly, while "The Ambitious Guest" embroiders on the true tale of the ill-fated Willeys, a pioneer family destroyed by a landslide in the Crawford Notch in 1826.

Sarah Josepha Hale, the author of the third selection in this book, blended fiction and nonfiction in the same way: "The Romance of Travelling" (1835) begins as an essay and ends with a romantic tale. In between, Hale included a plea that goes a long way toward explaining the connection between literary fame and scenic touring. American scenery, Hale lamented, was "barren" and meaningless for visitors precisely because few American writers had yet poured out "the light of song" over American landscapes. Sketches, poetry, and tales attached to specific parts of the American landscape would bring fame not only to the scenery itself, she implied, but also to their authors.

Hale's plea for American authors to provide more poetic tales and legends to go with American scenery did not go unanswered. When Hawthorne made his trip through what is now called Crawford Notch in the White Mountains, the area was not yet part of the regular tourist's itinerary. Half-cleared fields, roughly built shacks, and a barely passable road marked it as an area only recently opened for white settlement. But along with Hawthorne, such other writers as Washington Irving, Ralph Waldo Emerson, Henry David Thoreau, and James Russell Lowell also made treks through the Notch during the 1830s. All these ambitious literary men were in the White Mountains because they hoped to hitch their own professional wagons to the rising star of American scenic writing.

By the 1840s, a full-blown scenic literary market had emerged for magazines, gift books, and picture books like the beautiful two-volume *American Scenery*, a product of the combined efforts of British engraver William Bartlett and American author Nathaniel P. Willis. By the 1850s, the White Mountains had become the preeminent scenic tourist region in the United States. And not only mountains attracted attention: the coastal scenery of Newport, Rhode Island, and Nahant, Massachusetts, drew tourists as well. Writers had helped to put these new scenic regions on the map.

In fact, the act of scenic touring itself was a profoundly literary experience. Scenic tourists did more writing and talking than they did hiking and climbing. They quoted poetry, sketched views, and talked with one another about their responses to the scenery. Like the "well-dressed young man" Hawthorne described in his sketch, they quoted extensively from "Byron's rhapsodies on mountain scenery," and like that same young man, they wrote their own verses in the guestbooks of hotels. But scenery was an acquired, not a natural, taste. Before travelers could appreciate scenery, they had to master its language.

According to the categories Americans adopted from English writers, a traveler would use the word "beautiful" to denote a scene of pastoral serenity: smooth meadows, rivers winding through pleasant valleys, quiet lakes. The "picturesque" was a catch-all category that included all kinds of "rough" or "irregular" landscapes: perhaps a grassy meadow bordered by rugged pines, or intersected by a rocky ledge or stone ruin. White Mountain scenery fell into a third category: the "sublime." Sublime scenes—towering mountains, crashing waves, thundering waterfalls—were distinguished primarily by the response they awakened in observers: terror, awe, dizziness, fear, reverence, astonishment. The untrained traveler might pass through the Notch with little more than a fear that dark would find him alone in those waste places. For the traveler with a trained eye and mind, the scene generated a different set of responses.

But knowing the language of the sublime was not sufficient. Scenic travelers needed imagination, graceful turns of phrase, and experience with both literary and visual arts. They must have read—and memorized—the poems of Byron, seen—and discussed—the paintings of the Italian landscape masters. In short, they needed both an elite education and the cultivation provided by the society of the drawing room. Elegant style *and* a heartfelt emotional response were required by stern scenic judges. Without training in both, scenic tourists would fear the judgment Hawthorne rendered against his fellow traveler, the Byronic young man whose verses he judged "elegant" but "cold."

For that reason, an ability to respond to and talk about scenery was powerful evidence of gentility. Susan Warner followed that reasoning in her novel *Nobody* (1882), landing her impoverished but refined heroine on the Isles of Shoals, off the coast of New Hampshire—a perfect test of her aesthetic sensibility. There this daughter of rural New England, inexperienced and virtually untaught, proved her superiority to the wealthiest men and women of New York City, and there they were found wanting precisely because they could not fathom her passionate response to the sublimity of the sea or match her endless fascination with the picturesque stones and wildflowers of barren Appledore Island.

But Susan Warner's descriptions of society were sadly out of date by the time *Nobody* was published in 1882. Already by the 1860s, the ability to respond properly to scenery was no longer the litmus test of gentility it had been in 1840. Tourism and its subsidiary literary businesses had become mass enterprises. Ambitious travelers could find out where to go, where to stay, how to go about getting to the scenic locations, and even what to say when they got there from the guidebooks and scenic literature they could find anywhere. And the advice was easy to follow.

Thomas Starr King, Unitarian minister and author of the elegant volume *The White Hills* (1859), helped would-be scenic travelers by arranging suitable quotations from poetry to match the various points of interest in the White Mountains. King even gave advice on how to respond: "The surprise to the senses in first looking upon a noble landscape, ought to show itself in childlike animation."[2] Easiest of all, one could follow the prescription of Samuel Eastman, whose guidebook offered this advice for the tourist atop Mount Washington: "Words fail to give adequate expression to the feeling that has come over you and you stand in mute silence before this awe-inspiring scene."[3]

The effect of this easy formula was predictable. By the time Charles Dudley Warner published his serial novel, "Their Pilgrimage," in *Harper's Monthly Magazine* in 1886, a nearly complete reversal had taken place. Constructed of a thin plot holding together a series of descriptions of vacation resorts, Warner's story made it clear that wealthy and privileged people no longer looked at scenery in the old way. Warner's genteel travelers understood that they must avoid at all costs the impression that they found anything about the White Mountains exciting or novel. Enthusiasm would now mark them as members of the masses to whom the guidebooks and advertisements catered: as one critical character put it, "people had become so cosmopolitan that they dared not enjoy anything."

Something else had changed by the late nineteenth century, too. Warner's note of elegy for the experience of an earlier, more primitive trip to the White Mountains captured a sense of loss and longing for the old romance and adventure of travel, before the modern luxuries of hotels and railroads had intervened. If scenery could no longer generate an intense emotional response, what could? "Their Pilgrimage" makes the answer explicit: the focus of this novel was not romantic scenery, but romantic love. Writing about traveling had become inextricably linked with the stories of love, rivalry, and social position that dominated late nineteenth-century fiction.

The second section of this collection, "Pleasure and Danger at New England Resorts," begins with two writers who address the same question: what is the significance of a waltz? Susan and Anna Warner's heroine (very oddly named Wych Hazel) has promised her lover, in a passage of suppressed erotic intensity, that she would never waltz with any man. But he has come to believe that she has done just that—on a vacation in Newport. And Emma Dunham Kelley's young heroine, Megda, appears to have committed the same indiscretion while vacationing in Cottage City, on Martha's Vineyard. Caught up in the pleasure of the music, which "entered her whole being, and took entire possession," she waltzed all night long, only to repent in bitter tears after the evening was over.

These two passages expose a profound tension at the heart of nineteenth-century vacationing. As the practice spread from the upper levels of society down toward the middle levels, a heated debate raged on the nature and morality of the vacation experience. More and more people were going on vacation in mid-century. In 1867, an *Atlantic Monthly* article reported that "even our farmers are beginning to have their little after-harvest trips to the sea-shore, the Hudson, Niagara or the west."[4] An editorial in the *Providence Journal* in August 1865 described the tremendous increase in the number of vacations taken by the "brain-workers" of the city—the bank cashiers, clerks, and bookkeepers—and applauded that habit. The editor attributed this new habit to the increasingly crowded and frantic city environment, and he argued that vacations had become essential to the health of (white-collar) city dwellers.[5]

That argument was heard increasingly often even from the pulpit. As early as the 1850s, some religious leaders had been extolling the practice of summer vacationing. Henry Ward Beecher, for example, argued that vacations in the country would allow the professional man to "forget the city and lay aside its excitements," and give him time he did not have in the city, time Beecher believed he would use for "the most earnest reflection, and for the most solemn resolutions for the future."[6] Religious leaders argued that relaxation and certain kinds of leisure activities, when used properly, were not dangerous to the character, but good for the soul.

It might seem surprising that anyone needed to be convinced. Wealthy, well-educated people were accustomed to summer leisure and travel by mid-century. At the other end of the spectrum, poor and working-class city dwellers were not likely to grudge themselves a hard-won Sunday afternoon at the beach. But habits of leisure were not deeply ingrained in the shopkeepers and bank clerks who were now being enjoined to take vacations. For them, long hours of work, years of patient saving, and habitual self-denial had been absolutely necessary to achieve modest success. And their religious and social training had been designed to encourage them in this behavior. Summer resorts seemed dangerous to them for the same reasons that gambling casinos and saloons seemed dangerous: they were the first step down a long slope toward poverty and hell—not necessarily in that order.

For hard-working people suspicious of the corruptions of wealth and leisure, no place symbolized that danger better than Newport, the Rhode Island seaport community that was fast becoming the most luxurious and best known resort in the Northeast. The temptations of Newport were so well understood that Harriet Beecher Stowe had only to mention that the wicked wife in *Pink and White Tyranny* (1871) had gone to Newport to reveal her true character. Her husband was surprised to find that his wife faked illness, smoked cigarettes, and entertained lovers on the side. Stowe's readers were not.

Susan and Anna Warner's heroine Wych Hazel was visiting Newport when she was seen in the waltz that led her lover to reject her. No one would be surprised that misunderstandings and temptations, if not actual sin, would find her there. But Emma Kelley's heroine Megda was dancing in a different resort, one that might have been expected to protect her from such temptations. Megda's situation was different in many ways, not least because she was African-American (although it is virtually impossible to discern that fact from the text of the novel itself). Her vacation took place, not in Newport, but just up the coast, on Martha's Vineyard, at the Methodist campground-turned-vacationland called Cottage City. Cottage City was *not* an elite resort. It was attractive to many respectable, pious vacationers precisely because it was not an elite resort. As Charles Dudley Warner described them in "Their Pilgrimage," Cottage City vacationers were "of a grave, severe type, plain and good, of the sort of people ready to die for a notion."[7] Among the cluster of communities at Cottage City was a well-known resort for African-American vacationers with family roots in the Methodist and Baptist camp meetings there.

Cottage City staked its success as a resort on its moral safety, a feature that placed it in marked contrast to a place like Newport. No alcohol was served in Cottage City. (Newport, in contrast, was well known for its defiance of the local liquor laws.) There was no horse racing or gambling as there was at Saratoga Springs; no "bad characters" lurked in corners. The young men who danced with Megda were respectable sons of families she knew at home; no one insulted her, no one threatened her. But her experience with dancing points out the tension that surrounded vacationing for many Americans; the camp meeting set the moral tone for Cottage City, but all around it were the trappings of the Victorian vacation, from the luxury hotel to the brass band, from croquet to dancing—not sins in themselves, perhaps, but enticing alternatives to a workaday world.

Vacations offered another kind of temptation, closely linked to the sensual fascination of dancing: the lure of marriage to an inappropriate mate. The plots of Charles Dudley Warner's "Their Pilgrimage," of Susan Warner's *Nobody*, and of many other nineteenth-century novels revolved around that possibility. Because vacationing offered the possibility, even the certainty, that one would meet people who were not precisely calibrated to one's background and class, it always harbored such dangers. On tour, characters necessarily encountered dangerous individuals from uncertain backgrounds: upper-class charmers who espoused atheistic views, desperate husband-chasers who were older than they looked, young men who appeared respectable but were not. Resort promoters did everything they could to enforce extremely fine distinctions of class and background at resorts. But the fear, and perhaps the allure, of dangerous encounters remained a central feature of the vacation experience.

There was yet another danger: the possibility of a romantic encounter between a "native" and a "summer person," almost by definition an alliance across class lines. Edward Bellamy's *Six to One: A Nantucket Idyl* (1878) (excerpted in the third section of this collection, in another context) tells the story of a journalist whose Nantucket vacation experience was shaped by six local women who had made a collective vow not to monopolize him. Since young men were so scarce on the island, the women would reserve the journalist as an escort for all six of them. Naturally, the hero faced problems when he decided to marry one of the six. One problem he did not face, though, was an insurmountable social or cultural gap between himself and his island bride.

In Bellamy's version of this often-told story, the social gulf between the New York journalist and the Nantucket women was a comical one, but it was neither broad nor deep. A more serious look at a relationship between a sophisticated urban vacationer and a New England "native" is Edith Wharton's novel *Summer* (1917), where such an encounter ended in predictable disaster for the young country woman. Wharton laid bare a stark contrast between the sentimentalism of city visitors returning home to rural "North Dormer" and the constricted and hopeless lives of those who still lived there. Wharton's young architect, visiting the area in search of old houses to sketch, was as alien to the local girl Charity Royall, whose life and imagination were bounded by the next town, as if he had come from a different planet. The difference between Bellamy's vision and Wharton's is rooted in how the two authors imagined New England "natives." In Bellamy's view, Nantucket natives were rural, but essentially middle-class equals of vacationers. In Wharton's depiction, the natives of North Dormer were not only poor, they were intellectually and morally stunted by the constraints of village life. And how these writers saw New England natives depended finally on how they interpreted New England itself.

Visions of New England's countryside were undergoing a radical transformation in the late nineteenth century. Scenic resorts like the White Mountains had relied heavily on a sense of place and landscape, but not on an image of the region itself. Early nineteenth-century tourists had thought of New England, when they thought of it at all, as the home of the most modern technological and social innovations of their day, a place where one might see factories, schools, new inventions, and new social reforms. In the years after the Civil War, tourists began to perceive the region very differently. Increasingly, New England appeared to visitors as though it were a kind of museum, a storehouse for a whole collection of old-fashioned ways of being, of old-fashioned values and beliefs.

That transformation seems particularly strange, since, by 1865, New England had become the most highly urbanized, industrialized, and ethnically diverse region of the United States. Rhode Island was the single most densely populated state in the Union, with Massachusetts coming in a strong second. Southern New England had become a region of large industrial cities, and manufacturing was spreading up the Merrimack River through New Hampshire, into the valleys of the Berkshires, up the great rivers of Maine. The population of New England was in flux. Two-thirds of the people of Boston in 1890 were first- or second-generation immigrants. In a mill town like Fall River, the percentage reached an amazing eighty-three percent. Even in relatively rural and ethnically homogeneous

Vermont, one-third of the people counted in the 1890 census were first- and second-generation French-Canadian immigrants.

But in these very years the tourist's vision of New England was taking a turn in the opposite direction. Many native-born New Englanders were not happy with the side effects of industrialization. The great and growing cities filled with immigrants were more disturbing than gratifying. Some native-born people worried that the hard work and sobriety of their New England ancestors had inadvertently created a region in which individual actions were lost in the industrial grind, the search for money replaced honesty and integrity, and immigrants with alien customs replaced traditional Yankees.

Urban tourists in the late nineteenth century increasingly looked for a "New England" that was not New England—Yankee, rural, simple, and peaceful. The demand for such a nostalgic tourist experience was rooted in the very changes that were sweeping the region. New England's new tourist economy offered balm for every anxiety associated with the Gilded Age. Worried about unassimilated immigrants with alien customs and languages? The Old Colony Railroad pamphlet promised that Nantucket's "population (was) not increased, nor has it ever been, by . . . discordant elements from varying climes and nationalities."[8] (Actually Nantucket's population *was* filled with "elements from varying climes and nationalities," but that is another story.) Worried that your health is breaking down under the strain of money-making and urban socializing? The Boston and Maine Railroad's promotional brochure *All Along Shore* reported in 1889 that Newburyport "is a place of simple habits and old-time virtues where frugality and sobriety supplant the anxiety and restlessness that so greatly cloud so many lives."[9]

The final section of this book, "A Visit to Old New England," explores the tourist's search for an experience of this imaginary nostalgic New England. Each of the selections here harbors a fantasy—a memory of something lost that might be found in rural New England. The section begins with Edward Bellamy's vision of Nantucket, an "out-of-the-way, switched off sort of place" perfect for a man recovering from a nervous breakdown. Bellamy's hero suffers from "nervous exhaustion," brought on by overwork and urban tension. Once, a visitor might have been overworked and stressed on Nantucket, too, but that was before the decline of the whaling industry. By the 1870s, the island's profound economic depression provided the peace and quiet that soothed urban stress.

Sarah Orne Jewett described her home town, South Berwick, Maine, in similar terms, blending nostalgia for the past with meticulous powers of observation. Jewett's first collection of stories, published as *Deephaven* in 1877, features two wealthy young Boston women who have decided to spend the summer together in a deceased aunt's colonial mansion in a small Maine town not unlike South Berwick. The visitors are fascinated with the house's architectural detail, with their quaint neighbors, and with the mix of seascape and landscape around them—all products of the region's economic decline. The village appears nearly untouched by modern industrialism. The people are quaint, old-fashioned, and filled with the Yankee virtues of earlier times—dignity, honor, scrupulous honesty. The landscape provides a mix of traditional settings and occupations: inland people farm the homesteads their families have owned for many generations; coastal people fish, mend nets, build boats using timeless methods. No one works in a factory or a shop.

"Miss Godwin's Inheritance," a short story by Thomas Nelson Page, is set in the same region. Page's central character, Mrs. Davison, has purchased an old house in a coastal Maine village. (In fact, Mrs. Davison was modeled on Emily Tyson, a friend of both Page and Jewett who restored a mansion in South Berwick.) Mrs. Davison is attracted to the region and to the house for reasons not unlike those that brought Bellamy's hero to Nantucket. She is exhausted by the pointless round of social obligations in her elegant urban drawing room: "'I feel so tired all the time—so dissatisfied. . . . It is all so hollow and unreal." Mrs. Davison hopes for a specifically "colonial" experience in her newly restored house: an antidote for a vague but powerful sense of loss—of authenticity, perhaps, or of intensity of experience.

Vacationers like Mrs. Davison found that their winter homes in Boston and New York were changing alarmingly fast: native-born

Americans were far outnumbered by immigrants; everywhere were scenes of appalling poverty and fierce class conflict. The towns of rural New England appeared harmonious, stable, and orderly—holdovers from an imaginary past. To recapture that past by restoring an old house (or by photographing or painting or writing about it) was in a sense to recapture the stability and harmony of a world without industrial conflict, the graciousness and dignity of aristocrats whose claims to authority had never been challenged. That is precisely what Mrs. Davison sets out to do—and her real-life counterparts pursued the same experience, in the handsome Federal buildings of old New England ports, the picturesque fishing villages of Maine, and the refurbished mansions of Litchfield, Connecticut.

A New England vacation offered the pleasures of a "colonial" fantasy of order and stability, the quiet and solitude of a place off the railroad grid. It also offered another sort of pleasure: *food*. William Dean Howells describes the search for good country food in *The Vacation of the Kelwyns*. (Howells was something of a one-man industry of vacation fiction: his first published work was an account of his tour of Italy; his second, *Their Wedding Journey*, was the story of a honeymoon tour.) *The Vacation of the Kelwyns*, his last novel, was based on the experience of the Howells family. In the summer of 1876, Howells had rented a house in Shirley, Massachusetts. In June, he wrote to his father that his family had the "promise of a very pleasant summer" before them. The local woman who cooked for them would have to be taught their "ideas of cooking," but she was willing to learn, and "so far, all goes well."

Six weeks later, Howells suddenly informed his father that the family had fled their summer home because of their "extreme discontent" with their landlord and his family. The landlady was not, after all, willing to learn their ideas of cooking. As Howells described it, "everything on the table was sour, dirty, or rancid."[10] The problem so intrigued Howells that thirty years later he framed *The Vacation of the Kelwyns* around his family's attempts to compel their summer landlady to give them "plain country fare, with plenty of milk and eggs and berries" in the place of the "cowy milk," bitter tea, greasy eggs, and rancid butter she provided.

City visitors like Howells were in search of good food of a very specific kind. "Plain country fare"—fresh cream and eggs and berries, simply prepared—was associated in the minds of vacationers like Howells and his family with an idealized rural life that awaited them somewhere beyond the suburbs of Boston. There, tired editors relaxed, and their children laughed and sang in the fields. There, the most cherished memories of one's own rural childhood could be relived. But in reality, "plain country fare" was not easy to come by in the country. Urban reformers recorded with repugnance the endless round of pork, biscuits, doughnuts, and pies the average farmer ate. And in reality, the New England countryside was neither so old-fashioned nor so comfortable as vacationers hoped.

A darker side of Howells's search for the purity and peace of rural life is explored in Edith Wharton's *Summer* (excerpted here in Section II in another context). There, Wharton describes an Old Home Week celebration—a ritual invented by New Hampshire governor Frank Rollins in 1898 to bring vacationers "home" to northern New England, and to shore up the sagging rural economy. Old Home Week catered to a widespread sense of unease among middle-class urbanites who had left the rural homes of their childhood to pursue jobs or education in cities. For such visitors, Old Home Week offered a potent brew of memories, guilt, and nostalgia. As Wharton tells the story, though, Old Home Week was simply another stage setting that revealed the trapped desperation of rural life. Only outsiders—or people who had found a way out—spoke sentimentally of "the old ideals, the family and the homestead, and so on."

Some vacationers searched for colonial villages, some for a return to childhood joys. And some looked for a return to an even more primitive past. By the turn of the century, wilderness camping and hiking had become very popular. Theodore Roosevelt's pronouncements on the "unhealthy softening and relaxation of fibre" among native-born Americans hit a raw nerve for some vacationers. "Overcivilized" men (and some women) yearned for contact with the primitive. Here, in the excerpt that closes this collection, Sinclair Lewis's well-known character George Babbitt searches for the primitive in the Maine woods. But Babbitt's longing for a return to Nature is disappointed. The sturdy backwoods guide, unresponsive to all Babbitt's remarks about nature, punctures Babbitt's romantic bubble by admitting that his own dearest wish is to "go down to Tinker's Falls and open a swell shoe store."

Sinclair Lewis made savage fun of Babbitt's naive imaginings about the Maine backwoods. But even Lewis could not turn his back entirely on the allure of the myth. In his vision, Babbitt joins the long parade of fictional characters who are purified and healed by their encounters with New England rural life, from Page's Mrs. Davison to Bellamy's Mr. Edgerton. Babbitt's wilderness vacation finally *did* help him: "At the end of the second week he began to feel calm, and interested in life. . . . He was curiously weak, yet cheerful, as though he had cleansed his veins of poisonous energy and was filling them with wholesome blood." That is as close as Babbitt would ever come to taking control of his own life.

Like Sinclair Lewis, twentieth-century tourists may have become more jaded about the New England myth. We may no longer seek out a purely "Yankee" New England. Perhaps we have become more aware of the poverty that often lies behind rural tranquility and mountain scenery. In any case, it is increasingly difficult to believe in a "New England" untouched by modern life: ski resorts, ATMs, and factory outlets have penetrated all but the most isolated areas. But like our nineteenth-century counterparts, we cannot resist the allure of the vision. "New England" still beckons.

Notes

1. Nathaniel Hawthorne, *The Letters, 1813–1843* (Ohio State University Press, 1984), 224.
2. Thomas Starr King, *The White Hills: Their Legends, Landscape, and Poetry* (Boston: Crosby, Nichols, and Co., 1860), 53.
3. Samuel C. Eastman, *The White Mountain Guide Book*, 3rd Ed. (Concord, N.H.: Edson C. Eastman, 1863), 271.
4. Bayard Taylor, "Travel in the United States," *Atlantic Monthly* 19 (April 1867): 477.
5. *Providence Journal*, 9 August 1865, 1.

6. Henry Ward Beecher, "The Mountain Farm to the Sea-Side Farm," *Eyes and Ears* (Boston: Ticknor and Fields, 1862), 53.
7. Charles Dudley Warner, "Their Pilgrimage," *Harper's New Monthly Magazine* 73 (July 1886): 173.
8. Old Colony Railroad, *The Old Colony: or, Pilgrim Land, Past and Present* (Boston, 1887), 67.
9. Moses Sweetser, *Here and There in New England and Canada: All Along Shore* (Boston: Boston and Main Railroad, 1889), 66.
10. William Dean Howells, *Selected Letters of W. D. Howells* (Boston: Twayne Publishers, 1979), volume 2, June 18, 1876, and July 30, 1876.

I

THE USES OF SCENERY

1

Nathaniel Hawthorne, from "Sketches from Memory" (1835)

Nathaniel Hawthorne (1804–1864) wrote these "Sketches from Memory" near the beginning of his literary career, after he made a tour in the summer of 1832. Hawthorne's trip, and this sketch, followed one of the routes of the newly fashionable "northern tour" to Niagara Falls and back. This excerpt describes the "Notch of the White Mountains" (now Crawford Notch), and Ethan Allen Crawford's inn, the point from which early White Mountain tourists ascended Mount Washington. The word "sketches" in the title led early nineteenth-century readers to expect what Hawthorne provides here: elaborate descriptions of scenery, along with legends, poetry, and fantasies attached to specific scenic locations.

In this sketch, one of Hawthorne's earliest published works, the writer tries his hand at the performances of scenic touring. All travelers attempted to describe the scenery in poetic terms, as Hawthorne does here with an elaborate image of the violent creation of the Notch by a "demon" or a "Titan." Scenic tourists often associated legends and tales with the scenery they viewed, as Hawthorne also does here with the "Indian" legend of the "great carbuncle," a legend he would later turn into a fictional story of his own, despite his claim that he "abhor[s] an Indian story." Here, too, Hawthorne describes other people responding to scenery—a common preoccupation of scenic tourists. Early nineteenth-century tourists understood that looking at, talking about, and writing about scenery were important demonstrations of their own sensitivity and refinement. Judging other people's reactions was just as important. Here, Hawthorne passes judgment on at least one fellow vacationer: the young man with the opera glasses, whose poetry he finds "elegant" but "cold."

SKETCHES FROM MEMORY

The Notch of the White Mountains

It was now the middle of September. We had come since sunrise from Bartlett, passing up through the valley of the Saco, which extends between mountainous walls, sometimes with a steep ascent, but often as level as a church-aisle. All that day and two preceding ones, we had been loitering towards the heart of the White Mountains—those old crystal hills, whose mysterious brilliancy had gleamed upon our distant wanderings before we thought of visiting them. Height after height had risen and towered one above another, till the clouds began to hang below the peaks. Down their slopes, were the red path-ways of the Slides, those avalanches of earth, stones and trees, which descend into the hollows, leaving vestiges of their track, hardly to be effaced by the vegetation of ages. We had mountains behind us and mountains on each side, and a group of mightier ones ahead. Still our road went up along the Saco, right towards the centre of that group, as if to climb above the clouds, in its passage to the farther region.

In old times, the settlers used to be astounded by the inroads of the northern Indians, coming down upon them from this mountain rampart, through some defile known only to themselves. It is indeed a wondrous path. A demon, it might be fancied, or one of the Titans, was travelling up the valley, elbowing the heights carelessly aside as he passed, till at length a great mountain took its stand directly across his intended road. He tarries not for such an obstacle, but rending it asunder, a thousand feet from peak to base, discloses its treasures of hidden minerals, its sunless waters, all the secrets of the mountain's inmost heart, with a mighty fracture of rugged precipices on each side. This is the Notch of the White Hills. Shame on me, that I have attempted to describe it by so mean an image—feeling, as I do, that it is one of those symbolic scenes, which lead the mind to the sentiment, though not to the conception, of Omnipotence.

We had now reached a narrow passage, which showed almost the appearance of having been cut by human strength and artifice in the solid rock. There was a wall of granite on each side, high and precipitous, especially on our right, and so smooth that a few evergreens could hardly find foothold enough to grow there. This is the entrance, or, in the direction we were going, the extremity of the romantic defile of the Notch. Before emerging from it, the rattling of wheels approached behind us, and a stage-coach rumbled out of the mountain, with seats on top and trunks behind, and a smart driver, in a drab great-coat, touching the wheel horses with the whipstock, and reining in the leaders. To my mind, there was a sort of poetry in such an incident, hardly inferior to what would have accompanied the painted array of an Indian war-party, gliding forth from the same wild chasm. All the passengers, except a very fat lady on the back seat, had alighted. One was a mineralogist, a scientific, green-spectacled figure in black, bearing a heavy hammer, with which he did great damage to the precipices, and put the fragments in his pocket. Another was a well-dressed young man, who carried an opera-glass set in gold, and seemed to be making a quotation from some of Bryon's rhapsodies on mountain scenery. There was also a trader, returning from Portland to the upper part of Vermont; and a fair young girl with a very faint bloom, like one of those pale and delicate flowers, which sometimes occur among Alpine cliffs.

They disappeared, and we followed them, passing through a deep pine forest, which, for some miles, allowed us to see nothing but its own dismal shade. Towards night-fall, we reached a level amphitheatre, surrounded by a great rampart of hills, which shut out the sunshine long before it left the external world. It was here that we obtained our first view, except at a distance, of the principal group of mountains. They are majestic, and even awful, when contemplated in a proper mood; yet, by their breadth of base, and the long ridges which support them, give the idea of immense bulk, rather than of towering height. Mount Washington, indeed, looked near to Heaven; he was white with snow a mile downward, and had caught the only cloud that was sailing through the atmosphere, to veil his head. Let us forget the other names of American statesmen, that have been stamped upon these hills, but still call the loftiest—Washington. Mountains are Earth's undecaying monuments. They must stand while she endures, and never should be consecrated to the mere great men of their own age and country, but to the mighty ones alone, whose glory is universal, and whom all time will render illustrious.

The air, not often sultry in this elevated region, nearly two thousand feet above the sea, was now sharp and cold, like that of a clear November evening in the low-lands. By morning, probably, there would be a frost, if not a snow-fall, on the grass and rye, and an icy surface over the standing water. I was glad to perceive a prospect of comfortable quarters, in a house which we were approaching, and of pleasant company in the guests who were assembled at the door.

Our Evening Party Among the Mountains

We stood in front of a good substantial farm-house, of old date in that wild country. A sign over the door denoted it to be the White Mountain Post-Office, an establishment which distributes letters and newspapers to perhaps a score of persons, comprising the population of two or three townships among the hills. The broad and weighty antlers of a deer, "a stag of ten," were fastened at a corner of the house; a fox's bushy tail was nailed beneath them; and a huge black paw lay on the ground, newly severed and still bleeding—the trophy of a bear-hunt. Among several persons collected about the door-steps, the most remarkable was a sturdy mountaineer, of six feet two and corresponding bulk, with a heavy set of features, such as might be moulded on his own blacksmith's anvil, but yet indicative of mother-wit and rough humor. As we appeared, he uplifted a tin trumpet, four or five feet long, and blew a tremendous blast, either in honor of our arrival, or to awaken an echo from the opposite hill.

Ethan Crawford's guests were of such a motley description as to form quite a picturesque group, seldom seen together, except at some place like this, at once the pleasure-house of fashionable tourists, and the homely inn of country travellers. Among the company at the door, were the mineralogist and the owner of the gold opera-glass, whom we had encountered in the Notch; two Georgian gentlemen, who had chilled their southern blood, that morning, on the top of Mount Washington; a physician and his wife, from Conway; a trader, of Burlington, and an old 'Squire, of the Green Mountains; and two young married couples, all the way from Massachusetts, on the matrimonial jaunt. Besides these strangers, the rugged county of Coos, in which we were, was represented by half a dozen wood-cutters, who had slain a bear in the forest and smitten off his paw.

I had joined the party, and had a moment's leisure to examine them, before the echo of Ethan's blast returned from the hill. Not one, but many echoes had caught up the harsh and tuneless sound, untwisted its complicated threads, and found a thousand aerial harmonies in one stern trumpet-tone. It was a distinct, yet distant and dreamlike symphony of melodious instruments, as if an airy band had been hidden on the hill-side, and made faint music at the summons. No subsequent trial produced so clear, delicate, and spiritual a concert as the first. A field-piece was then discharged from the top of a neighboring hill, and gave birth to one long reverberation, which ran round the circle of mountains in an unbroken chain of sound, and rolled away without a separate echo. After these experiments, the cold atmosphere drove us all into the house, with the keenest appetites for supper.

It did one's heart good to see the great fires that were kindled in the parlor and bar-room, especially the latter, where the fire-place was built of rough stone, and might have contained the trunk of an old tree for a back-log. A man keeps a comfortable hearth when his own forest is at his very door. In the parlor, when the evening was fairly set in, we held our hands before our eyes, to shield them from the ruddy glow, and began a pleasant variety of conversation. The mineralogist and the physician talked about the invigorating qualities of the mountain air, and its excellent effect on Ethan Crawford's father, an old man of seventy-five, with the unbroken frame of middle life. The two brides and the doctor's wife held a whispered discussion, which, by their frequent titterings and a blush or two, seemed to have reference to the trials or enjoyments of the matrimonial state. The bridegrooms sat together in a corner, rigidly silent, like Quakers whom the spirit moveth not, being still in the odd predicament of bashfulness towards their own young wives. The Green Mountain 'Squire chose me for his companion, and described the difficulties he had met with, half a century ago, in traveling from the Connecticut river through the Notch to Conway, now a single day's journey, though it had cost him eighteen. The Georgians held the album between them, and favored us with the few specimens of its contents, which they considered ridiculous enough to be worth hearing. One extract met with deserved applause. It was a "Sonnet to the Snow on Mount Washington," and had been contributed that very afternoon, bearing a signature of great distinction in magazines and annuals. The lines were elegant and full of fancy, but too remote from familiar sentiment, and cold as their subject, resembling those curious specimens of crystallized vapor, which I observed next day on the mountain-top. The poet was understood to be the young gentleman of the gold opera-glass, who heard our laudatory remarks with the composure of a veteran.

Such was our party, and such their ways of amusement. But, on a winter evening, another set of guests assembled at the hearth, where these summer travellers were now sitting. I once had it in contemplation to spend a month hereabouts, in sleighing-time, for the sake of studying the yeomen of New-England, who then elbow each other through the Notch by hundreds, on their way to Portland. There could be no better school for such a purpose than Ethan Crawford's inn. Let the student go thither in December, sit down with the teamsters at their meals, share their evening merriment, and repose with them at night, when every bed has its three occupants, and parlor, bar-room and kitchen are strewn with slumberers around the fire. Then let him rise before daylight, button his great-coat, muffle up his ears, and stride with the departing caravan a mile or two, to see how sturdily they make head against the blast. A treasure of characteristic traits will repay all inconveniences, even should a frozen nose be of the number.

The conversation of our party soon became more animated and sincere, and we recounted some traditions of the Indians, who believed that the father and mother of their race were saved from a deluge by ascending the peak of Mount Washington. The children of that pair have been overwhelmed, and found no such refuge. In the mythology of the savage, these mountains were afterwards considered sacred and inaccessible, full of unearthly wonders, illuminated at lofty heights by the blaze of precious stones, and inhabited by deities, who sometimes shrouded themselves in the snowstorm, and came down on the lower world. There are few legends more poetical than that of the "Great Carbuncle" of the White Mountains. The belief was communicated to the English settlers, and is hardly yet extinct, that a gem, of such immense size as to be seen shining miles away, hangs from a rock over a clear, deep lake, high up among the hills. They who had once beheld its splendor, were enthralled with an unutterable yearning to possess it. But a spirit guarded that inestimable jewel, and bewildered the adventurer with a dark mist from the enchanted lake. Thus, life was worn away in the vain search for an unearthly treasure, till at length the deluded one went up the mountain, still sanguine as in youth, but returned no more. On this theme, methinks I could frame a tale with a deep moral.

The hearts of the pale-faces would not thrill to these superstitions of the red men, though we spoke of them in the centre of their haunted region. The habits and sentiments of that departed people were too distinct from those of their successors to find much real sympathy. It has often been a matter of regret to me, that I was shut out from the most peculiar field of American fiction, by an inability to see any romance, or poetry, or grandeur, or beauty in the Indian character, at least, till such traits were pointed out by others. I do abhor an Indian story. Yet no writer can be more secure of a permanent place in our literature, than the biographer of the Indian chiefs. His subject, as referring to tribes which have mostly vanished from the earth, gives him a right to be placed on a classic shelf, apart from the merits which will sustain him there.

I made inquiries whether, in his researchers about these parts, our mineralogist had found the three "Silver Hills," which an Indian sachem sold to an Englishman, nearly two hundred years ago, and the treasure of which the posterity of the purchaser have been looking for ever since. But the man of science had ransacked every hill along the Saco, and knew nothing of these prodigious piles of wealth. By this time, as usual with men on the eve of great adventure, we had prolonged our session deep into the night, considering how early we were to set out on our six miles' ride to the foot of Mount Washington. There was now a general breaking-up. I scrutinized the faces of the two bridegrooms, and saw but little probability of their leaving the bosom of earthly bliss, in the first week of the honey-moon, and at the frosty hour of three, to climb above the clouds. Nor, when I felt how sharp the wind was, as it rushed through a broken pane, and eddied between the chinks of my unplastered chamber, did I anticipate much alacrity on my own part, though we were to seek for the "Great Carbuncle."

2

Nathaniel Hawthorne, "The Ambitious Guest"

(1835)

Hawthorne is best known today as one of the great novelists of the "American Renaissance," but he first became popular as the writer of fanciful tales like "The Ambitious Guest," one of several stories based on his experiences touring the White Mountains of New Hampshire. This one follows the story of the Willey family, destroyed by a landslide in Crawford Notch in 1826. The Willeys had been the victims of a particularly cruel joke of fate. The entire family had been killed when they fled their cabin—but the house itself was spared, a perfect monument to them and a perfect shrine for future tourists. By the time Hawthorne visited the site in 1832, it was already a popular tourist destination, and an equally popular subject for writers. In "The Ambitious Guest," Hawthorne heightens the irony by adding a wandering young traveler to the doomed household—a young man not unlike Hawthorne himself, with a "high and abstracted ambition" to leave a lasting monument to posterity.

THE AMBITIOUS GUEST

One September night, a family had gathered round their hearth, and piled it high with the driftwood of mountain-streams, the dry cones of the pine, and the splintered ruins of great trees, that had come crashing down the precipice. Up the chimney roared the fire, and brightened the room with its broad blaze. The faces of the father and mother had a sober gladness; the children laughed; the eldest daughter was the image of Happiness at seventeen; and the aged grandmother, who sat knitting in the warmest place, was the image of Happiness grown old. They had found the "herb, heart's ease," in the bleakest spot of all New-England. This family were situated in the Notch of the White Hills, where the wind was sharp throughout the year, and pitilessly cold in the winter—giving their cottage all its fresh inclemency, before it descended on the valley of the Saco. They dwelt in a cold spot and a dangerous one; for a mountain towered above their heads, so steep, that the stones would often rumble down its sides, and startle them at midnight.

The daughter had just uttered some simple jest, that filled them all with mirth, when the wind came through the Notch and seemed to pause before their cottage—rattling the door, with a sound of wailing and lamentation, before it passed into the valley. For a moment, it saddened them, though there was nothing unusual in the tones. But the family were glad again, when they perceived that the latch was lifted by some traveller, whose footsteps had been unheard amid the dreary blast, which heralded his approach, and wailed as he was entering, and went moaning away from the door.

Though they dwelt in such a solitude, these people held daily converse with the world. The romantic pass of the Notch is a great artery, through which the life-blood of internal commerce is continually throbbing, between Maine, on one side, and the Green Mountains and the shores of the St. Lawrence on the other. The stage-coach always drew up before the door of the cottage. The wayfarer, with no companion but his staff, paused here to exchange a word, that the sense of loneliness might not utterly overcome him, ere he could pass through the cleft of the mountain, or reach the first house in the valley. And here the teamster, on his way to Portland market, would put up for the night—and, if a bachelor, might sit an hour beyond the usual bed-time, and steal a kiss from the mountain-maid, at parting. It was one of those primitive taverns, where the traveller pays only for food and lodging, but meets with a homely kindness, beyond all price. When the footsteps were heard, therefore, between the outer door and the inner one, the whole family rose up, grandmother, children, and all, as if about to welcome some one who belonged to them, and whose fate was linked with theirs.

The door was opened by a young man. His face at first wore the melancholy expression, almost despondency, of one who travels a wild and bleak road, at night-fall and alone, but soon brightened up, when he saw the kindly warmth of his reception. He felt his heart spring forward to meet them all, from the old woman, who wiped a chair with her apron, to the little child that held out its arms to him. One glance and smile placed the stranger on a footing of innocent familiarity with the eldest daughter.

"Ah, this fire is the right thing!" cried he; "especially when there is such a pleasant circle round it. I am quite benumbed; for the Notch is just like the pipe of a great pair of bellows; it has blown a terrible blast in my face, all the way from Bartlett."

"Then you are going towards Vermont?" said the master of the house, as he helped to take a light knapsack off the young man's shoulders.

"Yes; to Burlington, and far enough beyond," replied he. "I meant to have been at Ethan Crawford's, to-night; but a pedestrian lingers along such a road as this. It is no matter; for, when I saw this good fire, and all your cheerful faces, I felt as if you had kindled it on purpose for me, and were waiting my arrival. So I shall sit down among you, and make myself at home."

The frank-hearted stranger had just drawn his chair to the fire, when something like a heavy footstep was heard without, rushing down the steep side of the mountain, as with long and rapid strides, and taking such a leap, in passing the cottage, as to strike the opposite precipice. The family held their breath, because they knew the sound, and their guest held his, by instinct.

"The old Mountain has thrown a stone at us, for fear we should forget him," said the landlord, recovering himself. "He sometimes nods his head, and threatens to come down; but we are old neighbors, and agree together pretty well, upon the whole. Besides, we have a sure place of refuge, hard by, if he should be coming in good earnest."

Let us now suppose the stranger to have finished his supper of bear's meat; and, by his natural felicity of manner, to have placed himself on a footing of kindness with the whole family—so that they talked as freely together, as if he belonged to their mountain brood. He was a proud, yet gentle spirit—haughty and reserved among the rich and great; but ever ready to stoop his head to the lowly cottage door, and be like a brother or a son at the poor man's fireside. In the household of the Notch, he found warmth and simplicity of feeling, the pervading intelligence of New-England, and a poetry, of native growth, which they had gathered, when they little thought of it, from the mountain-peaks and chasms, and at the very threshold of their romantic and dangerous abode. He had travelled far and alone; his whole life, indeed, had been a solitary path; for, with the lofty caution of his nature, he had kept himself apart from those who might otherwise have been his companions. The family, too, though so kind and hospitable, had that consciousness of unity among themselves, and separation from the world at large, which, in every domestic circle, should still keep a holy place, where no stranger may intrude. But, this evening, a prophetic sympathy impelled the refined and educated youth to pour out his heart before the simple mountaineers, and constrained them to answer him with the same free confidence. And thus it should have been. Is not the kindred of a common fate a closer tie than that of birth?

The secret of the young man's character was, a high and abstracted ambition. He could have borne to live an undistinguished life, but not to be forgotten in the grave. Yearning desire had been transformed to hope; and hope, long cherished, had become like certainty, that, obscurely as he journeyed now, a glory was to beam on all his path-way—though not, perhaps, while he was treading it. But, when posterity should gaze back into the gloom of what was now the present, they would trace the brightness of his footsteps, brightening as meaner glories faded, and confess, that a gifted one had passed from his cradle to his tomb, with none to recognize him.

"As yet," cried the stranger—his cheek glowing and his eye flashing with enthusiasm—"as yet, I have done nothing. Were I to vanish from the earth to-morrow, none would know so much of me as you; that a nameless youth came up, at night-fall, from the valley of the Saco, and opened his heart to you in the evening, and passed through the Notch, by sunrise, and was seen no more. Not a soul would ask—'Who was he?—Whither did the wanderer go?' But, I cannot die till I have achieved my destiny. Then, let Death come! I shall have built my monument!" There was a continual flow of natural emotion, gushing forth amid abstracted reverie, which enabled the family to understand this young man's sentiments, though so foreign from their own. With quick sensibility of the ludicrous, he blushed at the ardor into which he had been betrayed.

"You laugh at me," said he, taking the eldest daughter's hand, and laughing himself. "You think my ambition as nonsensical as if I were to freeze myself to death on the top of Mount Washington, only that people might spy at me from the country roundabout. And truly, that would be a noble pedestal for a man's statue!"

"It is better to sit here, by this fire," answered the girl, blushing, "and be comfortable and contented, though nobody thinks about us."

"I suppose," said her father, after a fit of musing, "there is something natural in what the young man says; and if my mind had been turned that way, I might have felt just the same. It is strange, wife, how his talk has set my head running on things, that are pretty certain never to come to pass."

"Perhaps they may," observed the wife. "Is the man thinking what he will do when he is a widower?"

"No, no!" cried he, repelling the idea with reproachful kindness. "When I think of your death, Esther, I think of mine, too. But I was wishing we had a good farm, in Bartlett, or Bethlehem, or Littleton, or some other township round the White Mountains; but not where they could tumble on our heads. I should want to stand well with my neighbors, and be called 'Squire, and sent to General Court, for a term or two; for a plain, honest man may do as much good there as a lawyer. And when I should be grown quite an old man, and you an old woman, so as not to be long apart, I might die happy enough in my bed, and leave you all crying around me. A slate grave-stone would suit me as well as a marble one—with just my name and age, and a verse of a hymn, and something to let people know, that I lived an honest man and died a Christian."

"There now!" exclaimed the stranger; "it is our nature to desire a monument, be it slate, or marble, or a pillar of granite, or a glorious memory in the universal heart of man."

"We're in a strange way, to-night," said the wife, with tears in her eyes. "They say it's a sign of something, when folks' minds go a wandering so. Hark to the children!"

They listened accordingly. The younger children had been put to bed in another room, but with an open door between, so that they could be heard talking busily among themselves. One and all seemed to have caught the infection from the fireside circle, and were outvying each other, in wild wishes, and childish projects of what they would do, when they came to be men and women. At length, a little boy, instead of addressing his brothers and sisters, called out to his mother.

"I'll tell you what I wish, mother," cried he. "I want you and father and grandma'm, and all of us, and the stranger too, to start right away, and go and take a drink out of the basin of the Flume!"

Nobody could help laughing at the child's notion of leaving a warm bed, and dragging them from a cheerful fire, to visit the basin of the Flume—a brook, which tumbles over the precipice, deep within the Notch. The boy had hardly spoken, when a wagon rattled along the road, and stopped a moment before the door. It appeared to contain two or three men, who were cheering their hearts with the rough chorus of a song, which resounded, in broken notes, between the cliffs, while the singers hesitated whether to continue their journey, or put up here for the night.

"Father," said the girl, "they are calling you by name."

But the good man doubted whether they had really called him, and was unwilling to show himself too solicitous of gain, by inviting people to patronize his house. He therefore did not hurry to the door; and the lash being soon applied, the travellers plunged into the Notch, still singing and laughing, though their music and mirth came back drearily from the heart of the mountain.

"There, mother!" cried the boy, again. "They'd have given us a ride to the Flume."

Again they laughed at the child's pertinacious fancy for a night-ramble. But it happened, that a light cloud passed over the daughter's spirit; she looked gravely into the fire, and drew a breath that was almost a sigh. It forced its way, in spite of a little struggle to repress it. Then starting and blushing, she looked quickly round the circle, as if they had caught a glimpse into her bosom. The stranger asked what she had been thinking of.

"Nothing," answered she, with a downcast smile. "Only I felt lonesome just then."

"Oh, I have always had a gift of feeling what is in other people's hearts," said he, half seriously. "Shall I tell the secrets of yours? For I know what to think, when a young girl shivers by a warm hearth, and complains of lonesomeness at her mother's side. Shall I put these feelings into words?"

"They would not be a girl's feelings any longer, if they could be put into words," replied the mountain-nymph, laughing, but avoiding his eye.

All this was said apart. Perhaps a germ of love was springing in their hearts, so pure that it might blossom in Paradise, since it could not be matured on earth; for women worship such gentle dignity as his; and the proud, contemplative, yet kindly soul is oftenest captivated by simplicity like hers. But, while they spoke softly, and he was watching the happy sadness, the lightsome shadows, the shy yearnings of a maiden's nature, the wind, through the Notch, took a deeper and dearier sound. It seemed, as the fanciful stranger said, like the choral strain of the spirits of the blast, who, in old Indian times, had their dwelling among these mountains, and made their heights and recesses a sacred region. There was a wail, along the road, as if a funeral were passing. To chase away the gloom, the family threw pine branches on their fire, till the dry leaves crackled and the flame arose, discovering once again a scene of peace and humble happiness. The light hovered about them fondly, and caressed them all. There were the little faces of the children, peeping from their bed apart, and here the father's frame of strength, the mother's subdued and careful mien, the high-browed youth, the budding girl, and the good old grandam, still knitting in the warmest place. The aged woman looked up from her task, and, with fingers ever busy, was the next to speak.

"Old folks have their notions," said she, "as well as young ones. You've been wishing and planning; and letting your heads run on one thing and another, till you've set my mind a wandering too. Now what should an old woman wish for, when she can go but a step or two before she comes to her grave? Children, it will haunt me night and day, till I tell you."

"What is it, mother?" cried the husband and wife, at once.

Then the old woman, with an air of mystery, which drew the circle closer round the fire, informed them that she had provided her grave-clothes some years before—a nice linen shroud, a cap with a muslin ruff, and everything of a finer sort than she had worn since her wedding day. But, this evening, an old superstition had strangely recurred to her. It used to be said, in her younger days, that, if anything were amiss with a corpse, if only the ruff were not smooth, or the cap did not set right, the corpse, in the coffin and beneath the clods, would strive to put up its cold hands and arrange it. The bare thought made her nervous.

"Don't talk so, grandmother!" said the girl, shuddering.

"Now,"—continued the old woman, with singular earnestness, yet smiling strangely at her own folly,—"I want one of you, my children—when your mother is drest, and in the coffin—I want one of you to hold a looking-glass over my face. Who knows but I may take a glimpse at myself, and see whether all's right?"

"Old and young, we dream of graves and monuments," murmured the stranger-youth. "I wonder how mariners feel, when the ship is sinking, and they, unknown and undistinguished, are to be buried together in the ocean—that wide and nameless sepulchre!"

For a moment, the old woman's ghastly conception so engrossed the minds of her hearers, that a sound, abroad in the night, rising like the roar of a blast, had grown broad, deep, and terrible, before the fated group were conscious of it. The house, and all within it, trembled; the foundations of the earth seemed to be shaken, as if this awful sound were the peal of the last trump. Young and old exchanged one wild glance, and remained an instant, pale, affrighted, without utterance, or power to move. Then the same shriek burst simultaneously from all their lips.

"The Slide! The Slide!"

The simplest words must intimate, but not portray, the unutterable horror of the catastrophe. The victims rushed from their cottage, and sought refuge in what they deemed a safer spot—where, in contemplation of such an emergency, a sort of barrier had been reared. Alas! they had quitted their security, and fled right into the pathway of destruction. Down came the whole side of the mountain, in a cataract of ruin. Just before it reached the house, the stream broke into two branches—shivered not a window there, but overwhelmed the whole vicinity, blocked up the road, and annihilated everything in its dreadful course. Long ere the thunder of that great Slide had ceased to roar among the mountains, the mortal agony had been endured, and the victims were at peace. Their bodies were never found.

The next morning, the light smoke was seen stealing from the cottage-chimney, up the mountain-side. Within, the fire was yet smouldering on the hearth, and the chairs in a circle round it, as if the inhabitants had but gone forth to view the devastation of the slide, and would shortly return, to thank Heaven for their miraculous escape. All had left separate tokens, by which those, who had known the family, were made to shed a tear for each. Who has not heard their name? The story has been told far and wide, and will forever be a legend of these mountains. Poets have sung their fate.

There were circumstances, which led some to suppose that a stranger had been received into the cottage on this awful night, and had shared the catastrophe of all its inmates. Others denied that there were sufficient grounds for such a conjecture. Wo, for the high-souled youth, with his dream of Earthly Immortality! His name and person utterly unknown; his history, his way of life, his plans, a mystery never to be solved; his death and his existence, equally a doubt! Whose was the agony of that death-moment?

3

Sarah Josepha Hale, "The Romance of Travelling," from *Traits of American Life*

(1835)

Sarah Josepha Hale (1788–1879) was a popular writer, but she is best remembered as the editor of Godey's Lady's Book, *an influential and long-lived women's magazine. Hale's sketch may seem a little odd at first, in part because it eludes any sort of genre classification. The sketch combines journalistic description with contemporary social commentary, and it offers an apparently endless sequence of digressions—about the dignity of farming as an occupation, and the beauty of a ship at sea. All this serves as a very long prelude to a very short romantic tale, which seems to be incongruously tacked on at the end. In fact, these kinds of wandering, discursive sketches were increasingly popular in the early nineteenth century. (This one is much like Hawthorne's "Sketches from Memory," published the same year. See p. 23.) But Hale provides an ideological rationale for the mixture of fact and fancy she offers: she suggests that American writers need to compensate for the "barrenness" and "vacancy" of American scenery, by creating poetry and legends whose emotional intensity can be associated with specific places in the landscape. Then she proceeds to do just that, by recounting the story of Peter Wood to accompany her description of the scenery of Lake Sunapee.*

THE ROMANCE OF TRAVELLING

We must travel, if we would be in the fashion. Men, women, and even children, are abroad to see the wonders of the grand canal, and the grander cataract. There is nothing like variety and change, for enlarging the mind, and furnishing subjects for conversation. Who can improve at home, where the same faces are seen, the same voices heard, and the same employments pursued, day after day, and year after year?

It seems, too, as if circumstances had almost inevitably designed us as a nation of travellers. We should be acquainted with our own country and people. It is only by such means, that errors will be corrected, prejudices removed, and that good feeling and liberality of sentiment cultivated, which are indispensable to the perpetuity of the Union.

What American does not wish it were in his power to examine his whole country? But to accomplish this, he must wend farther than ever did knight of chivalry in service of his mistress.

It may be doubted, however, whether the indulgence of this passion for sight-seeing, is really conducive to happiness or mental improvement. Content is not found in the bustle of a stage-coach; nor does the power of steam, though hurrying on the progress of the car or boat, have any influence to quicken the faculties of the mind. The rapidity with which travelling is now conducted, prevents the tourist, unless extremely active and inquisitive, from gaining much information, except what may be called the technicalities of journeying,—such as the best routes to be pursued; the expenses; the fatigues and the privations. He gains little knowledge of the country beyond what he sees from the path he is traversing, or of the people, except it be the inn-keepers, which he might not have obtained at home, in much less time and with less exertion than his excursion has cost him. But then he has seen the world, and that he thinks adds to his consequence in the opinion of those poor wights, whom untoward circumstances detain within the vulgar precincts of their own state.

It must, however, be confessed there is, as yet, but little in our country to attract the sentimental traveller, or make any one, except a naturalist or a philosopher, linger on his way. The former would find an exhaustless source of speculation and amusement in the examination of our new world, still so rich in its first created beauty; and the latter would rejoice to delay his steps to witness the exhibitions of human comfort on every side, and to seek the causes of those rapid improvements he sees, as it were, developing themselves around him. But he who goes abroad to awaken remembrances, or with the hope of feeling those strong emotions which are excited, when

"Full flashes on the soul the light of ages,"

may range from St. Croix to the Sabine, from the Connecticut to the Columbia, and with some truth cry "that all is barren." Barren, but not in historic or traditional recollections. Though the grand events which have occurred in America are few, yet they are of such a peculiar character, and in their consequences appear likely to be so stupendous, that they stamp themselves on the heart, the mind, with a strong and stirring moral interest, which is, with the exception of the events recorded in sacred history, not exceeded by any memorials of the old world. The barrenness, the vacancy, painfully felt by the traveller of taste and sentiment, arises from the want of intellectual and poetic associations with the scenery he beholds. Genius has not consecrated our mountains, making them high places from which the mind may see the horizon of thought widening and expanding around, over past ages,—they are nothing but huge piles of earth and rocks, covered with blighted firs and fern; the song has not named our streams—they are only celebrated for affording fine fish, good mill-seats or safe navigation. No fairies nor lovers have made our valleys their places of resort; neither green rings or flowery arbours have been allotted to the one or the other; but fertile meadows and fair fields are famed for affording the cultivator very profitable crops. It is therefore that, though reason sees and acknowledges the abundance afforded by our soil, yet fancy calls it barren; and European travellers, accustomed to a land where every place and object has its real or romantic legend, would pronounce a tour of the United States insufferably dull, and its inhabitants destitute of taste.

And we are ourselves sensible of this lack of sentimental interest, of heart-stirring recollections, when viewing the wild and beautiful scenery of our country. True it is, that in this working-day world of ours, where every thing is intended to be graduated to the standard of common sense and equal rights, it would be very difficult, even for the imagination of genius, to give to "airy nothing a local habitation and a name."

But still we have reason to believe that such attempts will be approved. Illustrations of American character, scenery and history, are demanded by the public; and who does not feel, that to fix a trait which shall be recognized as genuine, or a record that shall make one solitary place remembered, will be a reward for the effort? We want the light of song poured over our wide land, and its lonely and waste places "peopled with the affections." We want writers who can throw enchantment around rural scenes and rural life, and, like Burns,

> "Gar our streams and burnies shine,
> Up wi' the best!"

Great events or wondrous things are not necessary to furnish themes for genius. A "yellow cowslip," or a "mountain daisy," will be sufficient to waken the feelings, when hymned by the hand of a master. Marathon is not more the object of curiosity to the traveller of intelligence and taste than Lake Leman.

> "For the lore
> Of might minds, doth hallow in the core
> Of human hearts the ruin of a wall."

And who among my readers would not prefer, with the Lady of the Lake for a directory, a tour to "Ben-venue" and "Coilantogle ford," and "Loch-Katrine," rather than to explore the field of Waterloo, even though De Coster were the guide?

These observations are designed as the preface of a "true" story which I relate, to throw, if possible, somewhat of a romantic interest over a path which those who have journeyed from Boston to Windsor, Vt., by the way of Concord, N. H., will readily allow has few real beauties to attract curiosity or reward fatigue. We will pass the first eighty miles, or thereabouts, without remark, as the traveller probably would, except that the characteristics of the country were truly New England—a rough but sterile soil, rendered interesting chiefly by those indications of persevering industry which unequivocally show that man has there obtained his allotted dominion over the earth.

To a reflecting mind no sight is more gratifying. There are grander exhibitions of human skill. A ship under sail is one of these. We gaze on the vessel, "walking the waters, like a thing of life," with curiosity, wonder, awe, and we are proud of the power of man. We look on a fine and highly cultivated landscape with a calm, contented, approving admiration, and we rejoice in his happiness. Storms and danger are connected in idea with the vessel; sunshine and security seem to rest on the landscape.

There is around a snug country-seat, where the neat white house looks forth from amid a group of trees and shrubbery, like a lady in her best; and the two barns, like buxom damsels in their working-day colour, keep modestly back; and the full-leaved, and fruit-covered orchard, comes sweeping down from the southern side of a green hill, while the walled fields are rich with the growing harvest, and cattle are in the pastures that stretch away to the mountains, from which the rills descend that swell the stream, sparkling in the valley. There is around such a residence an air of honest contentment, of plenty and independence, that always makes me glad. New England has not a rich soil, but its natural scenery is bold, variegated and beautiful; and where it is cultivated with a careful industry, directed by good taste, no part of our wide republic presents more charming landscapes. But the improvement (or beautifying rather) of the country, is slow. Our young men are eager to be rich and great. They despise the pursuit of their fathers—agriculture. They crowd our colleges and cities, and struggle to enter the learned professions, or become merchants or book-makers, imaging they shall then be gentlemen.

There will be, ere the republic continues another half century, a revolution in public sentiment respecting agriculture. If the people remain sovereigns of this fair country, they will not see the occupation, in which much the largest number of individuals are and must be engaged, degraded. Nothing is now requisite to make the station of the agriculturalist as honourable as it is useful and independent, but that those who engage in it should possess intelligence. Only let our farmers educate themselves as they might do, and they would be inferior to no class in society. The country ladies must endeavour to promote that refinement of feeling and taste, which have such an influence in awakening the mind to exercise its powers. Young men of talents and education would then more willingly engage in a pursuit which is sure to give a competency to the industrious, and still leave them more leisure for mental improvement, than any other business that is not necessarily connected with study.

But unless a young man is a thorough-going and determined geologist, so as actually to love the faces of stones, I would not advise him to establish himself any where on the route from Hopkinton to Newport, N. H. It is a fine situation to study the character of the primary rocks, for the country looks as if a hail-storm of granite had been discharged thereon. There they lie, and probably have lain thousands of years, masses of moss-covered rocks and a multitude of stones, encumbering and nearly concealing the earth; and what is their use? is probably the first inquiry arising in the minds of nearly every person who views them. All that was created was pronounced *good*—so we know the sterile as well as the fertile places have their appropriate advantages, and where granite rocks abound, there the traveller may always expect to find good water and "good air;" and where sufficient industry has been exerted, a good road. And the last, when passing through a country where nothing invites us to linger, is no small advantage. But Nature always exhibits some lovely scene, even in her rudest mood; such an one occurs unexpectedly, and therefore more welcome, on this road, when Lake Sunapee opens abruptly on the sight. The placid beauty of the blue waters, contrasted with the uncivilized scenery on which the eye has been resting, gives to the heart a sensation like that of suddenly meeting the smiling face of a friend, while making our way through a crowd of strangers.

Why is it that water, so monotonous in its characteristics, should nevertheless possess a charm for every mind? I believe it is chiefly because it bears the impress of the Creator, which we feel neither the power of time or of man can efface or alter.

> "Such as creation's dawn beheld, *water*, thou rollest now."

Some one has called flowers the poetry of earth. They are only its lyrical poetry. Water is the grand epic of creation; and there is not a human soul but feels the influence of its majesty, its power, or its beauty. Sunapee lake has the latter quality in a softened perfection, which, in some respects, hardly appears like the work of nature. Its shore, especially on the eastern side, is low and level, and defined, as far as the eye can reach, by a line of white sand, so uniform and unbroken, as to appear like a regular embankment to an artificial basin. There the water lies, calm as sleeping infancy, apparently so near the *brim*, that a shower might make it overflow. The country on the east rises gradually, exhibiting cultivated fields, that look soft and fair (partly from the distance which clothes them in colours of air), when compared with the rude scenery through which the road, having the lake on the east and Sunapee mountain on the west, winds for several miles.

Should a geologist, of the Huttonian theory, enter the narrow path, his imagination would probably travel back to the era of that awful convulsion, when, by the action of subterranean fires, the huge mountain, preceded by a shower of rocks and stones, which cover that region, was upheaved, leaving a granite basin for the reception of the cool waters which should there gather together.

The interest of the scene rests chiefly on the majestic mountain and the placid lake; yet here and there may be seen verdant knolls, shaded by a few tall trees, or little quiet dells, which might tempt the sentimentalist to wish for a cottage (that perfection of romantic comfort), and "one fair spirit," and then dream how sweetly life would pass away on the shore of the quiet lake.

We have not many such dreamers in our bustling country. Profit, not peace, is the object of pursuit with us republicans. And the turmoil of the cataract, rather than the tranquillity of the lake, would be in unison with the spirit of American travellers.

There is a remembrance connected with the lake which may interest our stirring tourists, and admonish those (if there are any such) who are really in quest of a spot where they may hope to dwell in safety and retirement, that peace is not of this world. The borders of Sunapee offer retirement in perfection; but for safety, before deciding on that, look—no, you cannot see from the coach—but alight and search till you find, what seems an impenetrable wilderness of stumps, fallen and decayed trees, broken rocks and tall brambles; were not these intermingled, here and there, with an apple tree, which in our climate always denotes the agency of man, we might think no human footstep, except perhaps the hunter's, had ever penetrated that desolate looking place. Yet there was once a habitation in that valley. Peter Wood's house stood where those large stones and (if you search closely you may find a few) those broken bricks lie.

Mr. Wood had built his house in that valley to screen it from the bleak winds, that during winter sweep across the frozen lake; but, by ascending the swell of land, about twenty rods distant, he commanded a fine view of the water and the eastern shore, and had that desideratum of society for a New England farmer—neighbours within sight. Though separated by the lake, they seemed near, when he could see their dwellings. And truly, his eye rested much oftener, and with more satisfaction, on those plain farm-houses, than on the wild wonders of the land, or the softening aspect of the water; thus proving, that neither the taste for natural scenery, or the love of solitude, had been the cause of his selecting that particular spot for his residence. In truth, it was neither; but a taste for fishing and the love of fine trout, for which the lake is famed. I state this with more pride, since the recent opinion of a refined British traveller has pronounced a voyage across the Atlantic to be well repaid by a breakfast on our shad. The ability fully to appreciate good fish is, we see, a mark of having been accustomed to "good society." I presume, therefore, none of my fashionable readers will consider Peter Wood otherwise than as a gentleman. Certain I and many gentlemen would have enjoyed extremely an acquaintance with him and a sail in his boat, when he went forth to fish, with a determination not to return without some good luck. His perfect familiarity with the science of angling was really wonderful, considering he had never heard of Izaak Walton;—but then he was an original thinker, and such do not need to have recourse to the rules of others; they are a law unto themselves.

I have said Peter Wood liked to angle; it was his passion, and he never felt more dignified than when he returned home with a fine mess of trout. But his triumph would have been incomplete, had none but himself known his success. Man was most certainly created a social being, and it is necessary to the enjoyment of prosperity, that there should be participants. We do not need a crowd to make us happy; but friends, or *one*—at least *one*—must smile, or the sensations will lose their perception, the heart its gladness, and the mind its energy.

Peter Wood had one friend—a wife whom he loved, and who was worthy of his affection; and that is saying all that is requisite in her praise. I never think it necessary to describe elaborately the charms and graces of a married woman, if I can say her husband loves her.

Well, Peter loved his wife and his infant child; and when he could prevail on Betsey to take the baby and accompany him to a fishing-place, which was but a little way from their dwelling up the lake, he was happier, I dare say, than ever Bonaparte was with Josephine by his side; for they had no child. And when Peter had a good haul, how delighted he was to hold up the fish for his wife to view; and sometimes he would advance the struggling victim close to his little girl; and then both parents would smile at her fright, with as much "secret pleasure" as did Hector and Andromache, when their boy was "scared with dazzling plume and nodding crest." O, happiness is made up of trifles—it is only the heart that invests them with importance.

One Sabbath afternoon, in the month of September, 18—, Peter Wood and his wife took a walk along the margin of the lake. They had, as usual, their little girl with them; the father thinking, that to walk without her in his arms was really loss of time. There is hardly a more heart-thrilling pleasure enjoyed by mortals, than that which parents feel when seeing their child first begin to "catch knowledge of objects." Byron, in his allusion to that bliss, of which he had been deprived, shows how fully he had sounded the depths of human feeling. Mary Wood was only eleven months old; but, from the circumstance of having been often abroad, as well as from that innate love of freedom in the open air, which every living earthly creature seems to covet, she was in ecstacies with the excursion; and, her father thought, understood all that was said to her on the occasion. And he afterwards observed, "that the little creature then appeared to know so much, he felt fearful she was not long for this world."

The day was calm as sleep; not a cloud had been visible, and the thin white vapour, that was like melted light over all the horizon, seemed but the air resting in equilibrium;—not a breath moved the water or stirred a leaf. The stillness was so deep as almost to be melancholy; as if Nature had sunk to a repose from which she could hardly be awakened.

Our husband and wife sat down beneath the shade of a large fir-tree, and passed the time chiefly in amusing their child. They loved the scene around them, and yet it could hardly be said they relished or understood its peculiar beauties. Certain it is, they had never analyzed the sources of the satisfaction with which they gazed on the bright smooth waters, as contrasted with the broken and brown landscape beyond. Neither did they notice the adorning which the dark evergreen forest received, from being here and there interspersed with trees of a less sombre hue, particularly the white birch;

thus showing how much of beauty is owing to situation and contrast. There is hardly a more ugly native tree in our country, when standing singly and alone, than the white birch. Its thin, leper-like looking trunk, and scanty dingy green foliage, which early in autumn assumes a dirty yellow colour, cause it to be altogether disagreeable to the eye; and then the thought of the detestable fuel it makes—you may about as comfortably burn snow—sends a shivering disgust through the frame, very similar to what we feel on viewing an ugly reptile. But place that same birch amid a forest of firs, where we can just see its tall trunk, like a sunbeam, flashing through the dark foliage, while its leaves blend their softening tints above, and we call it a graceful tree, an ornament to the woods. So it is. And so there is an appropriate place for every thing and every person, a niche where all would appear to advantage. But all do not feel so contented to be happy there, as did honest Peter Wood and his wife. They, good souls, never dreamed but what the landscape appeared to others precisely as it did to them. With the lake came the thought of water and fishing; with the forest, of fuel and hunting; and with that lofty mountain, rivalling Ben Lomond or the Grampian hills in majesty, was connected the idea of gathering whortleberries. And over all was the charm of familiarity—of home—that made it lovely.

Where ignorance is bliss, it really does seem folly to be wise. Who that has a heart would have wished to awaken Peter and his wife to the full consciousness of all the horrors which a cultivated and refined person would have felt in their situation? To live on with no object in view but just to procure enough to eat and drink, and live too in a place where the only advantage possessed was, that they dwelt in safety. This advantage they seemed to enjoy in perfection; for, unless the mountain toppled down headlong, what could occur to disturb them there in a place, bidding defiance, apparently, to that spirit of improvement, which works such astonishing changes in our land, and in whose train follow ambition, envy, covetousness, luxury, as surely as wealth, knowledge and taste.

But the storm was at hand—though not of human passion.

"It grows dark as night—it is sundown, Betsey?" said Peter, suddenly rising up.

She could not tell—but both felt that the darkness or deep shadow increased with uncommon rapidity. They hurried along the shore to the path that led to their dwelling—Peter carrying the child, which had fallen asleep, carefully, for fear of awakening her, and his wife preceding him about ten steps. There was no wind felt, not a breath, and the water lay motionless; but, though calm, it was awful in its tranquillity; for, an "inky hue" was deepening and settling on its surface, and it looked, when a flash of lightning gleamed over it, and the flashes became frequent, more like black marble than water. And several times Peter, who was less agitated than his wife, thought he heard a low, deep sound, like a groan, that seemed to come from the recesses of the lake. When Mrs. Wood reached, through the narrow-wooded track, the top of the eminence that rose, as has been named, east of their dwelling, she stopped, and raised her hands high above her head, as if wildly frightened.

"What is the matter?" called out her husband.

But she did not reply; and when he reached the top, he did not need to repeat his question. Though a strong man, his knees trembled under him. What mortal would not tremble at the sight of the whirlwind approaching, as it were, in an embodied form? Nothing could be more terrible. The cloud that seemed moving towards them, with winged rapidity, was of a singular appearance; as it were, a thick sheet of darkness, black as a pall—the edges of which were tinged with a brassy hue; and in the midst was an appearance, in shape like an inverted pyramid, whirling like the vortex of an eddying gulf, and sending out incessant and vivid flashes of lightning, which only prevented the horizon in the north and east from being dark as midnight.

There are no appearances or events in the natural world which men feel are so certainly connected with Almighty power, as signs in the air. "The heavens shall be rolled together as a scroll," thought Peter; for he had read his Bible (almost the only book he did read), and he trembled, lest the end of the world was at hand. But deep must be the sin, suffering and despair, of that man, who does not feel a sense of safety connected with the ideas of home.

"Home!—let us go home,"—said Peter Wood.

His wife started at the word, and they rushed towards the house as to a refuge. They reached it, and at the entrance Peter laid his little girl, still sleeping, into her mother's arms, in order to secure the doors and windows, as far as he could, to resist the fury of the coming storm. As yet, no gust, nor even a breeze, had been felt; the tempest, wrapped in the wings of the cloud, came on in silence; the moving darkness only giving warning that it was approaching.

Mrs. Wood, agitated and exhausted as she was, could hardly sustain the weight of the infant; and she carried her to a bed, thinking the little creature would sleep easier there than in her arms. The mother laid down her child, covering her with care: and stooped, with the mother's blessing in her heart, to kiss the forehead of her darling. As her lips touched the soft face of her babe—she felt a rush, a crash that shook the building to its foundation—and then seemed to gather up, crumbling, tossing, whirling, scattering all like atoms in its fury—trees, rocks, timber, furniture, were mingled, and driven, and dashed against each other, in the vortex of the cloud, that rose and descended alternately; when rising, it discharged from its centre a shower of shivered limbs of trees, leaves, gravel, and other spoils of its ravage; then sinking, it again swept up, as in revenge, all that lay in its path, tossing the huge rocks, as though they had been marbles, heaving up the foundations of buildings, breaking down, splintering, overturning acres and acres of the forest that lay in its desolating course. There was no thunder accompanied it—no sound but the crash of the destroying, till the tornado entered the lake; and then the tremendous conflict of the wind and water might be known by the hollow roaring that was sent forth. The winds triumphed—the waters, boiling and foaming, were forced upward in the cloud, till the column seemed to touch the sky—laying bare the banks of the lake, as though the secrets of the hidden springs were about to be revealed!

I have not time to follow the track of the tornado after it had passed the lake. A volume might be filled with the awful description—and the sufferings of those who were the victims of its fury, on the western shore; but I must return to that solitary family, who bore the first bursting of the storm.

Neither Peter Wood or his wife were injured; though how they escaped was wonderful. They were both lifted up by the power of the wind, and carried across a field and over fences, amidst the driving and dashing fragments of ruin contained in the cloud; yet they came to the earth without wound. But their Mary, their sweet babe—where was she? The gown of the tender sufferer was found on the borders of the lake, close by the spot where she had been playing during the afternoon—the bedstead on which she lay was found nearly a mile distant in the woods, in an opposite direction from the general track of the wind. But her body was never found. Whether her little form was reduced to atoms by the grinding storm, or thrown by the wind into the lake, or carried into the wilderness, is a secret the last trumpet only can reveal.

The parents looked on the destruction of their dwelling with indifference, when compared with the desolation their hearts felt in the loss of that child. They were surrounded with ruin. A few stones marked the site of their late residence; a broken chair, a bureau without drawers, and a few articles of hollow ware, was all that remained of their property.

Reader, should you ever sail down the Ohio—you may, if you please, see a small yankee-looking house, in the retired nook, a little way from the margin of the river. And then, if you see in a boat, not far from the shore, a square-built, spare-boned, black-bearded man, angling with that deep abstractedness which proves the devotee in his art,—that man is the original of Peter Wood. Should you address him by that name, he might not answer to the cognomen—but what's in a name? He will confirm the truth of my story, except, perhaps, in some trifling particulars respecting himself and wife. And he will describe the tempest as more terrific than I have done. He will tell you that his infant was swept away, and that he never could endure the thought of again casting a line into the water where she might be slumbering; that he could not bear to eat the fish of the lake, for fear they might have been fattening on the flesh of his child—and so he removed to the Ohio.

4

Susan Warner, from *Nobody*

(1882)

Susan Warner (1819–1885) is best known as the author of a runaway best seller, The Wide, Wide World *(1850), but she was a prolific writer. In* Nobody, *Warner revisits a favorite theme: the contrast between poor New England villagers and rich Manhattan socialites. (Warner grew up in a wealthy Manhattan family, but her father's bad business decisions had forced the family onto a farm on an island in the Hudson River—and had relegated Susan and her sister Anna to a life of unremitting literary toil.) Lois Lothrop, the heroine of* Nobody, *lives in a New England village, but has traveled to New York to visit her elegant cousin Mrs. Wishart. Predictably, a rich young man, Tom Caruthers, has fallen in love with her, in spite of her unfashionable religious convictions and her ignorance of French.*

In the chapters excerpted here, Mrs. Wishart has taken Lois to the Isles of Shoals off the coast of New Hampshire. Although Lois has had few opportunities for a genteel education, her natural refinement is expressed through her love of scenery. Lois's passionate love of the beauties of Nature highlights the coarseness and ignorance of the wealthy people around her. Tom Caruthers, for example, indicates that he has had some training in how to talk about scenery, asking Lois to help him to achieve a "sense of the beautiful." But Tom was evidently not listening when he was taught the scenic categories of the "sublime," the "beautiful," and the "picturesque," since he asks Lois a laughably ignorant question about the rocky coast of the Isles of Shoals: "Is it the beautiful, by the way, or is it something else?"

CHAPTER XII. APPLEDORE

It was a very bright, warm August day when Mrs. Wishart and her young companion steamed over from Portsmouth to the Isles of Shoals. It was Lois's first sight of the sea, for the journey from New York had been made by land; and the ocean, however still, was nothing but a most wonderful novelty to her. She wanted nothing, she could well nigh attend to nothing, but the movements and developments of this vast and mysterious Presence of nature. Mrs. Wishart was amused and yet half provoked. There was no talk in Lois; nothing to be got out of her; hardly any attention to be had from her. She sat by the vessel's side and gazed, with a brow of grave awe and eyes of submissive admiration; rapt, absorbed, silent, and evidently glad. Mrs. Wishart was provoked at her, and envied her.

"What *do* you find in the water, Lois?"

"Oh, the wonder of it!"—said the girl with a breath of rapture.

"Wonder? what wonder? I suppose everything is wonderful, if you look at it. What do you see there that seems so very wonderful?"

"I don't know, Mrs. Wishart. It is so great! and it is so beautiful! and it is so awful!"

"Beautiful?" said Mrs. Wishart. "I confess I do not see it. I suppose it is your gain, Lois. Yes, it is awful enough in a storm, but not to-day. The sea is quiet."

Quiet! with those low-rolling, majestic soft billows. The quiet of a lion asleep with his head upon his paws. Lois did not say what she thought.

"And you have never seen the sea-shore yet," Mrs. Wishart went on. "Well, you will have enough of the sea at the Isles. And those are they, I fancy, yonder. Are those the Isles of Shoals?" she asked a passing man of the crew; and was answered with a rough voiced, "Yaw, mum; they be th' oisles."

Lois gazed now at those distant brown spots, as the vessel drew nearer and nearer. Brown spots they remained, and to her surprise *small* brown spots. Nearer and nearer views only forced the conviction deeper. The Isles seemed to be merely some rough rocky projections from old Ocean's bed, too small to have beauty, too rough to have value. Were those the desired Isles of Shoals? Lois felt deep disappointment. Little bits of bare rock in the midst of the sea; nothing more. No trees, she was sure; as the light fell she could even see no green. Why would they not be better relegated to Ocean's domain, from which they were only saved by a few feet of upheaval? why should anybody live there? and still more, why should anybody make a pleasure visit there?

"I suppose the people are all fishermen?" she said to Mrs. Wishart.

"I suppose so. O there is a house of entertainment—a sort of hotel."

"How many people live there?"

"My dear, I don't know. A handful, I should think by the look of the place. What tempts *them*, I don't see."

Nor did Lois. She was greatly disappointed. All her fairy visions were fled. No meadows, no shady banks, no soft green dales; nothing she had ever imagined in connection with country loveliness. Her expectations sank down, collapsed, and vanished for ever.

She shewed nothing of all this. She helped Mrs. Wishart gather her small baggage together and followed her on shore, with her usual quiet thoughtfulness; saw her established in the hotel and assisted her to get things a little in order. But then, when the elder lady lay down to "catch a nap," as she said, before tea, Lois seized her flat hat and fled out of the house.

There was grass around it, and sheep and cows to be seen. Alas, no trees. But there were bushes certainly growing here and there, and Lois had not gone far before she found a flower. With that in her hand she sped on, out of the little grassy vale, upon the rocks that surrounded it, and over them, till she caught sight of the sea. Then she made her way, as she could, over the roughnesses and hindrances of the rocks, till she got near the edge of the island at that place; and sat down a little above where the billows of the Atlantic were rolling in. The wide sea line was before her, with its mysterious and infinite depth of colour; at her feet the waves were coming in and breaking, slow and gently to-day, yet every one seeming to make an invasion of the little rocky domain which defied it and to retire unwillingly, foiled, beaten, and broken, to gather new forces and come on again for a new attack. Lois watched them, fascinated by their persistence, their sluggish power, and yet their ever recurring discomfiture; admired the changing colours and hues of the water, endlessly varying, cool and lovely and delicate, contrasting with the wet washed rocks and the dark line of sea weed lying where high tide had cast it up. The breeze blew in her face, gently, but filled with freshness, life, and pungency of the salt air; sea birds flew past hither and thither, sometimes uttering a cry; there was no sound in earth or heaven but that of the water and the wild birds. And by and by, the silence, and the broad freedom of nature, and the sweet freshness of the life-giving breeze, began to take effect upon the watcher. She drank in the air in deep breaths; she watched with growing enjoyment the play of light and colour which offered such an endless variety; she let slip, softly and insensibly, every thought and consideration which had any sort of care attached to it; her heart grew light, as her lungs took in the salt breath, which had upon her somewhat the effect of champagne. Lois was at no time a very heavy-hearted person; and I lack a similitude which should fitly image the elastic bound her spirits made now. She never stirred from her seat, till it suddenly came into her head to remember that there might be dinner or supper in prospect somewhere. She rose then and made her way back to the hotel, where she found Mrs. Wishart just arousing from her sleep.

"Well, Lois—" said the lady, with the sleep still in her voice,—"where have you been? and what have you got? and what sort of a place have we come to?"

"Look at that, Mrs. Wishart!"

"What's that? A white violet! Violets here, on these rocks?"

"Did you ever see *such* a white violet? Look at the size of it, and the colour of it. And here's pimpernel. And O, Mrs. Wishart, I am so glad we came here that I don't know what to do! It is just delightful. The air is the best air I ever saw."

"Can you *see* it, my dear? Well, I am glad you are pleased. What's that bell for, dinner or supper? I suppose all the meals here are alike. Let us go down and see."

Lois had an excellent appetite.

"This fish is very good, Mrs. Wishart."

"O my dear, it is just fish! You are in a mood to glorify everything. I am envious of you, Lois."

"But it is really capital; it is so fresh. I don't believe you can get such blue fish in New York."

"My dear, it is your good appetite. I wish I was as hungry, for anything, as you are."

"Is it Mrs. Wishart?" asked a lady who sat opposite them at the table. She spoke politely with an accent of hope and expectation. Mrs. Wishart acknowledged the identity.

"I am very happy to meet you. I was afraid I might find absolutely no one here that I knew. I was saying only the other day—three days ago: this is Friday, isn't it? yes; it was last Tuesday. I was saying to my sister after our early dinner—we always have early dinner at home, and it comes quite natural here—we were sitting together after dinner, and talking about my coming. I have been meaning to come ever since three years ago; wanting to make this trip, and never could get away, until this summer things opened out to let me. I was saying to Lottie, I was afraid I should find nobody here that I could speak to; and when I saw you, I said to myself, Can that be Mrs. Wishart?—I am so very glad. You have just come?"

"To-day,"—Mrs. Wishart assented.

"Came by water?"

"From Portsmouth."

"Yes—ha, ha!" said the affable lady. "Of course. You could not well help it. But from New York?"

"By railway. I had occasion to come by land."

"I prefer it always. In a steamer you never know what will happen to you. If it's good weather, you may have a pleasant time; but you never can tell. I took the steamer once to go to Boston—I mean, to Stonington, you know; and the boat was so loaded with freight of some sort or other that she was as low down in the water as she could be and be safe; and I didn't think she was safe. And we went *so* slowly! and then we had a storm, a regular thunderstorm and squall, and the rain poured in torrents, and the Sound was rough, and people were sick, and I was very glad and thankful when we got to Stonington. I thought it would never be for pleasure that I would take a boat again."

"The Fall River boats are the best."

"I dare say they are, but I hope to be allowed to keep clear of them all. You had a pleasant morning for the trip over from Portsmouth."

"Very pleasant."

"It is such a gain to have the sea quiet! It roars and beats here enough in the best of times. I am sure I hope there will not a storm come while we are here; for I should think it must be dreadfully dreary. It's all sea here, you know."

"I should like to see what a storm here is like," Lois remarked.

"O don't wish that!" cried the lady, "or your wish may bring it. Don't think me a heathen," she added laughing; "but I have known such queer things. I must tell you—"

"You never knew a wish bring fair weather?" said Lois smiling, as the lady stopped for a mouthful of omelet.

"O no, not fair weather; I am sure, if it did, we should have fair weather a great deal more than we do. But I was speaking of a storm, and I must tell you what I have seen.—These fish are very deliciously cooked!"

"They understand fish, I suppose, here," said Lois.

"We were going down the bay, to escort some friends who were going to Europe. There was my cousin Llewellyn and his wife, and her sister, and one or two others in the party; and Lottie and I went to see them off. I always think it's rather a foolish thing to do, for why shouldn't one say good bye at the water's edge, when they go on board, instead of making a journey of miles out to sea to say it there?—but this time Lottie wanted to go. She had never seen the ocean, except from the land; and you know that is very different; so we went. Lottie always likes to see all she can, and is never satisfied till she has got to the bottom of everything—"

"She would be satisfied with something less than that in this case?" said Lois.

"Hey? She was satisfied," said the lady, not apparently catching Lois's meaning; "she was more delighted with the sea than I was; for though it was quiet, they said, there was unquietness enough to make a good deal of motion; the vessel went sailing up and down a succession of small rolling hills, and I began to think there was nothing steady *in*side of me, any more than *out*side. I never can bear to be rocked, in any shape or form."

"You must have been a troublesome baby," said Lois.

"I don't know how that was; naturally I have forgotten; but since I have been old enough to think for myself I never could bear rocking chairs. I like an easy chair—as easy as you please—but I want it to stand firm upon its four legs. So I did not enjoy the water quite as well as my sister did. But she grew enthusiastic; she wished she was going all the way over, and I told her she would have to drop *me* at some wayside station—"

"Where?" said Lois, as the lady stopped to carry her coffee cup to her lips. He question seemed not to have been heard.

"Lottie wished she could see the ocean in a mood not quite so quiet; she wished for a storm; she said she wished a little storm would get up before we got home, that she might see how the waves looked. I begged and prayed her not to say so, for our wishes often fulfil themselves. Isn't it extraordinary how they do? Haven't you often observed it, Mrs. Wishart?"

"In cases where wishes could take effect," returned that lady. "In the case of the elements, I do not see how they could do that."

"But I don't know how it is," said the other; "I have observed it so often."

"You call me by name," Mrs. Wishart went on rather hastily; "and I have been trying in vain to recall yours. If I had met you anywhere else, of course I should be at no loss; but at the Isles of Shoals one expects to see nobody, and one is surprised out of one's memory."

"I am never surprised out of my memory," said the other chuckling. "I am poor enough in all other ways, I am sure, but my memory is good. I can tell you where I first saw you. You were at the

Catskill House, with a large party; my brother-in-law, Dr. Salisbury, was there, and he had the pleasure of knowing you. It was two years ago."

"I recollect being at the Catskill House very well," said Mrs. Wishart, "and of course it was there I became acquainted with you; but you must excuse me, at the Isles of Shoals, for forgetting all my connections with the rest of the world."

"O I am sure you are very excusable," said Dr. Salisbury's sister-in-law. "I am delighted to meet you again. I think one is particularly glad of a friend's face where one had not expected to see it; and I really expected nothing at the Isles of Shoals—but sea air."

"You came for sea air?"

"Yes, to get it pure. To be sure, Coney Island beach is not far off— for we live in Brooklyn; but I wanted the sea air wholly sea air—quite unmixed; and at Coney Island, somehow New York is so near, I couldn't fancy it would be the same thing. I don't want to smell the smoke of it. And I was curious about this place too; and I have so little opportunity for travelling, I thought it was a pity now when I *had* the opportunity, not to take the utmost advantage of it. They laughed at me at home, but I said no, I was going to the Isles of Shoals or nowhere. And now I am very glad I came."—

"Lois," Mrs. Wishart said when they went back to their own room, "I don't know that woman from Adam. I have not the least recollection of ever seeing her. I know Dr. Salisbury—and he might be anybody's brother-in-law. I wonder if she will keep that seat opposite us? Because she is worse than a smoky chimney!"

"O no, not that," said Lois. "She amuses me."

"Everything amuses you, you happy creature! You look as if the fairies that wait upon young girls had made you their special care. Did you ever read the 'Rape of the Lock'?"

"I have never read anything"—Lois answered, a little soberly.

"Never mind; you have so much the more pleasure before you. But the 'Rape of the Lock'—in that story there is a young lady, a famous beauty, whose dressing-table is attended by sprites or fairies. One of them colours her lips; another hides in the folds of her gown; another tucks himself away in a curl of her hair.—You make me think of that young lady."

CHAPTER XIV. WATCHED

"Have I found you, Miss Lothrop?"

Looking over her shoulder, Lois saw the handsome features of Mr. Caruthers, wearing a smile of most undoubted satisfaction. And to the scorn of all her previous considerations, she was conscious of a flush of pleasure in her own mind. This was not suffered to appear.

"I thought I was where nobody could find me," she answered.

"Do you think there is such a place in the whole world?" said Tom gallantly. Meanwhile he scrambled over some inconvenient rocks to a place by her side. "I am very glad to find you, Miss Lothrop, both ways,—first at Appledore, and then here."

To this compliment Lois made no reply.

"What has driven you to this little out-of-the-way nook?"

"You mean Appledore?"

"No, no! this very uncomfortable situation among the rocks here? What drove you to it?"

"You think there is no attraction?"

"I don't see what attraction there is here for *you.*"

"Then you should not have come to Appledore."

"Why not?"

"There is nothing here for you."

"Ah, but! What is there for you? Do you find anything here to like now, really?"

"I have been down in this 'uncomfortable place' ever since near five o'clock—except while we were at breakfast."

"What for?"

"What for?" said Lois laughing. "If you ask, it is no use to tell you, Mr. Caruthers."

"Ah, be generous!" said Tom. "I'm a stupid fellow, I know; but do try and help me a little to a sense of the beautiful. *Is* it the beautiful, by the way, or is it something else?"

Lois's laugh rang softly out again. She was a country girl, it is true; but her laugh was as sweet to hear as the ripple of the waters among the stones. The laugh of anybody tells very much of what he is, making revelations undreampt of often by the laugher. A harsh croak does not come from a mind at peace, nor an empty clangour from a heart full of sensitive happiness; nor a coarse laugh from a person of refined sensibilities, nor a hard laugh from a tender spirit. Moreover, people cannot dissemble successfully in laughing; the truth comes out in a startling manner. Lois's laugh was sweet and musical; it was a pleasure to hear. And Tom's eyes said so.

"I always knew I was a stupid fellow," he said; "but I never felt myself so stupid as to-day! What is it, Miss Lothrop?"

"What is what, Mr. Caruthers?—I beg your pardon."

"What is it you find in this queer place?"

"I am afraid it is waste trouble to tell you."

"Good morning!" cried a cheery voice here from below them; and looking towards the water they saw Mr. Lenox, making his way as best he could over slippery seaweed and wet rocks.

"Hollo, George!" cried Tom in a different tone—"What are you doing there?"

"Trying to keep out of the water, don't you see?"

"To an ordinary mind that object would seem more likely to be attained if you kept further away from it."

"May I come up where you are?"

"Certainly!" said Lois. "But take care how you do it."

A little scrambling and the help of Tom's hand accomplished the feat; and the new comer looked about him with much content.

"You came the other way," he said. "I see. I shall know how next time. What a delightful post, Miss Lothrop!"

"I have been trying to find what she came here for; and she won't tell me" said Tom.

"You know what *you* came here for," said his friend. "Why cannot you credit other people with as much curiosity as you have yourself?"

"I credit them with more," said Tom. "But curiosity on Appledore will find itself baffled, I should say."

"Depends on what curiosity is after," said Lenox. "Tell him, Miss Lothrop; he will not be any the wiser."

"Then why should I tell him?" said Lois.

"Perhaps I shall!"

Lois's laugh came again.

"Seriously. If any one were to ask me, not only what we but what anybody should come to this place for, I should be unprepared with an answer. I am forcibly reminded of an old gentleman who went up Mount Washington on one occasion when I also went up. It came on to rain—a sudden summer gust and downpour; hiding the very mountain itself from our eyes; hiding the path, hiding the members of the party from each other. We were descending the mountain by that time, and it was ticklish work for a nervous person; every one was committed to his own sweet guidance; and as I went blindly stumbling along, I came every now and then upon the old gentleman, also stumbling along, on his donkey. And whenever I was near enough to him I could hear him dismally soliloquizing, 'Why am I here!'—in a tone of mingled disgust and self-reproach which was in the highest degree comical."

"So that is your state of mind now, is it?" said Tom.

"Not quite yet, but I feel it is going to be. Unless Miss Lothrop can teach me something."

"There are some things that cannot be taught," said Lois.

"And people—hey? But I am not one of those, Miss Lothrop."

He looked at her with such a face of demure innocence that Lois could not keep her gravity.

"Now Tom *is*," Lenox went on. "You cannot teach him anything, Miss Lothrop. It would be lost labour."

"I am not so stupid as you think," said Tom.

"He's not stupid,—he's obstinate," Lenox went on, addressing himself to Lois. "He takes a thing in his head. Now that sounds intelligent; but it isn't, or *he* isn't; for when you try, you can't get it out of his head again. So he took it into his head to come to the Isles of Shoals, and hither he has dragged his mother and his sister, and hither by consequence he has dragged me. Now I ask you, as one who can tell—what have we all come here for?"

Half quizzically, half inquisitively, the young man put the question, lounging on the rocks and looking up into Lois's face. Tom grew impatient. But Lois was too humble and simple-minded to fall into the snare laid for her. I think she had a half discernment of a hidden intent under Mr. Lenox's words; nevertheless in the simple dignity of truth she disregarded it, and did not even blush, either with consciousness or awkwardness. She was a little amused.

"I suppose experience will have to be your teacher, as it is other people's."

"I have heard so; I never *saw* anybody who had learned much that way."

"Come, George, that's ridiculous. Learning by experience is proverbial," said Tom.

"I know!—but it's a delusion nevertheless. You sprain your ankle among these stones, for instance. Well—you won't put your foot in that particular hole again; but you will in another. That's the way you do, Tom. But to return—Miss Lothrop, what has experience done for you in the Isles of Shoals?"

"I have not had much yet."

"Does it pay, to come here?"

"I think it does."

"How came anybody to think of coming here at first? that is what I should like to know. I never saw a more uncompromising bit of barrenness. Is there no desolation anywhere else, that men should come to the Isles of Shoals?"

"There was quite a large settlement here once," said Lois.

"Indeed! When?"

"Before the war of the revolution. There were hundreds of people; six hundred, somebody told me."

"What became of them?"

"Well," said Lois smiling, "as that is more than a hundred years ago, I suppose they all died."

"And their descendants?—"

"Living on the mainland, most of them. When the war came, they could not protect themselves against the English."

"Fancy, Tom," said Lenox. "People liked it so well on these rocks that it took ships of war to drive them away!"

"The people that live here now are just as fond of them, I am told."

"What earthly or heavenly inducement?—"

"Yes, I might have said so too, the first hour of my being here, or the first day. The second, I began to understand it."

"Do make me understand it!"

"If you will come here at five o'clock to-morrow, Mr. Lenox—in the morning, I mean,—and will watch the wonderful sunrise, the waking up of land and sea; if you will stay here then patiently till ten o'clock, and see the changes and the colours on everything—let the sea and the sky speak to you, as they will; then they will tell you—all you can understand!"

"All I can understand. H'm! May I go home for breakfast?"

"Perhaps you must; but you will wish you need not."

"Will *you* be here?"

"No," said Lois. "I will be somewhere else."

"But I couldn't stand such a long talk with myself as that," said the young man.

"It was a talk with Nature I recommended to you."

"All the same. Nature says queer things, if you let her alone."

"Best listen to them, then."

"Why?"

"She tells you the truth."

"Do you like the truth?"

"Certainly. Of course. Do not you?"

"*Always?*"

"Yes, always. Do not you?"

"It's fearfully awkward!" said the young man.

"Yes, isn't it?" Tom echoed.

"Do you like falsehood, Mr. Lenox?"

"I dare not say what I like—in this presence. Miss Lothrop, I am very much afraid you are a Puritan."

"What is a Puritan?" asked Lois simply.

"He doesn't know!" said Tom. "You needn't ask him."

"I will ask you then, for I do not know. What does he mean by it?"

"He doesn't know that," said Lenox laughing. "I will tell you, Miss Lothrop—if I can. A Puritan is a person so much better than the ordinary run of mortals that she is not afraid to let Nature and

Solitude speak to her—dares to look roses in the face, in fact;—has no charity for the crooked ways of the world or for the people entangled in them; a person who can bear truth and has no need of falsehood, and who is thereby lifted above the multitudes of this world's population, and stands as it were alone."

"I'll report that speech to Julia," said Tom laughing.

"But that is not what a 'Puritan' generally means, is it?" said Lois. They both laughed now at the quaint simplicity with which this was spoken.

"That is what it *is*," Tom answered.

"I do not think the term is complimentary," Lois went on, shaking her head; "however Mr. Lenox's explanation may be. Isn't it ten o'clock?"

"Near eleven."

"Then I must go in."

The two gentlemen accompanied her, making themselves very pleasant by the way. Lenox asked her about flowers; and Tom, who was something of a naturalist, told her about mosses and lichens, more than she knew; and the walk was too short for Lois. But on reaching the hotel she went straight to her own room and staid there. So also after dinner, which of course brought her to the company, she went back to her solitude and her work. She must write home, she said. Yet writing was not Lois's sole reason for shutting herself up.

She would keep herself out of the way, she reasoned. Probably this company of city people with city tastes would not stay long at Appledore; while they were there she had better be seen as little as possible. For she felt that the sight of Tom Caruthers' handsome face had been a pleasure; and she felt, and what woman does not? that there is a certain very sweet charm in being liked, independently of the question how much you like in return. And Lois knew, though she hardly in her modesty acknowledged it to herself, that Mr. Caruthers liked her. Eyes and smiles and manner shewed it; she could not mistake it; nay, engaged man though he was, Mr. Lenox liked her too. She did not quite understand him or his manner; with the keen intuition of a true woman she felt vaguely what she did not clearly discern, and was not sure of the colour of his liking, as she was sure of Tom's. Tom's—it might not be deep, but it was true, and it was pleasant; and Lois remembered her promise to her grandmother. She even, when her letter was done, took out her Bible and opened it at that well known place in 2nd Corinthians; 'Be not unequally yoked together with unbelievers'—and she looked hard at the familiar words. Then, said Lois to herself, it is best to keep at a distance from temptation. For these people were unbelievers. They could not understand one word of Christian hope or joy, if she spoke them. What had she and they in common?

Yet Lois drew rather a long breath once or twice in the course of her meditations. These "unbelievers" were so pleasant. Yes, it was an undoubted fact; they were pleasant people to be with and to talk to. They might not think with her, or comprehend her even, in the great questions of life and duty; in the lesser matters of every day experience they were well posted. They understood the world and the things in the world, and the men; and they were skilled and deft and graceful in the arts of society. Lois knew no young men,—nor old, for that matter,—who were, as gentlemen, as social companions, to be compared with these and others their associates in graces of person and manner, and interest of conversation. She went over again and again in memory the interview and the talk of that morning; and not without a secret thrill of gratification, although also not without a vague half perception of something in Mr. Lenox's manner that she could not quite read and did not quite trust. What did he mean? He was Miss Caruthers' property; how came he to busy himself at all with her own insignificant self? Lois was too innocent to guess; at the same time too finely gifted as a woman to be entirely hoodwinked. She rose at last with a third little sigh, as she concluded that her best way was to keep as well away as she could from this pleasant companionship.

But she could not stay in-doors. For once in her life she was at Appledore; she must not miss her chance. The afternoon was half gone; the house all still; probably everybody was in his room and she could slip out safely. She went down on soft feet; she found nobody on the piazza, not a creature in sight; she was glad; and yet, she would not have been sorry to see Tom Caruthers' genial face, which was always so very genial towards her. Inconsistent!—but who is not inconsistent? Lois thought herself free, and had half descended the steps from the verandah, when she heard a voice and her own name. She paused and looked round.

"Miss Lothrop!—are you going for a walk? may I come with you?"—and therewith emerged the form of Miss Julia from the house. "Are you going for a walk? will you let me go along?"

"Certainly," said Lois.

"I am regularly cast away here," said the young lady joining her. "I don't know what to do with myself. *Is* there anything to do or to see in this place?"

"I think so. Plenty."

"Then do shew me what you have found. Where are you going?"

"I am going down to the shore somewhere. I have only begun to find things yet; but I never in my life saw a place where there was so much to find."

"What, pray? I cannot imagine. I see a little wild bit of ground, and that is all I see; except the sea beating on the rocks. It is the forlornest place of amusement I ever heard of in my life!"

"Are you fond of flowers, Miss Caruthers?"

"Flowers? No, not very. O I like them to dress a dinner table, or to make rooms look pretty, of course; but I am not what you call 'fond' of them. That means, loving to dig in the dirt, don't it?"

Lois presently stooped and gathered a flower or two.

"Did you ever see such lovely white violets?" she said; "and is not that eyebright delicate, with its edging of colour? There are quantities of flowers here. And have you noticed how deep and rich the colours are? No, you have not been here long enough perhaps; but they are finer than any I ever saw of their kinds."

"What do you find down at the shore?" said Miss Caruthers, looking very disparagingly at the slight beauties in Lois's fingers. "There are no flowers there, I suppose?"

"I can hardly get away from the shore, every time I go to it," said Lois. "O I have only begun to explore yet. Over on that end of Appledore there are the old remains of a village, where the people used to live, once upon a time. I want to go and see that, but I haven't got there yet. Now take care of your footing, Miss Caruthers—"

They descended the rocks to one of the small coves of the island. Out of sight now of all save rocks and sea and the tiny bottom of the cove filled with mud and sand. Even the low bushes which grow so thick on Appledore were out of sight, huckleberry and bayberry and others; the wildness and solitude of the spot were perfect. Miss Caruthers found a dry seat on a rock. Lois began to look carefully about in the mud and sand.

"What are you looking for?" her companion asked somewhat scornfully.

"Anything I can find!"

"What *can* you find in that mud?"

"*This* is gravel; where I am looking now."

"Well what is in the gravel?"

"I don't know," said Lois, in the dreamy tone of rapt enjoyment. "I don't know yet. Plenty of broken shells."

"Broken shells!" ejaculated the other. "Are you collecting broken shells?"

"Look,"—said Lois coming to her and displaying her palm full of sea treasures. "See the colours of those bits of shell—that's a bit of a mussel; and that is a piece of a snail shell, I think; and aren't those little stones lovely?"

"That is because they are wet!" said the other in disgust. "They will be nothing when they are dry."

Lois laughed and went back to her search; and Miss Julia waited awhile with impatience for some change in the programme.

"Do you enjoy this, Miss Lothrop?"

"Very much! More than I can in any way tell you!" cried Lois, stopping and turning to look at her questioner. Her face answered for her; it was all flushed and bright with delight and the spirit of discovery; a pretty creature indeed she looked as she stood there on the wet gravel of the cove; but her face lost brightness for a moment, as Lois discerned Tom's head above the herbs and grasses that bordered the bank above the cove. Julia saw the change, and then the cause of it.

"Tom!" said she.—"What brought you here?"

"What brought you, I suppose," said Mr. Tom, springing down the bank. "Miss Lothrop, what can you be doing?" Passing his sister he went to the other girl's side. And now there were *two* searching and peering into the mud and gravel which the tide had left wet and bare; and Miss Caruthers, sitting on a rock a little above them, looked on; much marvelling at the follies men will be guilty of when a pretty face draws them on.

"Tom—Tom!—what do you expect to find?" she cried after awhile. But Tom was too busy to heed her. And then appeared Mr. Lenox upon the scene.

"You too!" said Miss Caruthers. "Now you have only to go down into the mud like the others and complete the situation. Look at Tom! Poking about to see if he can find a whole snail shell in the wet stuff there. Look at him! George, a brother is the most vexatious thing to take care of in the world. Look at Tom!"

Mr. Lenox did, with an amused expression of feature.

"Bad job, Julia—" he said.

"It is in one way, but it isn't in another, for I am not going to be baffled. He shall not make a fool of himself with that girl."

"*She* isn't a fool."

"What then?" said Julia sharply.

"Nothing. I was only thinking of the materials upon which your judgment is made up."

"Materials!" echoed Julia. "Yours is made up upon a nice complexion. That bewilders all men's faculties. Do *you* think she is very pretty, George?"

Mr. Lenox had no time to answer, for Lois, and of course Tom, at this moment left the cove bottom and came towards them. Lois was beaming, like a child, with such bright, pure pleasure; and coming up, shewed upon her open palm a very delicate little white shell, not a snail shell by any means. "I have found that!" she proclaimed.

"What is that?" said Julia disdainfully, though not with rudeness.

"You see. Isn't it beautiful? And isn't it wonderful that it should not be broken? If you think of the power of the waves here, that have beat to pieces almost everything—rolled and ground and crushed everything that would break—and this delicate little thing has lived through it."

"There is a power of life in some delicate things," said Tom.

"Power of fiddlestick!" said his sister. "Miss Lothrop, I think this place is a terrible desert!"

"Then we will not stay here any longer," said Lois. "I am very fond of these little coves."

"No, no, I mean Appledore generally. It is the stupidest place I ever was in my life. There is nothing here."

Lois looked at the lady with an expression of wondering compassion.

"Your experience does not agree with that of Miss Caruthers?" said Lenox.

"No," said Lois. "Let us take her to the place where you found me this morning; maybe she would like that."

"We must go, I suppose," groaned Julia, as Mr. Lenox helped her up over the rocks after the lighter-footed couple that preceded them. "George, I believe you are in the way."

"Thanks!" said the young man laughing. "But you will excuse me for continuing to be in the way?"

"I don't know—you see, it just sets Tom free to attend to her. Look at him—picking those purple irises—as if iris did not grow anywhere else! And now elderberry blossoms! And he will give her lessons in botany, I shouldn't wonder. O Tom's a goose!"

"That disease is helpless," said Lenox laughing again.

"But George, it is madness!"

Mr. Lenox's laugh rang out heartily at this. His sovereign mistress was not altogether pleased.

"I do certainly consider—and so do you,—I do certainly consider unequal marriages to be a great misfortune to all concerned."

"Certainly—inequalities that cannot be made up. For instance, too tall and too short do not match well together. Or for the lady to be rich and the man to be poor; that is perilous."

"Nonsense, George! don't be ridiculous! Height is nothing, and money is nothing; but family—and breeding—and habits—"

"What is her family?" asked Mr. Lenox, pursing up his lips as if for a whistle.

"No family at all. Just country people, living at Shampuashuh."

"Don't you know, the English middle class is the finest in the world?"

"No! no better than ours."

"My dear, we have no middle class."

"But what about the English middle class? why do you bring it up?"

"It owes its great qualities to its having the mixed blood of the higher and the lower."

"Ridiculous! What is that to us, if we have no middle class? But don't you *see*, George, what an unhappy thing it would be for Tom to marry this girl?"

Mr. Lenox whistled slightly, smiled, and pulled a purple iris blossom from a tuft growing in a little spot of wet ground. He offered it to his disturbed companion.

"There is a country flower for you—" he observed.

But Miss Caruthers flung the flower impatiently away, and hastened her steps to catch up with her brother and Lois who made better speed than she. Mr. Lenox picked up the iris and followed, smiling again to himself.

They found Lois seated in her old place, where the gentlemen had seen her in the morning. She rose at once to give the seat to Miss Caruthers, and herself took a less convenient one. It was almost a new scene to Lois, that lay before them now. The lights were from a different quarter; the colours those of the sinking day; the sea, from some inexplicable reason, was rolling higher than it had done six hours ago, and dashed on the rocks and on the reef in beautiful breakers, sending up now and then a tall jet of foam or a shower of spray. The hazy mainland shore line was very indistinct under the bright sky and lowering sun; while every bit of west-looking rock, and every sail, and every combing billow was touched with warm hues or gilded with a sharp reflection. The air was like the air nowhere but at the Isles of Shoals; with the sea's salt strength and freshness, and at times a waft of perfumes from the land side. Lois drank it with an inexpressible sense of exhilaration; while her eye went joyously roving from the lovely light on a sail, to the dancing foam of the breakers, to the colours of driftwood or seaweed or moss left wet and bare on the rocks, to the line of the distant ocean, or the soft vapoury racks of clouds floating over from the west. She well nigh forgot her companions altogether; who however were less absorbed. Yet for a while they all sat silent, looking partly at Lois, partly at each other, partly no doubt at the leaping spray from the broken waves on the reef. There was only the delicious sound of the splash and gurgle of waters—the scream of a gull—the breath of the air—the chirrup of a few insects; all was wild stillness and freshness and pureness, except only that little group of four human beings. And then, the puzzled vexation and perplexity in Tom's face, and the impatient disgust in the face of his sister, were too much for Mr. Lenox's sense of the humorous; and the silence was broken by a hearty burst of laughter, which naturally brought all eyes to himself.

"Pardon!" said the young gentleman. "The delight in your face, Julia, was irresistible."

"Delight!" she echoed. "Miss Lothrop, do you find something here in which you take pleasure?"

Lois looked round. "Yes," she said simply. "I find something everywhere to take pleasure in."

"Even at Shampuashuh?"

"At Shampuashuh of course. That is my home."

"But I never take pleasure in anything at home. It is all such an old story. Every day is just like any other day, and I know beforehand exactly how everything will be; and one dress is like another, and one party is like another. I must go away from home to get any real pleasure."

Lois wondered if she succeeded.

"That's a nice look-out for you, George," Caruthers remarked.

"I shall know how to make home so agreeable that she will not want to wander any more," said the other.

"That is what the women do for the men, down our way," said Lois smiling. She began to feel a little mischief stirring.

"What sort of pleasures do you find, or make, at home, Miss Lothrop?" Julia went on. "You are very quiet, are you not?"

"There is always one's work," said Lois lightly. She knew it would be in vain to tell her questioner the instances that came up in her memory; the first dish of ripe strawberries brought in to surprise her grandmother; the new potatoes uncommonly early; the fine yield of her raspberry bushes; the wonderful beauty of the early mornings in her garden; the rarer, sweeter beauty of the Bible reading and talk with old Mrs. Armadale; the triumphant afternoons on the shore, from which she and her sisters came back with great baskets of long clams; and countless other visions of home comfort and home peace, things accomplished and the fruit of them enjoyed. Miss Caruthers could not understand all this; so Lois answered simply,

"There is always one's work."

"Work! I hate work," cried the other woman. "What do you call work?"

"Everything that is to be done," said Lois. "Everything, except what we do for mere pleasure. We keep no servant; my sisters and I do all that there is to do, in doors and out."

"*Out* of doors!" cried Miss Caruthers. "What do you mean? You cannot do the farming?"

"No," said Lois smiling merrily; "no; not the farming. That is done by men. But the gardening I do."

"Not seriously?"

"Very seriously. If you will come and see us, I will give you some new potatoes of my planting. I am rather proud of them. I was just thinking of them."

"Planting potatoes!" repeated the other lady, not too politely. "Then *that* is the reason why you find it a pleasure to sit here and see those waves beat."

The logical concatenation of this speech was not so apparent but that it touched all the risible nerves of the party; and Miss Caruthers could not understand why all three laughed so heartily.

"What did you expect when you came here?" asked Lois, still sparkling with fun.

"Just what I found!" returned the other rather grumbly.

5

Charles Dudley Warner, from *Their Pilgrimage*

(1886)

Charles Dudley Warner (1829–1900) wrote "Their Pilgrimage" for serial publication in Harper's New Monthly Magazine. *The plot is thin: a young man of elite background falls in love with a Midwestern woman whose parents are rich, but not cultivated. She discovers that his relatives (particularly a cousin named "Mrs. Bartlett-Glow") would disapprove of a match with her, so she flees his courtship, moving from one summer resort to another, up and down the eastern United States. His pursuit of her affords Charles Dudley Warner a convenient opportunity to describe the attractions of all those resorts, and the social classes and fashions to which they cater. In this excerpt, near the end of "their pilgrimage" in late summer, Stanhope King pursues Irene Benson into the White Mountains, the premier resort region of New England, at the most fashionable time of the year.*

Charles Dudley Warner's serial came out only a few years after Susan Warner's Nobody, *but he was much better attuned to the shifting fashions of the Gilded Age. (In fact, he wrote the book on it: Warner's best-known work was another novel,* The Gilded Age, *which he co-authored with Mark Twain.) Quotations from Byron and passionate love of scenery are clearly no longer in style in "Their Pilgrimage." In this selection, for example, Stanhope King recommends the Crawford House to his friends: "a delightful place to stay in a region full of associations, Willey House, avalanche, and all that"—effectively summing up with "and all that" his light-hearted dismissal of the serious concerns of earlier tourists.*

CHAPTER XVII

The White Mountains are as high as ever, as fine in sharp outline against the sky, as savage, as tawny; no other mountains in the world of their height so well keep, on acquaintance, the respect of mankind. There is a quality of refinement in their granite robustness; their desolate, bare heights and sky-scraping ridges are rosy in the dawn and violet at sunset, and their profound green gulfs are still mysterious. Powerful as man is, and pushing, he cannot wholly vulgarize them. He can reduce the valleys and the show "freaks" of nature to his own moral level, but the vast bulks and the summits remain for the most part haughty and pure.

Yet undeniably something of the romance of adventure in a visit to the White Hills is wanting, now that the railways penetrate every valley, and all the physical obstacles of the journey are removed. One can never again feel the thrill that he experienced when, after a weary all-day jolting in the stage-coach, or plodding hour after hour on foot, he suddenly came in view of a majestic granite peak. Never again by the new rail can he have the sensation that he enjoyed in the ascent of Mount Washington by the old bridlepath from Crawford's, when, climbing out of the woods and advancing upon that marvellous backbone of rock, the whole world opened upon his awed vision, and the pyramid of the summit stood up in majesty against the sky. Nothing, indeed, is valuable that is easily obtained. This modern experiment of putting us through the world—the world of literature, experience, and travel—at excursion rates is of doubtful expediency.

I cannot but think that the White Mountains are cheapened a little by the facilities of travel and the multiplication of excellent places of entertainment. If scenery were a sentient thing, it might feel indignant at being vulgarly stared at, overrun and trampled on, by a horde of tourists who chiefly value luxurious hotels and easy conveyance. It would be mortified to hear the talk of the excursionists, which is more about the quality of the tables and the beds, and the rapidity with which the "whole thing can be done," than about the beauty and the sublimity of nature. The mountain, however, was made for man, and not man for the mountain; and if the majority of travellers only get out of these hills what they are capable of receiving, it may be some satisfaction to the hills that they still reserve their glories for the eyes that can appreciate them. Perhaps nature is not sensitive about being run after for its freaks and eccentricities. If it were, we could account for the catastrophe, a few years ago, in the Franconia Notch flume. Everybody went there to see a bowlder which hung suspended over the stream in the narrow cañon. This curiosity attracted annually thousands of people, who apparently cared more for this toy than for anything else in the region. And one day, as if tired of this misdirected adoration, nature organized a dam on the site of Mount Lafayette, filled it with water, and then suddenly let loose a flood which tore open the cañon, carried the bowlder away, and spread ruin far and wide. It said as plainly as possible, You must look at me, and not at my trivial accidents. But man is an ingenious creature, and nature is no match for him. He now goes, in increasing number, to see where the bowlder once hung, and spends his time in hunting for it in the acres of wreck and débris. And in order to satisfy reasonable human curiosity, the proprietors of the flume have been obliged to select a bowlder and label it as the one that was formerly the shrine of pilgrimage.

In his college days King had more than once tramped all over this region, knapsack on back, lodging at chance farmhouses and second-class hotels, living on viands that would kill any but a robust climber, and enjoying the life with a keen zest only felt by those who are abroad at all hours, and enabled to surprise Nature in all her varied moods. It is the chance encounters that are most satisfactory; Nature is apt to be whimsical to him who approaches her of set purpose at fixed hours. He remembered also the jolting stage-coaches, the scramble for places, the exhilaration of the drive, the excitement of the arrival at the hotels, the sociability engendered by this juxtaposition and jostle of travel. It was therefore with a sense of personal injury that, when he reached Bethlehem Junction, he found a railway to the Profile House, and another to Bethlehem. In the interval of waiting for his train he visited Bethlehem Street, with its mile of caravansaries, big boarding-houses, shops, and city veneer, and although he was delighted, as an American, with the "improvements" and with the air of refinement, he felt that if he wanted retirement and rural life, he might as well be with the hordes in the depths of the Adirondack wilderness. But in his impatience to reach his destination he was not sorry to avail himself of the railway to the Profile House. And he admired the ingenuity which had carried this road through nine miles of shabby firs and balsams, in a way absolutely devoid of interest, in order to heighten the effect of the surprise at the end in the sudden arrival at the Franconia Notch. From whichever way this vast, white hotel establishment is approached, it is always a surprise. Midway between Echo Lake and Profile Lake, standing in the very jaws of the Notch, overhung on the one side of Cannon Mountain and on the other by a bold spur of Lafayette, it makes a contrast between the elegance and order of civilization and the untouched ruggedness and sublimity of nature scarcely anywhere else to be seen.

The hotel was still full, and when King entered the great lobby and office in the evening a very animated scene met his eye. A big fire of logs was blazing in the ample chimney-place; groups were seated about at ease, chatting, reading, smoking; couples promenaded up and down; and from the distant parlor, through the long passage, came the sound of the band. It was easy to see at a glance that the place had a distinct character, freedom from conventionality, and an air of reposeful enjoyment. A large proportion of the assembly being residents for the summer, there was so much of the family content that the transient tourists could little disturb it by the introduction of their element of worry and haste.

King found here many acquaintances, for fashion follows a certain routine, and there is a hidden law by which the White Mountains break the transition from the sea-coast to Lenox. He was therefore not surprised to be greeted by Mrs. Cortlandt, who had arrived the day before with her usual train.

"At the end of the season," she said, "and alone?"

"I expect to meet friends here."

"So did I; but they have gone, or some of them have."

"But mine are coming to-morrow. Who has gone?"

"Mrs. Pendragon and the Bensons. But I didn't suppose I could tell you any news about the Bensons."

"I have been out of the way of the newspapers lately. Did you happen to hear where they have gone?"

"Somewhere around the mountains. You need not look so indifferent; they are coming back here again. They are doing what I must do; and I wish you would tell me what to see. I have studied the guide-books till my mind is a blank. Where shall I go?"

"That depends. If you simply want to enjoy yourselves, stay at this hotel—there is no better place—sit on the piazza, look at the mountains, and watch the world as it comes round. If you want the best panoramic view of the mountains, the Washington and Lafayette House. If you are after the best single limited view in the mountains, drive up to the top of Mount Willard, near the Crawford House—a delightful place to stay in a region full of associations, Willey House, avalanche, and all that. If you would like to take a walk you will remember forever, go by the carriage road from the top of Mount Washington to the Glen House, and look into the great gulfs, and study the tawny sides of the mountains. I don't know anything more impressive hereabouts than that. Close to, those granite ranges have the color of the hide of the rhinoceros; when you look up to them from the Glen House, shouldering up into the sky, and rising to the cloud-capped summit of Washington, it is like a purple highway into the infinite heaven. No, you must not miss either Crawford's or the Glen House; and as to Mount Washington, that is a duty."

"You might personally conduct us and expound by the way."

King said he would like nothing better. Inquiry failed to give him any more information of the whereabouts of the Bensons; but the clerk said they were certain to return to the Profile House. The next day the party which had been left behind at Alexandria Bay appeared, in high spirits, and ready for any adventure. Mrs. Farquhar declared at once that she had no scruples about going up Washington, commonplace as the trip was, for her sympathies were now all with the common people. Of course Mount Washington was of no special importance, now that the Black Mountains were in the Union, but she hadn't a bit of prejudice.

King praised her courage and her patriotism. But perhaps she did not know how much she risked. He had been talking with some *habitués* of the Profile, who had been coming here for years, and had just now for the first time been up Washington, and they said that while the trip was pleasant enough, it did not pay for the exertion. Perhaps Mrs. Farquhar did not know that mountain-climbing was disapproved of here as sea-bathing was at Newport. It was hardly the thing one would like to do, except, of course, as a mere lark, and, don't you know, with a party.

Mrs. Farquhar said that was just the reason she wanted to go. She was willing to make any sacrifice; she considered herself just a missionary of provincialism up North, where people had become so cosmopolitan that they dared not enjoy anything. She was an enemy of the Boston philosophy. What is the Boston philosophy? Why, it is not to care about anything you do care about.

The party that was arranged for this trip included Mrs. Cortlandt and her bevy of beauty and audacity, Miss Lamont and her uncle, Mrs. Farquhar, the artist, and the desperate pilgrim of love. Mrs. Farquhar vowed to Forbes that she had dragged King along at the request of the proprietor of the hotel, who did not like to send a guest away, but he couldn't have all the trees at Profile Lake disfigured with his cutting and carving. People were running to him all the while to know what it meant with "I. B.," "I. B.," "I. B.," everywhere, like a grove of Baal.

From the Junction to Fabyan's they rode in an observation car, all open, and furnished with movable chairs, where they sat as in a balcony. It was a picturesque load of passengers. There were the young ladies in trim travelling suits, in what is called compact fighting trim; ladies in mourning; ladies in winter wraps; young men with shawl-straps and opera-glasses, standing, legs astride, consulting maps and imparting information; the usual sweet pale girl with a bundle of cat-tails and a decorative intention; and the *nonchalant* young man in a striped English boating cap, who nevertheless spoke American when he said anything.

As they were swinging slowly along the engine suddenly fell into a panic, puffing and sending up shrill shrieks of fear in rapid succession. There was a sedate cow on the track. The engine was agitated, it shrieked more shrilly, and began backing in visible terror. Everybody jumped and stood up, and the women clung to the men, all frightened. It was a beautiful exhibition of the sweet dependence of the sex in the hour of danger. The cow was more terrible than a lion on the track. The passengers all trembled like the engine. In fact, the only calm being was the cow, which, after satisfying her curiosity, walked slowly off, wondering what it was all about.

The cog-wheel railway is able to transport a large number of excursionists to the top of the mountain in the course of the morning. The tourists usually arrive there about the time the mist has crept up from the valleys and enveloped everything. Our party had the common experience. The Summit House, the Signal Station, the old Tip-top House, which is lashed down with cables, and rises ten feet higher than the highest crag, were all in the clouds. Nothing was to be seen except the dim outline of these buildings.

"I wonder," said Mrs. Farquhar, as they stumbled along over the slippery stones, "what people come here for?"

"Just what we came for," answered Forbes—"to say they have been on top of the mountain."

They took refuge in the hotel, but that also was invaded by the damp chill atmosphere, wrapped in and pervaded by the clouds. From the windows nothing more was to be seen than is visible in a Russian steam bath. But the tourists did not mind. They addressed themselves to the business in hand. This was registering their names. A daily newspaper called *Among the* Clouds is published here, and every person who gets his name on the register in time can see it in print before the train goes. When the train descends, every passenger has one of these two-cent certificates of his exploit. When our party entered, there was a great run on the register, especially by women who have a repugnance, as is well known, to seeing their names in print. In the room was a hot stove, which was more attractive than the cold clouds, but unable to compete in interest with the register. The artist, who seemed to be in a sardonic mood, and could get no chance to enter his name, watched the scene, while his friends enjoyed the view of the stove. After registering, the visitors all bought note-paper with a chromo heading, "Among the Clouds," and a natural wild flower stuck on the corner, and then rushed to the writing-room in order to indite an epistle "from the summit." This is indispensable.

After that they were ready for the Signal Station. This is a great attraction. The sergeant in charge looked bored to death, and in the mood to predict the worst kind of weather. He is all day beset with a crowd craning their necks to look at him, and bothered with ten thousand questions. He told King that the tourists made his life miserable; they were a great deal worse than the blizzards in the winter. And the government, he said, does not take this into account in his salary.

Occasionally there was an alarm that the mist was getting thin, that the clouds were about to break, and a rush was made out-of-doors, and the tourists dispersed about on the rocks. They were all on the *qui vive* to see the hotel or the boarding-house they had left in the early morning. Excursionists continually swarmed in by rail or by carriage road. The artist, who had one of his moods for wanting to see nature, said there were too many women; he wanted to know why there were always so many women on excursions. "You can see nothing but excursionists; whichever way you look, you see their backs." These backs, looming out of the mist, or discovered in a rift, seemed to enrage him.

At length something actually happened. The curtain of cloud slowly lifted, exactly as in a theatre; for a moment there was a magnificent view of peaks, forests, valleys, a burst of sunshine on the lost world, and then the curtain dropped, amid a storm of "Ohs!" and "Ahs!" and intense excitement. Three or four times, as if in response to the call of the spectators, this was repeated, the curtain lifting every time on a different scene, and then it was all over, and the heavy mist shut down on the registered and the unregistered alike. But everybody declared that they preferred it this way; it was so much better to have these wonderful glimpses than a full view. They would go down and brag over their good fortune.

The excursionists by-and-by went away out of the clouds, gliding breathlessly down the rails. When snow covers this track, descent is sometimes made on a toboggan, but it is such a dangerous venture that all except the operatives are for now forbidden to try it. The velocity attained of three and a half miles in three minutes may seem nothing to a locomotive engineer who is making up time; it might seem slow to a lover whose sweetheart was at the foot of the slide; to ordinary mortals a mile a minute is quite enough on such an incline.

Our party, who would have been much surprised if any one had called them an excursion, went away on foot down the carriage road to the Glen House. A descent of a few rods took them into the world of light and sun, and they were soon beyond the little piles of stones which mark the spots where tourists have sunk down bewildered in the mist and died of exhaustion and cold. These little mounds help to give Mount Washington its savage and implacable character. It is not subdued by all the roads and rails and scientific forces. For days it may lie basking and smiling in the sun, but at any hour it is liable to become inhospitable and pitiless, and for a good part of the year the summit is the area of elemental passion.

How delightful it was to saunter down the winding road into a region of peace and calm; to see from the safe highway the great giants in all their majesty; to come to vegetation, to the company of men! As they reached the Glen House all the line of rugged mountain peaks was violet in the reflected rays. There were people on the porch who were looking at this spectacle. Among them the eager eyes of King recognized Irene.

"Yes, there she is," cried Mrs. Farquhar, "and there—oh, what a treacherous North—is Mr. Meigs also."

It was true. There was Mr. Meigs apparently domiciled with the Benson family. There might have been a scene, but fortunately the porch was full of loungers looking at the sunset, and other pedestrians in couples and groups were returning from afternoon strolls. It might be the crisis of two lives, but to the spectator nothing more was seen than the everyday meeting of friends and acquaintances. A couple say good-night at the door of a drawing-room. Nothing has happened—nothing except a look, nothing except the want of pressure of the hand. The man lounges off to the smoking-room, cool and indifferent; the women, in her chamber, falls into a passion of tears, and at the end of a wakeful night comes into a new world, hard and cold and uninteresting. Or the reverse happens. It is the girl who tosses the thing off with a smile, perhaps with a sigh, as the incident of a season, while the man, wounded and bitter, loses a degree of respect for woman, and pitches his life henceforth on a lower plane.

In the space of ten steps King passed through an age of emotions, but the strongest one steadied him. There was a general movement, exclamations, greetings, introductions. King was detained a moment by Mr. and Mrs. Benson; he even shook hands with Mr. Meigs, who had the tact to turn immediately from the group and talk with somebody else; while Mrs. Farquhar and Miss Lamont and Mrs. Cortlandt precipitated themselves upon Irene in a little tempest of cries and caresses and delightful feminine fluttering. Truth to say, Irene was so overcome by these greetings that she had not the strength to take a step forward when King at length approached her. She stood with one hand grasping the back of her chair. She knew that that moment would decide her life. Nothing is more admirable in woman, nothing so shows her strength, as her ability to face in public such a moment. It was the critical moment for King—how critical the instant was, luckily, he did not then know. If there had been in his eyes any doubt, any wavering, any timidity, his cause would have been lost. But there was not. There was infinite love and tenderness, but there was also resolution, confidence, possession, mastery. There was that that would neither be denied nor turned aside, nor accept any subterfuge. If King had ridden up on a fiery steed, felled Meigs with his "mailed hand," and borne away the fainting girl on his saddle pommel, there could have been no more doubt of his resolute intention. In that look all the mists of doubt that her judgment had raised in Irene's mind to obscure love vanished. Her heart within her gave a great leap of exultation that her lover was a man strong enough to compel, strong enough to defend. At that instant she knew that she could trust him against the world. In that moment, while he still held her hand, she experienced the greatest joy that woman ever knows—the bliss of absolute surrender.

"I have come," he said, "in answer to your letter. And this is my answer."

She had it in his presence, she read it in his eyes. With the delicious sense thrilling her that she was no longer her own master there came a new timidity. She had imagined that if ever she should meet Mr. King again, she should defend her course, and perhaps appear in his eyes in a very heroic attitude. Now she only said, falteringly, and looking down, "I—I hoped you would come."

That evening there was a little dinner given in a private parlor by Mr. Benson in honor of the engagement of his daughter. It was great larks for the young ladies whom Mrs. Cortlandt was chaperoning, who behaved with an elaboration of restraint and propriety that kept Irene in a flutter of uneasiness. Mr. Benson, in mentioning the reason for the "little spread," told the story of Abraham Lincoln's sole response to Lord Lyons, the bachelor Minister of her Majesty, when he came officially to announce the marriage of the Prince of Wales—"Lord Lyons, go thou and do likewise," and he looked at Forbes when he told it, which made Miss Lamont blush, and appear what the artist had described her to King—the sweetest thing in life. Mrs. Benson beamed with motherly content, and was quite as tearful as ungrammatical, but her mind was practical and forecasting. "There'll have to be," she confided to Miss Lamont, "more curtains in the parlor, and I don't know but new paper." Mr. Meigs was not present. Mrs. Farquhar noticed this, and Mrs. Benson remembered that he had said something about going down to North Conway, which gave King an opportunity to say to Mrs. Farquhar that she ought not to despair, for Mr. Meigs evidently moved in a circle, and was certain to cross her path again. "I trust so," she replied. "I've been his only friend through all this miserable business." The dinner was not a great success. There was too much self-consciousness all round, and nobody was witty and brilliant.

The next morning King took Irene to the Crystal Cascade. When he used to frequent this pretty spot as a college boy, it had seemed to him the ideal place for a love scene—much better than the steps of a hotel. He said as much when they were seated at the foot of the fall. It is a charming cascade fed by the water that comes down Tuckerman's Ravine. But more beautiful than the fall is the stream itself, foaming down through the bowlders, or lying in deep limpid pools which reflect the sky and the forest. The water is as cold as ice and as clear as cut glass; few mountain streams in the world, probably, are so absolutely without color. "I followed it up once," King was saying, by way of filling in the pauses with personal revelations, "to the source. The woods on the side are dense and impenetrable, and the only way was to keep in the stream and climb over the bowlders. There are innumerable slides and cascades and pretty falls, and a thousand beauties and surprises. I finally came to a marsh, a thicket of alders, and around this the mountain closed in an amphitheatre of naked perpendicular rock a thousand feet high. I made my way along the stream through the thicket till I came to a great bank and arch of snow—it was the last of July—from under which the stream flowed. Water dripped in many little rivulets down the face of the precipices—after a rain there are said to be a thousand cascades there. I determined to climb to the summit, and go back by the Tip-top House. It does not look so from a little distance, but there is a rough zigzag sort of path on one side of the amphitheatre, and I found this, and scrambled up. When I reached the top the sun was shining, and although there was nothing around me but piles of granite rocks, without any sign of a path, I knew that I had my bearings so that I could either reach the house or a path leading to it. I stretched myself out to rest a few moments, and suddenly the scene was completely shut in by a fog. [Irene put out her hand and touched King's.] I couldn't tell where the sun was, or in what direction the hut lay, and the danger was that I would wander off on a spur, as the lost usually do. But I knew where the ravine was, for I was still on the edge of it."

"Why," asked Irene, trembling at the thought of that danger so long ago—"why didn't you go back down the ravine?"

"Because," and King took up the willing little hand and pressed it to his lips, and looked steadily in her eyes—"because that is not my way. It was nothing. I made what I thought was a very safe calculation, starting from the ravine as a base, to strike the Crawford bridle-path at least a quarter of a mile west of the house. I hit it—but it shows how little one can tell of his course in a fog—I struck it within a rod of the house! It was lucky for me that I did not go two rods further east."

Ah me! how real and still present the peril seemed to the girl! "You will solemnly promise me, solemnly, will you not, Stanhope, never to go there again—never—without me?"

The promise was given. "I have a note," said King, after the promise was recorded and sealed, "to show you. It came this morning. It is from Mrs. Bartlett-Glow."

"Perhaps I'd rather not see it," said Irene, a little stiffly.

"Oh, there is a message to you. I'll read it."

It was dated at Newport.

"MY DEAR STANHOPE,—The weather has changed. I hope it is more congenial where you are. It is horrid here. I am in a bad humor, chiefly about the cool. Don't think I'm going to inflict a letter on you. You don't deserve it besides. But I should like to know Miss Benson's address. We shall be at home in October, late, and I want her to come and make me a little visit. If you happen to see her, give her my love, and believe me your affectionate cousin, Penelope."

The next day, they explored the wonders of the Notch, and the next were back in the serene atmosphere of the Profile House. How lovely it all was; how idyllic; what a bloom there was on the hills; how amiable everybody seemed; how easy it was to be kind and considerate! King wished he could meet a beggar at every turn. I know he made a great impression on some elderly maiden ladies at the hotel, who thought him the most gentlemanly and good young man they had ever seen. Ah! if one could always be in love and always young!

II

PLEASURE AND DANGER AT NEW ENGLAND RESORTS

6

Emma Dunham Kelley, from *Megda*

(1891)

Emma Dunham Kelley's Megda *traces the psychological and spiritual development of three girls, Megda, Dell, and Laurie, who are just graduating from high school. In this chapter, the girls take a vacation to Cottage City, on Martha's Vineyard—a plot that is echoed in Kelley's later novel,* Four Girls at Cottage City. *The title character, Megda, is a true heroine—dashing, determined, independent—but this vacation comes just after Megda's discovery that the man she loves is about to marry one of her friends. The discovery has begun a process of repentance and conversion for Megda, and that process is now brought to a crisis at Cottage City. Most immediately, the scene revolves around the choice of whether or not to go to a dance—and whether to dance once she is there. In this vacation setting, the waltz is alluring, but the emotional intensity of prayer and repentance is ultimately even more seductive.*

Cottage City caught Kelley's attention as a setting for her novels because of its peculiar origins. For one thing, it was a vacation resort of a very special kind, grown up around the Methodist summer camp meeting of Wesleyan Grove. It provided an appropriate setting for Megda's soul-searching. Equally important for Kelley's purposes is the fact that the nearby Baptist camp meeting welcomed African-Americans, who established a vibrant resort community of their own there in the late nineteenth century. Megda, Dell, and Laurie, like Emma Dunham Kelley herself, are African-American, although it would be difficult to glean that fact from the text of the novel alone, which is insistent in its description of their pale skin, blue eyes, and golden hair.

XX. A VISIT

Meg, Dell and Laurie were seated in Mrs. Randal's sitting-room, in earnest discussion. Meg had the chair of state, the large, old-fashioned, softly-cushioned "rocker." Dell sat very upright in a straight-backed chair. Laurie, as usual, on an ottoman, but so excited was she over what they were talking about, that half the time she was on the floor.

One whole hour they sat there, and when Dell and Laurie at last rose to go, Meg followed them out of the house, and even half way down the shady walk; and when she left them it was with the impressive words: "Remember, Saturday morning at ten minutes past eight—rain or shine. Sure!"

"Sure," repeated both the girls, as impressively.

This was on Wednesday afternoon. On Saturday morning, at eight o'clock, precisely, a gurney drove up to Mrs. Randal's door. It was raining, probably as hard as it ever had rained, and looked, as Meg said rather petulantly, as if it might rain forever and the day afterward. But for all that she was dressed for traveling, and waiting when the gurney stopped at the gate. Her trunk was taken out by Hal and the driver, and strapped in its place. Then Meg, closely attended by mother and sister, stepped out upon the piazza.

Meg wore a plain, tight-fitting flannel dress—the loveliest shade of gray. A peasant cape of the same color, and a pretty shirred tennis cap. She wore a small white vail over her face, and had her gossamer on her arm.

"Put your gossamer on, Girlie," said Hal, clearing the space from the gate to the piazza, in about two steps.

He took it from her arm and wrapped it, with loving care, about her. Then he took her reticule, opened his umbrella, and escorted her to the gurney—lifted her in and sprang in after her. In another moment, mother and sister were straining their eyes to catch a last glimpse of the gurney, as it was fast disappearing from their sight in a mist of driving rain.

"What a long week it will be!" sighed the mother.

"Dreadfully long," echoed the sister.

"Oh Meg, you darling! I knew you would come, but I was so afraid you wouldn't."

Hal laughed outright, and several people standing near, smiled "openly" in spite of themselves, as Laurie gave expression to her joy, fear and relief, in this rather contradictory manner. Meg laughed and returned the kiss heartily. "Let us be thankful that madam is not present, Laurie. Dell, you look most provokingly calm and undisturbed. Doesn't this storm effect you in the least?"

"Well, yes, I can't deny that it does," replied Dell, who always told the strict truth even on the smallest occasion. "I always did dislike wearing a gossamer—they wet the ankles so; but that is all that I complain of. We shan't be out in it much."

"I know it," said Meg, "but it is too bad it isn't pleasant; it will be so dull on the boat."

"Haven't you brought your book?" asked Laurie, "I have, and so has Dell."

"Yes," answered Meg; "I have brought 'John Ward, Preacher.' What have you?"

"I have 'Ester Ried'."

"And you, Dell?"

"Oh, I have 'Johnstown Horrors.' I had not decided what book to take until this morning, and then the weather decided for me. Quite appropriate, isn't it? Didn't know but we might have a flood before it got through."

Both girls laughed at Dell's choice and her reason for making such an one. Then Hal, who had gone to buy Meg's ticket and get her trunk checked, came up and asked them what they were laughing at.

"Dell is in a watery frame of mind," said Meg. "She thinks there is nothing like adaptability."

"She is referring to my choice," explained Dell, holding up her book for Hal to read its title. "Do you not think it an appropriate one?"

"Very. Have you seen hers?"—and Hal took Meg's book from under her arm and held it gravely up. "'John Ward, Preacher.' She is in a theological frame of mind which is almost as bad as that of which she accuses you. I do not know but the book may change her religious views entirely. She may come back to us a thorough Presbyterian."

"Never," said Meg firmly. "Their creed is too—too"—

"Are you quoting Oscar to us?" inquired Hal severely.

"I can't find words to express my opinion of it," finished Meg, not heeding the interruption.

"Then don't try," said Dell dryly. "You ought not to allow yourself to read such books, Meg."

"Why not?"

"Because they do you no good. It is no matter if you do not understand the different beliefs; what do they amount to? There is but one Bible; take that for your guide and be satisfied. What do you care for different people's different opinions? Reading them up is only liable to throw you in a very undecided and dissatisfied frame of mind, which is much worse than a 'watery' one, I assure you."

"For when you are in the latter, you are supposed to be all right," laughed Meg. "Oh, Dell, you have any amount of logic, but it is all as dry as saw-dust."

"It is very good logic," said Hal seriously; "the very best kind—good, common-sense."

Just then the whistle sounded, and the girls had barely time to gather up their "traps" before the train steamed into the station. Hal kissed Meg tenderly, and said, "Be a good girl, and don't forget the postal." Then he shook hands with Dell and then fell behind with Laurie to say his good-by to her in a low tone.

Meg and Dell hurried out together, good girls as they were, but Hal was beside them to help them into the car, and when the "all-aboard" was shouted, and the train moved slowly at first, then faster and faster, he stood on the platform and watched it out of sight.

For the first half-hour the girls talked and laughed very quietly together, but after that they settled back in their seats, opened their books and began to read. Meg and Laurie found theirs very interesting, and were very soon oblivious to everything and everybody about them. Dell's eyes were constantly wandering here, there and everywhere. Now she would look dreamily out of the window at the gray, misty, rain-drenched country through which they were passing, an inclination probably derived from the sight of the book she held open before her, and then she would allow her eyes to wander carelessly around her at her fellow-passengers.

During one of these "eye excursions" a young gentleman, sitting two or three seats in front of her on the opposite side of the car, happened to look up from the paper he was reading, just as Dell was looking at him. She was looking at him, and still *not* looking at him; that is, she was looking at him without seeing him, for she was thinking deeply of something that happened at home that morning before she left, and as she thought a smile curved her lips. The young man returned the look with interest. He had never before beheld such a beautiful face. She did not seem to resent his admiring gaze, but on the contrary, judging from her continued stare, appeared to like and encourage it. He laid aside his paper and proceeded at once to "business." Poor, unconscious Dell was literally miles away. The young gentleman (?) assumed his most fascinating (?) manner; he leaned back in his seat easily and gracefully, and allowed a smile, half pensive, half amused, to steal over his countenance. Presently he took courage to raise his hat, hardly decided as to how the young lady would take that. Eureka! She smiled! Alas, it was to her father that the smile was really given. Without more ado, the young gent rose from his seat and skipped jauntily up the aisle. Her focus being thus abruptly removed, Dell came to herself with a little start. She looked up, surprised, to see a strange young man partly leaning over the arm of her seat, with a smile on his face. The look of surprise was so genuine, that the young man paused, hardly knowing what to do. The smile faded, and he looked—alas for him! downright foolish.

"I beg your pardon," he stammered at last, "but, did—did—I thought—did you not wish me to sit beside you?"

Dell stared at him. But Dell was not entirely ignorant of some of the follies of the age, if she had lived out of the city all her life. She determined to give the young man a little lesson.

"Is there anything the matter with the seat you have just left?" she asked curiously, as if really thinking there might be.

He smiled a sickly smile as if to say, "Oh, of course you are only joking."

"Is there?" repeated Dell, with the manner of one who meant just what she says.

"No—no—not that I am aware of."

"Then I advise you to go back to it," she said, calmly; and resumed her reading without so much as a flicker of a smile.

Down went Meg's head into her own book, and she laughed until the tears came; she could not help it. Laurie tried hard not to laugh, but it was too much. As for the young man—the way in which he went out of the car, and made his way to the "smoker," was a caution. Dell put the "finishing touch" to it all, by saying—when the young man had disappeared—"Time for refreshments," and gravely fished out from some hidden region a bag of brambles.

When Meg and Laurie had gotten over their laughing, they commended Dell most highly on her "manner of treatment." "It is just what he deserved," said Meg indignantly, but always careful to speak in a low tone. "I never heard of such impudence. Perhaps he will not be quite so eager to indulge in such unpardonable conduct at another time. I only wish all such 'upstarts' would meet with like treatment in like instances."

At New Bedford they took the steamer for Cottage City. The rain still came down in torrents, but they pinned their dresses up underneath their gossamers, took their reticules under their arms, raised their umbrellas, and hurried as fast as they could in the little way they had to go.

I shall not say anything of the "sail down," for after two or three ineffectual attempts to sit on deck under the awning, and view the scenery, our girls made their way to the saloon, settled themselves in easy-chairs, and gave themselves up to the only pleasure that presented itself—reading—while the rain came pouring down, wrapping earth and sky in a thick, gray cloud.

At half-past two they reached Cottage City, the boat being over an hour late. The rain had ceased to a considerable extent, but it was foggy, cold and most disagreeably damp.

"Not much like the second of August," said Meg, as they made their way through the pushing, struggling crowd to a "son of the South," who was proclaiming in stentorian tones "that he carried luggage to all parts of the city."

"He may as well carry ours then," said Dell.

The girls decided to walk to the cottage at which they were to stop. A fifteen-minutes' walk brought them to it. It was a pretty white cottage situated on the corner of Trinity Park and Montgomery Square. Right opposite the front entrance was the Methodist Tabernacle. Around the corner and about two minutes' walk, was the Casino, in which were the Post-Office and free library. But what the girls rejoiced in most, was what they called "the little green pump." Never had water tasted so deliciously pure and cool. They were soon on the most intimate terms with "the little green pump." Three times every day, and often four and five, the three girls might be seen walking, arm in arm, in the direction of their invaluable friend.

The cottage was owned and let by a superannuated preacher and his wife—Rev. and Mrs. ———, of Cambridge—and the people stopping there were all pleasant, educated, and refined; though our girls saw little of them, as they spent the evening in their own rooms. On the front and back of the house were wide piazzas, and it was on them that the girls passed some of their pleasantest hours. The street cars passed the front of the house, and there was a great deal of foot-passing. The electric lights on the Tabernacle grounds shone through the branches of the large trees, and lighted the front piazzas and the girls' room, which opened out on a balcony facing the park in which the Tabernacle was situated, with its beautiful, soft, moon-like radiance. Withal, it was a most beautiful place, and our girls daily and hourly congratulated themselves on their good fortune in procuring such a desirable situation. Their meals they procured at the "B— House," which was situated immediately back of the cottage.

But to go back to the "night of arrival." The girls were glad enough when they found themselves in their pleasant, comfortable room. I am not going to enter into details in the least, so I shall say nothing of how the room was furnished, except that there were two beds in it, and the question as to who should occupy one bed alone, was at once brought up, discussed and decided upon in this wise: they would "take turns." So far so good.

The time between three o'clock and five was given to the transferring of dresses, etc., from their trunks to the two clothes-presses in which the room rejoiced, putting the bottles of camphor, glycerine, bay-rum, eau de cologne, vaseline, etc., etc., on the wash-stand and toilet-table. Then Meg threw herself down on the bed with a sigh of relief.

"I'll sleep in this bed to-night, girls," she said. "So please do not make any objections to my tossing about on it as much as I please."

"We have no objections," replied Dell, coolly possessing herself of the other. "Come up here, Laurie, and get rested."

So Laurie accordingly "came up."

"Let us map out a plan of action for our week of pleasure," suggested Meg, "beginning with to-morrow morning."

"Map out all the plans of action you please," said Dell, closing her eyes; "I'm going to sleep."

"You lazy thing!" exclaimed Meg, throwing a pillow at her, and hitting the foot-board. "If we don't plan to suit you, don't complain."

"No," murmured Dell, already half asleep; "anything will be agreeable to me."

To give the "plan of action" as it was really carried out: Every morning they arose at sunrise and took a long, pleasant walk along the shore. When they came back Meg and Dell went immediately to breakfast; Laurie went to morning prayers at the church near by.

Meg and Dell loitered over their breakfast that Laurie might get back from prayers before they finished. Two or three times during the week they accompanied Laurie. After breakfast they made their beds, set their room in order, took their books or crocheting and sat out on the front piazza. Sometimes they went to the beach and watched the bathers, but never indulged in that pastime themselves. At one they went to dinner, came home and had their siestas, as Meg called it. Between three and four o'clock they took a promenade, sometimes in one place, and sometimes in another. Toward sunset they strolled along the beach again. Between six and seven o'clock they went to supper, and after that, every night, to the band concert. At ten they went to bed, and slept soundly all night.

Meg was changed. Dell did not notice it, but Laurie's loving, watchful eyes saw it, and she grieved in secret over it. Meg was restless and had spasmodic fits of gaiety followed by one of deep depression. At times she would keep Dell and Laurie in a perfect gale of laughter half an hour at a time; then, when she thought herself unobserved, she would sit quietly by herself, looking before her with sad, wistful, dreamy eyes, until, suddenly thinking her silence might be noticed, she would give expression to some ludicrous thought, and jump up and catch one of them around the waist, and waltz her madly around the room.

Thursday morning as they were sitting out on the front piazza, reading, a party of bicycle-riders passed the cottage. The girls looked up from their books, and watched them absently. There were about a dozen of them, and they presented quite a gay appearance in their gray bicycle suits and bright-red sashes.

One of the riders said something to the one beside him in a low tone. The one addressed turned his eyes toward the cottage where our girls were. The look of careless indifference gave place to one of pleased surprise, and murmuring a word or two of apology to his astonished companion, he wheeled his bicycle sharply around, and rode up to the gate.

Exclamations of a very complimentary nature escaped our three girls, as they recognized him, and hastened down the walk to meet him. "Why, Mr. Blanding, is it possible!" "Why, Mr. Blanding, how came you here?" "Why, Mr. Blanding, how glad we are to see you!" And Mr. Blanding laughed, as he raised his cap and shook hands with the girls, as if he were very glad to be there.

"I came down with the Club of which I am a member," he explained. "Did not get here until last night. We rode our machines as far as New Bedford, and then took the boat. Where were you last evening?"

"We were at the concert," answered Dell; while Meg offered him a chair on the piazza.

"Were you?" he said, as he took his seat. "I did not see you. I was riding around there, too."

"We did not walk about any," said Meg.

Then they asked about the folks at home, and he answered, "They are all well."

"I tried to get Will and Ed to run down with me," he added, looking slyly at Meg and Dell; "but they said they couldn't spare the time."

"Where are you stopping?" asked Laurie.

"At the 'Sea View,'" he answered.

The girls opened their eyes at this.

"We are not going to stay later than Saturday," Ray hastened to explain with a laugh, "so we can afford to pay high board for that short time. And that reminds me, there is to be a 'Hop' at the 'Sea View' this evening. Would you like to attend? I should be very happy to have the honor of your company."

He looked at all three as he spoke. Meg's eyes shone with pleasure, Dell smiled her assent, and only Laurie looked disturbed.

"I shall be most happy," said Meg. "You are very kind."

"I should like to attend very much, thank you," said Dell.

Ray looked inquiringly at Laurie. Her face was suffused with blushes, but her blue eyes looked steadily back at him.

"Thank you very much, Mr. Blanding," she said in a low, trembling voice; "but I do not think I care to go."

Ray understood and respected her reason. He only bowed, and said kindly, "I should be very happy to have you go, Miss Ray, but you know best."

Laurie's grateful look thanked him. As for Meg, she felt irritably, but unreasonably, angry toward Laurie for refusing to go with them. Does anyone know why?

Dell took Laurie's reason calmly, as a "matter of course." She was not at all surprised, much less angry. Laurie was doing what she thought was right; Dell did not consider it any of her business to question that right. Besides, she fully understood Laurie, as well as the rest did, and she respected her for not doing what she thought she ought not. But then, Dell's conscience was not troubling her, and Meg's was; had been for the past four weeks. She determined to drown it to-night if it were a possible thing.

Poor Meg!

In the afternoon, great clouds came rolling up from the West, covering the bright-blue of the sky, and hiding the sun from sight. At six o'clock it commenced to rain—not hard, but in a most provoking, misty, drizzling way. The girls went to supper and came back again in their gossamers with the hoods pulled up over their heads. At quarter past seven Meg and Dell commenced to dress, Laurie serving as waiting-maid. Meg spoke sharply to her now and then—she had been very cross with her all the afternoon—but Laurie bore it meekly and patiently. She was going to have her revenge on her after they had gone and she was there alone. She was going to spend the evening in prayer for Meg; she could afford to bear with her patiently now.

"Of course we shall go in a carriage," said Meg, standing in the door of the clothes-press, and looking at her dresses hanging up inside; "so I shall dress as I should have done if it had been pleasant."

"And that is?" said Dell, interrogatively, looking up through the meshes of her long, golden hair which she was brushing.

"In my white mull."

"Very well; so shall I."

At eight o'clock Ray came for them. The girls wrapped their peasant-capes about them, put their lace scarfs over their hair, and glided down the stairs. Laurie held the lamp over the balcony railing to light the way from the door to the carriage. Ray helped them in and away they went.

Meg was feeling feverishly unhappy. She was doing what she knew to be a weak thing. Where was all her boasted "strength of character"? Laurie had proved herself worthy, and she—Meg—was fast proving herself most unworthy. So she told herself, bitterly, as she leaned back in the carriage.

"But it is easy for Laurie to be good," she said to herself, in self-defense. "She has everything to encourage her. A lovely home, all the money she wants, a father to take care of her; and then Hal"— Here Meg found her thoughts intolerable. She sat up straight in her seat and commenced to talk vivaciously with Ray.

When Meg went into the large, brilliantly-lighted ball-room, and took her seat, she thought: "If I have been weak enough to come, I need not dance. I will surely be strong enough to resist that temptation."

So she smilingly declined Ray's request that she should dance the Lanciers with him, on the plea that she wanted to watch the others a while. So Dell went off with him instead, and Meg sat and watched the gay crowd. But when the first, clear, beautiful strains of music burst upon the air, Meg felt herself tremble all over. Her cheeks flushed, her eyes shone, her heart beat quickly. Before the first figure was finished, she was almost wild to get up and take part in the intricate mazes of the dance. She kept time with the music softly with her hands and feet, and when the dance was over, and Ray led Dell to a seat beside her, Meg greeted them with, "What perfect music!"

"Isn't it?" replied Ray, unfurling Dell's fan and fanning himself and Dell with it. "The next number is a waltz. Surely you will not be content to watch that?" he asked lightly.

Meg smiled—she wasn't quite sure.

The music commenced—soft, dreamy, intoxicating—"Flowers of St. Petersburg." When had Meg ever been proof against her favorite waltz? The music entered her whole being, and took entire possession. She looked up into Ray's face bending over her, with shining eyes. He smiled and held out his hand. The next moment she had risen to her feet, his arm clasped her lightly, but firmly, and together they went swaying down the long, smooth floor.

"You are a perfect waltzer," whispered Ray, but Meg scarcely heard him.

After that until twelve o'clock, Meg did not miss one number. Ray brought up several of his "bicycle acquaintances"—all pleasant, refined, intelligent, but worldly, young men—and introduced them. Meg did not have time to think, but did want to think. The gentlemen coaxed and pleaded that they would stay "just one hour longer"—"just one dance more," but the girls were inexorable. At twelve o'clock they bade them good-night, and were driven back to their cottage.

When Meg and Dell entered their room—softly, for fear of waking Laurie—they found the lamp burning dimly on the table, and beside it was Laurie's little Bible with her handkerchief put between the leaves. Meg stood looking at it for a moment, then she opened it slowly to the place where Laurie's handkerchief held it, and her eyes fell upon these words: "The Lord loveth whom He chasteneth."

Meg closed the book and stepped to the bed where Laurie lay, fast asleep. How pure and sweet and untroubled looked the pretty, flower-like face! A smile parted the pretty lips; the whole expression was one of simple trust and perfect peace. Meg turned away with an aching heart. Dell was shaking out the folds of her white dress, with a rueful face.

"We shan't be able to wear these dresses here again, Meg," she said, going into the closet to hang hers up. "They are crushed beyond redemption."

The words were thoughtless, and were thoughtlessly spoken, but they went through Meg's heart like a dart. Oh, to be alone once more; to fall upon her knees and ask God to forgive her for all her bitter feelings for the past weeks; her weak, sinful yielding to temptation; her bitter complaining against her Heavenly Father's will, before she was lost "beyond redemption." Her sin looked terrible to her that night. She had dared to question God's goodness; she had dared to rebel against His righteous will.

"Father, forgive me," was the prayer she said that night, and said it many times over, before she fell into a deep, untroubled sleep. She had put herself altogether, in His strong, merciful hands;

she had prayed for strength to say from the heart, "Thy will be done." She had simply "gone back" to Him—to the shelter of His dear, loving arms, and He was holding her firm and sure. After that night, the lamp of Faith burned more brightly before Meg in her path through life, driving away the mists and shadows of uncertainty and doubt, and making all clear before her.

Saturday morning found "our girls" all ready to go home. They had had a delightful time, but still they were ready to go home. Ray and his friends had made the remaining time pass very swiftly and pleasantly. They went as far as New Bedford with the girls, and then left them to make the rest of the distance home on their wheels.

The day was beautiful, clear, cool and sunshiny. The young people found comfortable seats on the upper deck and enjoyed the sail home in a degree that made up for the sail down. As the girls settled themselves in their seats in the train after bidding the gentlemen good-by, Meg looked at Laurie's pretty, unconscious face bent over her book with a loving, peaceful smile.

"Darling Laurie," she said to herself. "What a lesson you have taught me! You have taught me the meaning of that prayer, 'Lead us not into temptation.'"

7

Susan and Anna Warner, from *The Gold of Chickaree* (1876)

Susan and Anna Warner's The Gold of Chickaree *is the sequel to* Wych Hazel, *a novel whose plot rests on a rather strange family situation. Wych Hazel, an orphaned heiress, has been officially "willed" to two guardians. The younger guardian, Dane Rollo (nicknamed "Duke"), is intended to marry her. If she marries him, she will inherit her fortune immediately; if she refuses, she will not inherit until she turns twenty-five. That first novel explores the young woman's attempt to come to terms with the humiliation of having been given away by a document, and the even greater humiliation of discovering that she actually loves the man to whom she has been given. At the end of the first novel, Rollo agrees with Wych Hazel that he will give her one year to decide what she wants to do. They will meet on September 25, and he will ask her again to marry him. In the meantime, he asks for only one thing, as a sign of her sexual purity and her religious convictions: that she will promise not to waltz.* The Gold of Chickaree *opens during the year of waiting: Wych Hazel takes a vacation, and a rumor surfaces (Chapter 1 is called "On Dit," French for "they say") that she has been seen waltzing at Newport.*

THE GOLD OF CHICKAREE

Chapter I. On Dit

"Papa," said Primrose, very thoughtfully, "do you think Hazel will marry Duke?"

Dr. Maryland and his daughter were driving homeward after some business which had taken them to the village.

"She will if she knows what is good for her," the doctor answered decidedly.

"But she has been away from Chickaree now nearly a year."

"I don't know what her guardian is thinking of," Dr. Maryland said, somewhat discontentedly.

"Duke is her guardian too," remarked Primrose.

"You land a fish sometimes best with a long line, my dear."

"People say she has been very gay at Newport."

"I am sorry to hear it."

"Do you think, papa, she would ever settle down and be quiet and give all such gayety up?"

"The answer to that lies in what I do not know, my dear."

"Papa," Primrose went on, after the pause of a minute, "don't you think the will was rather hard upon Hazel?"

"No," said the doctor, decidedly. "What can a girl want more?"

"But if she does not like Duke?"

"She is not obliged to marry him."

"But she can't marry anybody else, papa, without losing all her fortune, that is—"

"'Till she is twenty-five, my dear; only till she is twenty-five. She is not obliged to wait any longer than that, and no woman need be married before she is twenty-five."

Primrose laughed a little privately at the statement which she did not combat. She was thinking that Duke did not look at all depressed, and querying whether it was because he knew more than she did, or because he did not care. The old buggy stopped before the door of the long, low, stone house, and the conversation went no further.

Meanwhile, far away in the city, the young lady in question had discovered what nobody knew, and at last had unveiled her own secret. Not doubtingly, as she had glanced at it before, but beyond question, as an accepted fact. She hid it well from other people; she was at no pains to hide it from herself. Pains would have been of no use. If, in the somewhat secluded quiet of the first part of the winter, she had contrived a little to confuse things, it was no longer possible the moment she was out in the world again. Well she knew that she would rather live over three minutes in the red room when she had unconsciously pleased Mr. Rollo's taste, than to dance the gayest dance with such men as Stuart Nightingale, or do miles of promenading with the peers of Mr. May. For to Wych Hazel, to care for anybody *so*, was to care not two straws for anybody else. The existence, almost, of other men sank out of sight. She heard their compliments, she laughed at their talk, but through it all neither eye nor ear would have missed the faintest token of Mr. Rollo's presence; and since he was not there, she amused herself with mental comparisons not very flattering to the people at hand. She could not escape their admiration, but it was rather a bore. She *care* to have them stand round her, and join her in the street, and ask her to drive? She *enjoy* their devotion? "In idea" she belonged to somebody else, some time ago; now, the idea was her own; and she cared no more for the rest of the world than if they had been so many [c]lay figures. It was not too easy, sometimes, to hide this; not easy always to look long enough at the hearts laid at her feet, to give them the sympathetic courtesy which was their due. She never had tried her hand at flirting; but it was left for this season to stamp Miss Kennedy as "the most unapproachable woman in town." Which, however, unfortunately, made her more popular than ever. She was so lovely in her shy reserve; the hardwon favours were so delightful; the smiles so witching when they came; and nobody ever suspected that what she did with all her triumphs was to mentally bestow them on somebody else. They belonged to him, now, not to her, and for her had no other value.

It was a very timid consciousness of all this Hazel allowed herself, even yet. Thoughts were scolded out of sight and shut up and hushed; but none the less they had their way; and the sudden coming of forbidden thoughts, and the half oblivion of things at hand, made the prettiest work that could be in face and manner. A sweeter shyness than that of the girl who had nothing to hide watched all doors that led to her secret; a fairer reserve than mere timidity kept back what belonged to one man alone. A certain womanly veil over the girlish face but made the beautiful life changes more beautiful still. If anything, she looked younger than she had done the year before.

All this being true, why then did Miss Kennedy throw herself into the whirl of society, and carry her elder guardian about with her from place to place, till they had nearly made the round of all the gay scenes of winter and summer? Very simply and plainly, she said to herself, because there was nothing else to do. Of course she could not settle down permanently away from home; and as to going to Chickaree—to rides, and walks, and talks—with September hurrying on as if everybody was in a hurry to have it—*that* was out of the question. The very idea took her breath away. Till September Mr. Rollo had pledged himself to be quiet; longer it could not be expected of him. No, she must keep her distance, and keep moving; and if she had to meet her fate, meet it at least on a sudden. She could not sit still and watch it coming, step by step; she could not even sit still and think about it. If she could have persuaded Mr. Falkirk, Hazel would have gone straight to Europe, and stayed there till—she did not know when. She had an overpowering dread of going home, and seeing Mr. Rollo, and having herself and her secret brought out into the open day. So she rushed about from one gay place to another, and hid herself in the biggest crowds she could find; and all the while went to his "penny readings" (in imagination), and counted the days that were yet left before the end of September. But the tension began to tell upon her, and her face took a delicate look that Mr. Falkirk did not like to see, in spite of the ready colour that flickered there in such fitful fashion. And then, Dr.

Arthur Maryland, watching her one night at the Ocean House, with his critical eyes, gave his opinion, unasked. All that appeared was purely professional.

"She would be better at home, Mr. Falkirk, with different surroundings, and more quiet. Just now she is attempting too much. But do not tell her I say so."

The advice chimed in well with Mr. Falkirk's own private notions and opinions. It pleased him not to have his ward so given up to society, so engrossed with other people, as for months he had been obliged to see her. Mr. Falkirk had a vague sense of danger, comparable to the supposed feelings of a good mother-hen which has followed her brood of ducklings to the edge of the water. For Mr. Falkirk's attendance seemed to himself not much more valuable or efficient to guard from evil than the said mother-hen's clucking round the pond. True, he stood by, and saw that Wych Hazel was there; he went and came with her; but the waves of the social entertainment floated her hither and thither, and he could scarce follow at a distance, much less navigate for her. What she was doing, or saying, or engaging to do, was quite beyond his ken or his management. Besides, Mr. Falkirk thought it ill that the beautiful home at Chickaree should be untenanted; and ill that Wych Hazel's tastes and habits should be permanently diverted from home joys and domestic avocations. He was very much in the dark about Rollo; but, knowing nothing about the secret compact for the year, and seeing that Rollo did not of late seek his ward's society, and that Wych Hazel shunned to come near his neighbourhood, and affected any other place rather, he half comforted himself with the thought that as yet his little charge was his only, and her sweet trust and affection unshared by anybody who had a greater claim.

So Mr. Falkirk issued his decree, and made his arrangements; that is, he told Wych Hazel he thought she ought to go to Chickaree for the rest of the season; and, seeing that she must, Wych Hazel agreed.

It came to be now the end of August. And all through the season, Rollo had kept at his work or his play in the Hollow, and he had not sought out Wych Hazel in her various abiding places. Perhaps he was too busy; perhaps he was constantly expecting that her wanderings would cease, and she would return to her own home. Perhaps he guessed partly at the reason for her keeping at a distance, and would not hurry her by any premature importunity. And, perhaps—for some men are so—he was willing that she should run to the end of her line, see all that she cared to see, and find, if she could find, anything that she liked better than him. It might have been patiently or impatiently; but Rollo waited, and did not recall—did not go after her. And now she was coming home.

It was September and one week of it gone. Rollo had ridden over to Dr. Maryland's to dinner, and the little party were just sitting down to the table, when Dr. Arthur arrived. He had been, we know, at Newport, on business of his own, where Wych Hazel and Mr. Falkirk were, and was just returned after an absence of some weeks. He was a lion, of course, as any one is in a country home who has ventured out into the great sea of the world and come home again; and his sisters could hardly serve him fast enough, or listen eagerly enough to his talk at the dinner-table. Though Prim cared most for the sound of his voice, and Mrs. Coles for what it had to tell.

"And you saw Miss Kennedy, Arthur, did you?" this latter lady asked, with a view to getting intelligence through various channels at once, keeping her ears for him and her eyes for Rollo.

"I saw Miss Kennedy."

"How was she looking, Arthur?" said Prim.

"Not very well, I thought. That is, well according to you ladies, but not according to us doctors."

"*Not* well?" echoed Prim in dismay; while Rollo said nothing and did not even look.

"Rather delicate, it seemed to me," said Dr. Arthur. "But she is coming to-morrow, Prim, so you can judge for yourself."

"Is she as much admired as ever?" quoth Mrs. Coles, eyeing Rollo hard by stealth and not making much of him.

"More. And deserves it."

"How does she deserve more?" said Rollo.

"I am not good at descriptions," Dr. Arthur answered, somewhat briefly.

"I suppose she takes all she gets?" said Prudentia.

"Difficult to do anything else with it."

"Who is her special admirer now, or the most remarkable? for she reckons them by scores."

"All seemed to be special. One or two young Englishmen made themselves pretty prominent."

"That Sir Henry something—was *he* one of them? Is he there?"

"Crofton? Yes, he was there."

"What do people say, Arthur? Who of them is going to have her?"

"People say everything. And know nothing."

"That's true—sometimes. But whom does she dance with oftenest? Did you notice?"

"I saw her dance but once, and so could not notice," said Dr. Arthur.

"Well, what was that? and whom with? If you saw her dance only once, that might tell something."

"No, it might not; for I never went into the ball-room. This once that I spoke of was at a private party, and the dancing was on the lawn. Crofton was her partner then."

"Crofton was her partner! Sir Henry Crofton. Waltzing with her? Then he'll be the man, you see if he won't. Was he waltzing with her?"

"Nonsense, Prudentia!" said her sister. "He won't be the one; and it proves nothing if she was waltzing with him. Why shouldn't she waltz with him, as well as with anybody else?"

"You'll see," said Prudentia. "Answer my question, Arthur. Was it a waltz?"

"A waltz they call it," said Dr. Arthur, with considerable disgust. "I should choose a longer name, and call it an abomination."

"I don't believe Arthur is a good witness, Prim," said Rollo. "His testimony gets confused. Does he ever go walking in his sleep in these days—nights, I mean?"

"I was awake then," said Dr. Arthur. "And why you women don't put that thing down!"—

"Arthur!" said Prim, half laughing but half fearful too, "it's rather hard on the people who don't go, to tell them they ought to put a stop to it; and the people who do go, some of them, do it very innocently."

"Yes!" said Dr. Arthur, "and any man who takes such a young, pure face into that whirligig ought to be shot!"

"I daresay she'll marry Sir Henry Crofton," said Mrs. Coles.

But Rollo did not seem terrified, and did not seem to pay much attention to the whole thing, she thought. He was rather silent the rest of the dinner; but so he had been the former part of it, ever since Dr. Arthur had come home to talk. To Prudentia he never said more words than were civilly necessary. As soon as dinner was over he mounted and rode away.

Chapter II. What Comes of On Dit

Wych Hazel had not wanted to come home. But neither did she at all wish to arouse Mr. Falkirk's suspicions by a too strenuous resistance; and besides, when he really made up his mind to a thing, she had to yield; so, with much secret trepidation, and a particularly wayward outside development, she made the journey; and late the next night after Dr. Arthur's revelations, laid her head on the pillows in her own room at Chickaree, with a strange little feeling of gladness, that half began to take the trepidation in hand. Well—it was not the end of September yet: she would have a little breathing space. And then—Wych Hazel dropped asleep.

Things "happen," as we say, strangely sometimes. Threads which should lie smooth and straight alongside of each other and make no confusion, get all snarled, and twisted, and thrown crosswise of each other by just a little breeze of influence, or some slight impulse on one side. And so it fell next day.

Mrs. Powder, who had also been at Newport, and left it three days before Wych Hazel, had engaged her and Mr. Falkirk to lunch for this very day, the next after their arrival. That was one thread, not necessarily touching, one would say, the grand event of the day, which was Rollo's coming and [his] visit at Chickaree. For that visit was to have been made right early in the morning, and Collingwood was ordered, and even mounted, when there came a message from the mills. Some complication or accident of business made the master's presence necessary. Rollo went to the Hollow, and stayed there till he had but just time left to get to Chickaree before luncheon. This thread was twisted.

The carriage at the door. Rollo threw himself off his horse and went in. He was too late. Just within the door he met the little lady he came to see, standing in her pretty draperies of mantle and veil, ready for her drive; and Mr. Falkirk was behind her.

"O Mr. Rollo!" she said (fortified with this last fact) "you have come for lunch!"

"Have I?" said he, as he took her hand in the old-fashioned way. "I see I shall not get it."

"Will getting it to-morrow help you to dispense with it to-day? We are engaged at Mrs. Powder's. You see I *must* go."

"I see you must go. I have been delayed."

Mr. Falkirk, according to his accustomed tactics, passed out upon the veranda after giving his own greeting, leaving the others alone. Rollo had come in with a face flushed with pleasure and riding; now a certain shade fell upon it; his brow grew grave, as if with sudden thought.

"I will not detain you," he said, after seeing that Mr. Falkirk was at a safe distance; "only let me ask you one question. Arthur Maryland says he saw you waltzing with that English Crofton. I know it is not true; but tell me so, that I may contradict him. He was mistaken."

"Dr. Arthur! was *he* there?" voice and face too shewed a sudden check.

"But he did not see that?" said Rollo, with eyes which seemed as if they would deny the fact by sheer force of will.

Her eyes had no more than glanced at him hitherto, shyly withholding themselves. But now they looked full into his face, using the old, wistful, girlish right of search; watching him as keenly as sometimes he watched her. She answered gravely:

"How could Dr. Arthur be mistaken in what he says he saw?"

"Is it *true*?" came with an astonished, fiery glance of the gray eyes. She drew herself up a little, stepping back.

"It is true—since he says so—that he saw me among the rest."

It is not often that we see a man lose colour from intense feeling. Wych Hazel's eyes saw it now. Rollo stood still before her, quite still, for a space of time that neither could measure, growing very pale, while at the same time the lines on lip and brow gradually took a firmer and firmer set. Motionless as an iron statue, and assuming more and more the fixedness of one, he stood, while minute after minute slipped by. To Wych Hazel the time probably seemed measureless and endless; while to Rollo, in the struggle and tumultuous whirl of feeling, it was only a single sharp point of existence. He stood with his eyes cast down; and without raising them, without uttering another syllable, for which I suppose he had not self-control, at last he bowed gravely and low, and turned away. In another minute, the bay house and his rider went past the door and were gone.

On her part, Wych Hazel had stood waiting, expecting him to speak, scanning his face with eager scrutiny. Then, with a grave shadow of disappointment upon her own, looked down again, nerving herself for the words of anger which must follow such a look. But when he turned, she raised her head quickly and looked after him, following with her eyes as long as eyes could follow, listening as long as ears could hear—then drew her veil over her face and went down and entered the carriage. Answering, somehow, Mr. Falkirk's words; and, somehow, taking her part in Mrs. Powder's festivities.

O the interminable length of those bridges from life-point to life-point, over which we must sometimes pass at a foot-pace! Is anything more intolerable than the monotonous tramp, tramp, of the meaningless steps? Is anything more sickening than the easy sway of the bridge, which seems to make the whole world reel, while in truth it is only ourselves? If Wych Hazel had been asked afterwards who was at Mrs. Powder's, and what was said, and when she came home, she could not have told a word. She came home with a scarlet spot on either cheek, burning brighter and brighter. They were very beautiful, people said.

But to-morrow he would come, when his anger was cooled down. What if he did?—for pain this time had used a trident. He had doubted her. Then he *could* doubt her! *Then*, he never could trust. And what was anything after that? Not her discretion merely, as before; not her obedience; but her word! Well, he would come, and she would tell him—that would be one little shred of comfort, at least. But he had looked at her *so*! and then—he had turned his eyes away. And no matter what she told him, or what he might believe then, that look had gone down to the depths of her heart. He had doubted her!—

Well, the night wore away, somehow, between bitter waking pain and snatches of exhausted sleep; and then the morning—as mornings sometimes will—seemed to speak comfort. He would come, and she would tell him.

But he did not come. And one day followed another, and still there came not even a message; and Wych Hazel waited. No one guessed how little she ate in those days, no one guessed how little she slept; the one thing she knew of herself was, that no earthly temptation could have made her leave the house for five minutes. She rose up early—for he might come then; and she sat up till impossible hours, lest they might be the only ones left free by business. But under all this watching, the keen, three-pointed pain never relaxed its pressure. What was the use of anything, after that? and yet she longed for his coming with an intensity that could not be measured.

Earlier in the year,—certainly before his declaration,—she would not have waited so long, without taking the matter into her own hands and writing. But the twenty-fifth was close at hand; how could she do anything to bring herself to his notice, or call him to her side? And he was almost a stranger now; she had seen him but once since near a year ago. And on the twenty-fifth, at least, she *must* see him. Alas! what could she say to him then? unless—that—. But she could not think of it now. Her mind clasped hold of just one thought: he will come then: "He wants me to understand how angry he is," thought Hazel to herself as the tenth day crept slowly by. "Does he think I am made of iron, like himself, I wonder?"

And so we judge and misjudge each other, the best of us; and how can we help it? Misjudgments will be, must be; the only thing left to human finiteness and short-sightedness is frank dealing. There is one possible remedy in that.

Rollo did not come to Chickaree, and he did not write. How long Wych could have borne to wait without herself writing, to clear herself, it is difficult to say. A week passed, the second week was in progress, the twenty-fifth was not more than a week off, when Mr. Falkirk announced at dinner one day that Rollo was just setting off upon a journey.

"He's going to see some great manufacturing establishment in the northeast somewhere, and can't attend to my business, he tells me, before the fifth or sixth of next month; he hopes to be back by that time."

Mr. Falkirk thought the non-intercourse between the Hollow and Chickaree a very significant fact; but it was not his plan to annoy his ward by seeming to see anything it was not necessary he should see. It cannot be said that he was quite satisfied with the condition of things, indeed; however, he knew it was hopeless to attack Wych Hazel in the hope of getting information; and with what patience he might, he waited too; the third in that unrestful attitude.

With that strange double life which she had been leading of late, Wych Hazel heard Mr. Falkirk's announcement and poured out his "after-dinner coffee" with a steady hand. Then asked when Mr. Rollo was to go. He had gone already, that very day. And till when must this other business wait? Till the second week of October. Then she knew that he had thrown her off. No other earthly thing would have kept him away on the twenty-fifth, without even a word. Could he have done it, unless his liking for her had changed? *Would* he have done it, caring for her as—she thought—he had cared a year ago? With these questions beating back and forth in her mind,—so she went through the rest of the day. Receiving visitors, giving Mr. Falkirk his tea, sitting with him through the evening; until, at last, it was done and he had gone, and she could be alone. It never even crossed her mind to go to bed that night.

Whatever the new day may do with things that are sure, it is yet rather gentle with uncertainties; making fair little suggestions, and giving stray touches of light, in a way that is altogether hopeful and beguiling. And so, when that weary moonlight night had spent its glitter, and the tender dawn came up, Hazel breathed freer over a new thought. Mr. Falkirk might be mistaken! His own business might fill Mr. Rollo's hands until the second week in October,—that word proved nothing at all about his staying away. She would wait and see. No use in trusting people just while you can keep watch. And so, though the secret pain at her heart did never disappear, and though at best her next meeting with Mr. Rollo could not be very pleasant, still Hazel did hold up her head, and hope, and wait, with a woman's ready faith, and a courage that died out in the twilight and revived in the dawn, and kept her in a fever of suspense and expectation. It wearied her so unspeakably, in the long hours of practical daylight and unmanageable night, that sometimes she could hardly bear it. The world seemed to turn round till she could not catch her thoughts; and nerves overstrung and on the watch, made her start and grow pale with the commonest little sounds of every day and every night.

She had never had many people to love; she had never (before) loved anybody very much; and the truth and dignity which had kept her from all forms of love-trifling, so kept the hidden treasures of her heart all sparkling with their own freshness. They had never been passed about from hand to hand; no weather-stains, no worn-out impressions were there. What the amount might be, Wych Hazel had never guessed until in these dark days she began to tell it over; making herself feel so poor! For, after all, what is the use of a treasure which nobody wants?

Not the least among her troubles was the painful hiding them all. She must laugh and talk and entertain Mr. Falkirk; she must guard her face when the mail-bag came in, and steady the little hand stretched out for her letters; must meet and turn off all Mrs. Bywank's looks and words; must dress and go out, and dress and receive people at home. Ah, how hard it was—and no one to whom she could speak, no lap where she could lay down her head, and pour out her sorrows.

Slowly, as the days went by, and hope grew fainter, and the dawn turned cold, there grew up in Wych Hazel's mind an intense longing to lay hold of something that was still; something that would stand; something beyond the wind and above the waves; and slowly, gradually, the words she had read to Gyda came back, and made themselves a power in her mind:

"I will be with him in trouble."

Oh for some one to be with her! Oh for something she could grasp, and stop this endless swaying and rocking and trembling of all things else! And then, following close, came other words, more lately learned. Not now read over, with those pencil marks beside them; but read often enough before, happily, to have been learned by heart; and now passing and re-passing in unceasing procession before her thoughts.

"For the love of Christ constraineth us."—

The love that could be counted on; the Presence that was sure!

And so, reaching her hands out blindly through the dark, the girl did now and then lay hold of the Eternal strength, and for a while sometimes found rest. But there came other days and hours when she seemed to be clinging to she hardly knew what, with the full rush and sweeping of the tide around her; conscious only that she was not quite swept away; until when at last the twenty-third was past, and three days of grace had followed suit, Hazel rose up one morning with this one thought: if she did not see somebody to speak to, she should die.

8

Harriet Beecher Stowe, from *Pink and White Tyranny: A Society Novel*

(1871)

In Uncle Tom's Cabin *(1852) and many other novels, Harriet Beecher Stowe (1811–1896) contributed as much as any writer to the nineteenth-century vision of women as gentle, loving, and angelically pious. Here, she takes another view.* Pink and White Tyranny *is one of a series of novels Stowe wrote in the 1870s, exploring the role of the "new woman." In* Pink and White Tyranny, *Stowe launched an attack on the "modern woman's" abuse of her sexual power. In fact, it was written partly in response to feminist attacks on the notorious adultery of her celebrity clergyman-brother Henry Ward Beecher. Poor John, an old-fashioned, upright New England man, has fallen prey to the wiles of a fashionable woman, whom he has married. Lillie (the spelling, with its "ie," is a suitably French affectation) is determined to live just as she pleases and to ignore John's old-fashioned house, his sister Gracie, and their expectations. But the central character in these chapters is the resort community of Newport, the very polar opposite of John's quiet New England town, a place where nouveau riche families flaunted their clothes, their carriages, and their careless morals. In Newport, Lillie's addiction to every vice allowed to women in respectable fiction—from flirtation to cigarettes to the use of cosmetics—finally comes to light.*

CHAPTER X. CHANGES

Scene.—A chamber at the Seymour House. Lillie discovered weeping. John rushing in with empressement.

"Lillie, you *shall* tell me what ails you."

"Nothing ails me, John."

"Yes, there does; you were crying when I came in."

"Oh, well, that's nothing!"

"Oh, but it *is* a great deal! What is the matter? I can see that you are not happy."

"Oh, pshaw, John! I am as happy as I ought to be, I dare say; there isn't much the matter with me, only a little blue, and I don't feel quite strong."

"You don't feel strong! I've noticed it, Lillie."

"Well, you see, John, the fact is, that I never have got through this month without going to the sea-side. Mamma always took me. The doctors told her that my constitution was such that I couldn't get along without it; but I dare say I shall do well enough in time, you know."

"But, Lillie," said John, "if you do need sea-air, you must go. I can't leave my business; that's the trouble."

"Oh, no, John! don't think of it. I ought to make an effort to get along. You see, it's very foolish in me, but places affect my spirits so. It's perfectly absurd how I am affected."

"Well, Lillie, I hope this place doesn't affect you unpleasantly," said John.

"It's a nice, darling place, John, and it's very silly in me; but it is a fact that this house somehow has a depressing effect on my spirits. You know it's not like the houses I've been used to. It has a sort of old look; and I can't help feeling that it puts me in mind of those who are dead and gone; and then I think I shall be dead and gone too, some day, and it makes me cry so. Isn't it silly of me, John?"

"Poor little pussy!" said John.

"You see, John, our rooms are lovely; but they are n't modern and cheerful, like those I've been accustomed to. They make me feel pensive and sad all the time; but I'm trying to get over it."

"Why, Lillie!" said John, "would you like the rooms refurnished? It can easily be done if you wish it."

"Oh, no, no, dear! You are too good; and I'm sure the rooms are lovely, and it would hurt Gracie's feelings to change them. No: I must try and get over it. I know just how silly it is, and I shall try to overcome it. If I had only more strength, I believe I could."

"Well, darling, you must go the sea-side. I shall have you sent right off to Newport. Gracie can go with you."

"Oh, no, John! not for the world. Gracie must stay, and keep house for you. She's such a help to you, that it would be a shame to take her away. But I think mamma would go with me,—if you could take me there, and engage my rooms and all that, why, mamma could stay with me, you know. To be sure, it would be a trial not to have you there; but then if I could get up my strength, you know,"—

"Exactly, certainly; and, Lillie, how would you like the parlors arranged if you had your own way?"

"Oh, John! I don't think of it."

"But I just want to know for curiosity. Now, how would you have them if you could?"

"Well, then, John, don't you think it would be lovely to have them frescoed? Did you ever see the Folingsbees' rooms in New York? They were so lovely!—one was all in blue, and the other in crimson, opening into each other; with carved furniture, and those *marquetrie* tables, and all sorts of little French things. They had such a gay and cheerful look."

"Now, Lillie, if you want our rooms like that, you shall have them."

"O John, you are so good! I couldn't ask such a sacrifice."

"Oh, pshaw! it isn't a sacrifice. I don't doubt I shall like them better myself. Your taste is perfect, Lillie; and, now I think of it, I wonder that I thought of bringing you here without consulting you in every particular. A woman ought to be queen in her own house, I am sure."

"But, Gracie! Now, John, I know she has associations with all the things in this house, and it would be cruel to her," said Lillie, with a sigh.

"Pshaw! Gracie is a good, sensible girl, and ready to make any rational changes. I suppose we have been living rather behind the times, and are somewhat rusty, that's a fact; but Gracie will enjoy new things as much as anybody, I dare say."

"Well, John, since you are set on it, there's Charlie Ferrola, one of my particular friends; he's an architect, and does all about arranging rooms and houses and furniture. He did the Folingsbees', and the Hortons', and the Jeromes', and no end of real nobby people's houses; and made them perfectly lovely. People say that one wouldn't know that they weren't in Paris, in houses that he does."

Now, our John was by nature a good solid chip of the old Anglo-Saxon block; and, if there was anything that he had no special affinity for, it was for French things. He had small opinion of French morals, and French ways in general; but then at this moment he saw his Lillie, whom, but half an hour before, he found all pale and tear-drenched, now radiant and joyous, sleek as a humming-bird, with the light in her eyes, and the rattle on the tip of her tongue; and he felt so delighted to see her bright and gay and joyous, that he would have turned his house into the Jardin Mabille, if that were possible.

Lillie had the prettiest little caressing tricks and graces imaginable; and she perched herself on his knee, and laughed and chatted so gayly, and pulled his whiskers so saucily, and then, springing up, began arraying herself in such an astonishing daintiness of device, and fluttering before him with such a variety of well-assorted plumage, that John was quite taken off his feet. He did not care so much whether what she willed to do were, "Wisest, virtuousest, discreetest, best," as feel that what she wished to do must be done at any rate.

"Why, darling!" he said in his rapture; "why didn't you tell me all this before? Here you have been growing sad and blue, and losing your vivacity and spirits, and never told me why!"

"I thought it was my duty, John, to try to bear it," said Lillie, with the sweet look of a virgin saint. "I thought perhaps I should get used to things in time; and I think it is a wife's duty to accommodate herself to her husband's circumstances."

"No, it's a husband's duty to accommodate himself to his wife's wishes," said John. "What's that fellow's address? I'll write to him about doing our house, forthwith."

"But, John, do pray tell Gracie that it's *your* wish. I don't want her to think that it's I that am doing this. Now, pray do think whether you really want it yourself. You see it must be so natural for you to like the old things! They must have associations, and I wouldn't for the world, now, be the one to change them; and, after all, how silly it was of me to feel blue!"

"Don't say any more, Lillie. Let me see,—next week," he said, taking out his pocket-book, and looking over his memoranda,—"next week I'll take you down to Newport; and you write to-day to your mother to meet you there, and be your guest. I'll write and engage the rooms at once."

"I don't know what I shall do without you, John."

"Oh, well, I couldn't stay possibly! But I may run down now and then, for a night, you know."

"Well, we must make that do," said Lillie, with a pensive sigh.

Thus two very important moves on Miss Lillie's checker-board of life were skillfully made. The house was to be refitted, and the Newport precedent established.

Now, dear friends, don't think Lillie a pirate, or a conspirator, or a wolf-in-sheep's-clothing, or any thing else but what she was,—a pretty little, selfish woman; undeveloped in her conscience and affections, and strong in her instincts and perceptions; in a blind way using what means were most in her line to carry her purposes. Lillie had always found her prettiness, her littleness, her helplessness, and her tears so very useful in carrying her points in life that she resorted to them as her lawful stock in trade. Neither were her blues entirely shamming. There comes a time after marriage, when a husband, if he be any thing of a man, has something else to do than make direct love to his wife. He cannot be on duty at all hours to fan her, and shawl her, and admire her. His love must express itself through other channels. He must be a full man for her sake; and, as a man, must go forth to a whole world of interests that takes him from her. Now what in this case shall a woman do, whose only life lies in petting and adoration and display?

Springdale had no *beau monde*, no fashionable circle, no Bois de Boulogne, and no beaux, to make amends for a husband's engrossments. Grace was sisterly and kind; but what on earth had they in common to talk about? Lillie's wardrobe was in all the freshness of bridal exuberance, and there was nothing more to be got, and so, for the moment, no stimulus in this line. But then where to wear all these fine French dresses? Lillie had been called on, and invited once to little social evening parties, through the whole round of old, respectable families that lived under the elm-arches of Springdale; and she had found it rather stupid. There was not a man to make an admirer of, except the young minister, who, after the first afternoon of seeing her, returned to his devotion to Rose Ferguson.

You know, ladies, Æsop has a pretty little fable as follows: A young man fell desperately in love with a cat, and prayed to Jupiter to change her to a woman for his sake. Jupiter was so obliging as to grant his prayer; and, behold, a soft, satin-skinned, purring, graceful woman was given into his arms.

But the legend goes on to say that, while he was delighting in her charms, she heard the sound of *mice* behind the wainscot, and left him forthwith to rush after her congenial prey.

Lillie had heard afar the sound of *mice* at Newport, and she longed to be after them once more. Had she not a prestige now as a rich young married lady? Had she not jewels and gems to show? Had she not any number of mouse-traps, in the way of ravishing toilets? She thought it all over, till she was sick with longing, and was sure that nothing but the sea-air could do her any good; and so she fell to crying, and kissing her faithful John, till she gained her end, like a veritable little cat as she was.

CHAPTER XI. NEWPORT; OR, THE PARADISE OF NOTHING TO DO

Behold, now, our Lillie at the height of her heart's desire, installed in fashionable apartments at Newport, under the placid chaperonship of dear mamma, who never saw the least harm in any earthly thing her Lillie chose to do.

All the dash and flash and furbelow of upper-tendom were there; and Lillie now felt the full power and glory of being a rich, pretty, young married woman, with oceans of money to spend, and nothing on earth to do but follow the fancies of the passing hour.

This was Lillie's highest ideal of happiness; and didn't she enjoy it?

Wasn't it something to flame forth in wondrous toilets in the eyes of Belle Trevors and Margy Silloway and Lottie Cavers, who were *not* married; and before the Simpkinses and the Tomkinses and the Jenkinses, who, last year, had said hateful things about her, and intimated that she had gone off in her looks, and was on the way to be an old maid?

And wasn't it a triumph when all her old beaux came flocking round her, and her parlors became a daily resort and lounging-place for all the idle swains, both of her former acquaintance and of the newcomers, who drifted with the tide of fashion? Never had she been so much the rage; never had she been declared so "stunning." The effect of all this good fortune on her health was immediate. We all know how the spirits affect the bodily welfare; and hence, my dear gentlemen, we desire it to be solemnly impressed on you, that there is nothing so good for a woman's health as to give her her own way.

Lillie now, from this simple cause, received enormous accessions of vigor. While at home with plain, sober John, trying to walk in the quiet paths of domesticity, how did her spirits droop! If you only could have had a vision of her brain and spinal system, you would have seen how there was no nervous fluid there, and how all the fine little cords and fibres that string the muscles were wilting like flowers out of water; but now she could bathe the longest and the strongest of any one, could ride on the beach half the day, and dance the German into the small hours of the night, with a degree of vigor which showed conclusively what a fine thing for her the Newport air was. Her dancing-list was always over-crowded with applicants; bouquets were showered on her; and the most superb "turn-outs," with their masters for charioteers, were at her daily disposal.

All this made talk. The world doesn't forgive success; and the ancients informed us that even the gods were envious of happy people. It is astonishing to see the quantity of very proper and rational moral reflection that is excited in the breast of society, by any sort of success in life. How it shows them the vanity of earthly enjoyments, the impropriety of setting one's heart on it! How does a successful married flirt impress all her friends with the gross impropriety of having one's head set on gentlemen's attentions!

"I must say," said Belle Trevors, "that dear Lillie does astonish me. Now, I shouldn't want to have that dissipated Danforth lounging in my rooms every day, as he does in Lillie's: and then taking her out driving day after day; for my part, I don't think it's respectable."

"Why don't you speak to her?" said Lottie Cavers.

"Oh, my dear! she wouldn't mind *me*. Lillie always was the most imprudent creature; and, if she goes on so, she'll certainly get awfully talked about. That Danforth is a horrid creature; I know all about him."

As Miss Belle had herself been driving with the "horrid creature" only the week before Lillie came, it must be confessed that her opportunities for observation were of an authentic kind.

Lillie, as queen in her own parlor, was all grace and indulgence. Hers was now to be the sisterly *rôle*, or, as she laughingly styled it, the maternal. With a ravishing morning-dress, and with a killing little cap of about three inches in extent on her head, she enacted the young matron, and gave full permission to Tom, Dick, and Harry to make themselves at home in her room, and smoke their cigars there in peace. She "adored the smell;" in fact, she accepted the present of a fancy box of cigarettes from Danforth with graciousness, and would sometimes smoke one purely for good company. She also encouraged her followers to unveil the tender secrets of their souls confidentially to her, and offered gracious mediations on their behalf with any of the flitting Newport fair ones. When they, as in duty bound, said that they saw nobody whom they cared about now she was married, that she was the only woman on earth for them,—she rapped their knuckles briskly with her fan, and bid them mind their manners. All this mode of proceeding gave her an immense success.

But, as we said before, all this was talked about; and ladies in their letters, chronicling the events of the passing hour, sent the tidings up and down the country; and so Miss Letitia Ferguson got a letter from Mrs. Wilcox with full pictures and comments; and she brought the same to Grace Seymour.

"I dare say," said Letitia, "these things have been exaggerated; they always are: still it does seem desirable that your brother should go there, and be with her."

"He can't go and be with her," said Grace, "without neglecting his business, already too much neglected. Then the house is all in confusion under the hands of painters; and there is that young artist up there,—a very elegant gentleman,—giving orders to right and left, every one of which involves further confusion and deeper expense; for my part, I see no end to it. Poor John has got 'the Old Man of the Sea' on his back in the shape of this woman; and I expect she'll be the ruin of him yet. I can't want to break up his illusion about her; because, what good will it do? He has married her, and must live with her; and, for Heaven's sake, let the illusion last while it can! I'm going to draw off, and leave them to each other; there's no other way."

"You are, Gracie?"

"Yes; you see John came to me, all stammering and embarrassment, about this making over of the old place; but I put him at ease at once. 'The most natural thing in the world, John,' said I. 'Of course Lillie has her taste; and it's her right to have the house arranged to suit it.' And then I proposed to take all the old family things, and furnish the house that I own on Elm Street, and live there, and let John and Lillie keep the house by themselves. You see there is no helping the thing. Married people must be left to themselves; nobody can help them. They must make their own discoveries, fight their own battles, sink or swim, together; and I have determined that not by the winking of an eye will I interfere between them."

"Well, but do you think John wants you to go?"

"He feels badly about it; and yet I have convinced him that it's best. Poor fellow! all these changes are not a bit to his taste. He liked the old place as it was, and the old ways; but John is so unselfish. He has got it in his head that Lillie is very sensitive and peculiar, and that her spirits require all these changes, as well as Newport air."

"Well," said Letitia, "if a man begins to say A in that line, he must say B."

"Of course," said Grace; "and also C and D, and so on, down to X, Y, Z. A woman, armed with sick-headaches, nervousness, debility, presentiments, fears, horrors, and all sorts of imaginary and real diseases, has an eternal armory of weapons of subjugation. What can a man do? Can he tell her that she is lying and shamming? Half the time she isn't; she can actually work herself into about any physical state she chooses. The fortnight before Lillie went to Newport, she really looked pale, and ate next to nothing; and she managed admirably to seem to be trying to keep up, and not to complain,—yet you see how she can go on at Newport."

"It seems a pity John couldn't understand her."

"My dear, I wouldn't have him for the world. Whenever he does, he will despise her; and then he will be wretched. For John is no hypocrite, any more than I am. No, I earnestly pray that his soap-bubble may not break."

"Well, then," said Letitia, "at least, he might go down to Newport for a day or two; and his presence there might set some things right: it might at least check reports. You might just suggest to him that unfriendly things were being said."

"Well, I'll see what I can do," said Grace.

So, by a little feminine tact in suggestion, Grace despatched her brother to spend a day or two in Newport.

His coming and presence interrupted the lounging hours in Lillie's room; the introduction to "my husband" shortened the interviews. John was courteous and affable; but he neither smoked nor drank, and there was a mutual repulsion between him and many of Lillie's *habitués*.

"I say, Dan," said Bill Sanders to Danforth, as they were smoking on one end of the veranda, "you are driven out of your lodgings since Seymour came."

"No more than the rest of you," said Danforth.

"I don't know about that, Dan. I think *you* might have been taken for master of those premises. Look here now, Dan, why didn't you *take* little Lill yourself? Everybody thought you were going to last year."

"Didn't want her; knew too much," said Danforth. "Didn't want to keep her; she's too cursedly extravagant. It's jolly to have this sort of concern on hand; but I'd rather Seymour'd pay her bills than I."

"Who thought you were so practical, Dan?"

"Practical! that I am; I'm an old bird. Take my advice, boys, now: keep shy of the girls, and flirt with the married ones,—then you don't get roped in."

"I say, boys," said Tom Nichols, "isn't she a case, now? What a head she has! I bet she can smoke equal to any of us."

"Yes; I keep her in cigarettes," said Danforth; "she's got a box of them somewhere under her ruffles now."

"What if Seymour should find them?" said Tom.

"Seymour? pooh! he's a muff and a prig. I bet you he won't find her out; she's the jolliest little hum-bugger there is going. She'd cheat a fellow out of the sight of his eyes. It's perfectly wonderful."

"How came Seymour to marry her?"

"He? Why, he's a pious youth, green as grass itself; and I suppose she talked religion to him. Did you ever hear her talk religion?"

A roar of laughter followed this, out of which Danforth went on. "By George, boys, she gave me a prayer-book once! I've got it yet."

"Well, if that isn't the best thing I ever heard!" said Nichols.

"It was at the time she was laying siege to me, you see. She undertook the part of guardian angel, and used to talk lots of sentiment. The girls get lots of that out of George Sand's novels about the *holiness* of doing just as you've a mind to, and all that," said Danforth.

"By George, Dan, you oughtn't to laugh. She may have more good in her than you think."

"Oh, humbug! don't I know her?"

"Well, at any rate she's a wonderful creature to hold her looks. By George! how she *does* hold out! You'd say, now, she wasn't more than twenty."

"Yes; she understands getting herself up," said Danforth, "and touches up her cheeks a bit now and then."

"She don't paint, though?"

"Don't paint! *Don't* she? I'd like to know if she don't; but she does it like an artist, like an old master, in fact."

"Or like a young mistress," said Tom, and then laughed at his own wit.

Now, it so happened that John was sitting at an open window above, and heard occasional snatches of this conversation quite sufficient to impress him disagreeably. He had not heard enough to know exactly what had been said, but enough to feel that a set of coarse, low-minded men were making quite free with the name and reputation of his Lillie; and he was indignant.

"She is so pretty, so frank, and so impulsive," he said. "Such women are always misconstrued. I'm resolved to caution her."

"Lillie," he said, "who is this Danforth?"

"Charlie Danforth—oh! he's a millionnaire that I refused. He was wild about me,—is now, for that matter. He perfectly haunts my rooms, and is always teasing me to ride with him."

"Well, Lillie, if I were you, I wouldn't have any thing to do with him."

"John, I don't mean to, any more than I can help. I try to keep him off all I can; but one doesn't want to be rude, you know."

"My darling," said John, "you little know the wickedness of the world, and the cruel things that men will allow themselves to say of women who are meaning no harm. You can't be too careful, Lillie."

"Oh! I am careful. Mamma is here, you know, all the while; and I never receive except she is present."

John sat abstractedly fingering the various objects on the table; then he opened a drawer in the same mechanical manner.

"Why, Lillie! what's this? what in the world are these?"

"O John! sure enough! well, there is something I was going to ask you about. Danforth used always to be sending me things, you know, before we were married,—flowers and confectionery, and one thing or other; and since I have been here now, he has done the same, and I really didn't know what to do about it. You know I didn't want to quarrel with him, or get his ill-will; he's a high-spirited fellow, and a man one doesn't want for an enemy; so I have just passed it over easy as I could."

"But, Lillie, a box of cigarettes!—of course, they can be of no use to you."

"Of course: they are only a sort of curiosity that he imports from Spain with his cigars."

"I've a great mind to send them back to him myself," said John.

"Oh, don't, John! why, how it would look! as if you were angry, or thought he meant something wrong. No; I'll contrive a way to give 'em back without offending him. I am up to all such little ways."

"Come, now," she added, "don't let's be cross just the little time you have to stay with me. I do wish our house were not all torn up, so that I could go home with you, and leave Newport and all its bothers behind."

"Well, Lillie, you could go, and stay with me at Gracie's," said John, brightening at this proposition.

"Dear Gracie,—so she has got a house all to herself; how I shall miss her! but, really, John, I think she will be happier. Since you would insist on revolutionizing our house, you know"—

"But, Lillie, it was to please you."

"Oh, I know it! but you know I begged you not to. Well, John, I don't think I should like to go in and settle down on Grace; perhaps, as I am here, and the sea-air and bathing strengthens me so, we may as well put it through. I will come home as soon as the house is done."

"But perhaps you would want to go with me to New York to select the furniture?"

"Oh, the artist does all that! Charlie Ferrola will give his orders to Simon & Sauls, and they will do every thing up complete. It's the way they all do—saves lots of trouble."

John went home, after three days spent in Newport, feeling that Lillie was somehow an injured fair one, and that the envious world bore down always on beauty and prosperity.

But incidentally, he heard and overheard much that made him uneasy. He heard her admired as a "bully" girl, a "fast one;" he heard of her smoking, he overheard something about "painting."

The time was that John thought Lillie an embryo angel,—an angel a little bewildered and gone astray, and with wings a trifle the worse for the world's wear,—but essentially an angel of the same nature with his own revered mother.

Gradually the mercury had been falling in the tube of his estimation. He had given up the angel; and now to himself he called her "a silly little pussy," but he did it with a smile. It was such a neat, white, graceful pussy; and all his own pussy too, and purred and rubbed its little head on no coat-sleeve but his,—of that he was certain. Only a bit silly. She would still *fib* a little, John feared, especially when he looked back to the chapter about her age,—and then, perhaps, about the cigarettes.

Well, she might, perhaps, in a wild, excited hour, have smoked *one or two*, just for fun, and the thing had been exaggerated. She had promised fairly to return those cigarettes,—he dared not say to himself that he feared she would not. He kept saying to himself that she would. It was necessary to say this often to make himself believe it.

As to painting—well, John didn't like to ask her, because, what if she shouldn't tell him the truth? And, if she did paint, was it so great a sin, poor little thing? he would watch, and bring her out of it. After all, when the house was all finished and arranged, and he got her back from Newport, there would be a long, quiet, domestic winter at Springdale; and they would get up their reading-circles, and he would set her to improving her mind, and gradually the vision of this empty, fashionable life would die out of her horizon, and she would come into his ways of thinking and doing.

But, after all, John managed to be proud of her. When he read in the columns of "The Herald" the account of the Splandangerous ball in Newport, and of the entrancingly beautiful Mrs. J. S., who appeared in a radiant dress of silvery gauze made *à la nuage*, &c., &c., John was rather pleased than otherwise. Lillie danced till daylight,—it showed that she must be getting back her strength,—and she was voted the belle of the scene. Who wouldn't take the comfort that is to be got in any thing? John owned this fashionable meteor,—why shouldn't he rejoice in it?

Two years ago, had anybody told him that one day he should have a wife that told fibs, and painted, and smoked cigarettes, and danced all night at Newport, and yet that he should love her, and be proud of her, he would have said, Is thy servant a dog? He was then a considerate, thoughtful John, serious and careful in his life-plans; and the wife that was to be his companion was something celestial. But so it is. By degrees, we accommodate ourselves to the actual and existing. To all intents and purposes, for us it is the inevitable.

9

Edith Wharton, from *Summer*

(1917)

Vacations offered a variety of dangers, but perhaps the greatest was the temptation of a romantic encounter with an inappropriate partner. Edith Wharton (1862–1939), the author of Summer, *provides a highly charged and tragic view of such an encounter. Lucius Harney, a young architect from New York City, is visiting a cousin in the remote northern New England hamlet of North Dormer. There he encounters Charity Royall, a village girl whose lineage cannot even be traced back to respectable New England villagers. Their socially impossible but passionate affair takes place amid the preparations for "Old Home Week," a real-life celebration created by the governor of New Hampshire, Frank Rollins, in 1898. Old Home Week was designed to draw former residents of northern New England towns back "home" to the village or farm for a week—to spread money around, to liven up the old places, and to boost morale. Here, the Old Home Week rhetoric rings hollow. The sentimental speechifying about "the old oaken bucket, patient white-haired mothers, and where the boys used to go nutting" only underscores Charity's helpless and desperate position.*

XII

One afternoon toward the end of August a group of girls sat in a room at Miss Hatchard's in a gay confusion of flags, turkey-red, blue and white paper muslin, harvest sheaves and illuminated scrolls.

North Dormer was preparing for its Old Home Week. That form of sentimental decentralization was still in its early stages, and, precedents being few, and the desire to set an example contagious, the matter had become a subject of prolonged and passionate discussion under Miss Hatchard's roof. The incentive to the celebration had come rather from those who had been obliged to stay there, and there was some difficulty in rousing the village to the proper state of enthusiasm. But Miss Hatchard's pale prim drawing-room was the centre of constant comings and goings from Hepburn, Nettleton, Springfield and even more distant cities; and whenever a visitor arrived he was led across the hall, and treated to a glimpse of the group of girls deep in their pretty preparations.

"All the old names . . . all the old names . . . " Miss Hatchard would be heard, tapping across the hall on her crutches. "Targatt . . . Sollas . . . Fry: this is Miss Orma Fry sewing the stars on the drapery for the organ-loft. Don't move, girls . . . and this is Miss Ally Hawes, our cleverest needle-woman . . . and Miss Charity Royall making our garlands of evergreen. . . . I like the idea of its all being home-made, don't you? We haven't had to call in any foreign talent; my young cousin Lucius Harney, the architect—you know he's up here preparing a book on Colonial houses—he's taken the whole thing in hand so cleverly; but you must come and see his sketch for the stage we're going to put up in the Town Hall."

One of the first results of the Old Home Week agitation had, in fact, been the reappearance of Lucius Harney in the village street. He had been vaguely spoken of as being not far off, but for some weeks past no one had seen him at North Dormer, and there was a recent report of his having left Creston River, where he was said to have been staying, and gone away from the neighbourhood for good. Soon after Miss Hatchard's return, however, he came back to his old quarters in her house, and began to take a leading part in the planning of the festivities. He threw himself into the idea with extraordinary good-humour, and was so prodigal of sketches, and so inexhaustible in devices, that he gave an immediate impetus to the rather languid movement, and infected the whole village with his enthusiasm.

"Lucius has such a feeling for the past that he has roused us all to a sense of our privileges," Miss Hatchard would say, lingering on the last word, which was a favourite one. And before leading her visitor back to the drawing-room she would repeat, for the hundredth time, that she supposed he thought it very bold of little North Dormer to start up and have a Home Week of its own, when so many bigger places hadn't thought of it yet; but that, after all, Associations counted more than the size of the population, didn't they? And of course North Dormer was so full of Associations . . . historic, literary (here a filial sigh for Honorius) and ecclesiastical . . . he knew about the old pewter communion service imported from England in 1769, she supposed? And it was so important, in a wealthy materialistic age, to set the example of reverting to the old ideals, the family and the homestead, and so on. This peroration usually carried her half-way back across the hall, leaving the girls to return to their interrupted activities.

The day on which Charity Royall was weaving hemlock garlands for the procession was the last before the celebration. When Miss Hatchard called upon the North Dormer maidenhood to collaborate in the festal preparations Charity had at first held aloof; but it had been made clear to her that her non-appearance might excite conjecture, and, reluctantly, she had joined the other workers. The girls, at first shy and embarrassed, and puzzled as to the exact nature of the projected commemoration, had soon become interested in the amusing details of their task, and excited by the notice they received. They would not for the world have missed their afternoons at Miss Hatchard's, and, while they cut out and sewed and draped and pasted, their tongues kept up such an accompaniment to the sewing-machine that Charity's silence sheltered itself unperceived under their clatter.

In spirit she was still almost unconscious of the pleasant stir about her. Since her return to the red house, on the evening of the day when Harney had overtaken her on her way to the Mountain, she had lived at North Dormer as if she were suspended in the void. She had come back there because Harney, after appearing to agree to the impossibility of her doing so, had ended by persuading her that any other course would be madness. She had nothing further to fear from Mr. Royall. Of this she had declared herself sure, though she had failed to add, in his exoneration, that he had twice offered to make her his wife. Her hatred of him made it impossible, at the moment, for her to say anything that might partly excuse him in Harney's eyes.

Harney, however, once satisfied of her security, had found plenty of reasons for urging her to return. The first, and the most unanswerable, was that she had nowhere else to go. But the one on which he laid the greatest stress was that flight would be equivalent to avowal. If—as was almost inevitable—rumours of the scandalous scene at Nettleton should reach North Dormer, how else would her disappearance be interpreted? Her guardian had publicly taken away her character, and she immediately vanished from his house. Seekers after motives could hardly fail to draw an unkind conclusion. But if she came back at once, and was seen leading her usual life, the incident was reduced to its true proportions, as the outbreak of a drunken old man furious at being surprised in disreputable company. People would say that Mr. Royall had insulted his ward to justify himself, and the sordid tale would fall into its place in the chronicle of his obscure debaucheries.

Charity saw the force of the argument; but if she acquiesced it was not so much because of that as because it was Harney's wish. Since that evening in the deserted house she could imagine no reason for doing or not doing anything except the fact that Harney wished or did not wish it. All her tossing contradictory impulses were merged in a fatalistic acceptance of his will. It was not that she felt in him any ascendency of character—there were moments already when she knew she was the stronger—but that all the rest of life had become a mere cloudy rim about the central glory of their passion. Whenever she stopped thinking about that for a moment she felt as she sometimes did after lying on the grass and staring up too long at the sky; her eyes were so full of light that everything about her was a blur.

Each time that Miss Hatchard, in the course of her periodical incursions into the work-room, dropped an allusion to her young cousin, the architect, the effect was the same on Charity. The hemlock garland she was wearing fell to her knees and she sat in a kind of trance. It was so manifestly absurd that Miss Hatchard should talk of Harney in that familiar possessive way, as if she had any claim on him, or knew anything about him. She, Charity Royall, was the only being on earth who really knew him, knew him from the soles of his feet to the rumpled crest of his hair, knew the shifting lights in his eyes, and the inflexions of his voice, and the things he liked and disliked, and everything there was to know about him, as minutely and yet unconsciously as a child knows the walls of the room it wakes up in every morning. It was this fact, which nobody about her guessed, or would have understood, that made her life something apart and inviolable, as if nothing had any power to hurt or disturb her as long as her secret was safe.

The room in which the girls sat was the one which had been Harney's bedroom. He had been sent upstairs, to make room for the Home Week workers; but the furniture had not been moved, and as Charity sat there she had perpetually before her the vision she had looked in on from the midnight garden. The table at which Harney had sat was the one about which the girls were gathered; and her own seat was near the bed on which she had seen him lying. Sometimes, when the others were not looking, she bent over as if to pick up something, and laid her cheek for a moment against the pillow.

Toward sunset the girls disbanded. Their work was done, and the next morning at daylight the draperies and garlands were to be nailed up, and the illuminated scrolls put in place in the Town Hall. The first guests were to drive over from Hepburn in time for the midday banquet under a tent in Miss Hatchard's field; and after that the ceremonies were to begin. Miss Hatchard, pale with fatigue and excitement, thanked her young assistants, and stood in the porch, leaning on her crutches and waving a farewell as she watched them troop away down the street.

Charity had slipped off among the first; but at the gate she heard Ally Hawes calling after her, and reluctantly turned.

"Will you come over now and try on your dress?" Ally asked, looking at her with wistful admiration. "I want to be sure the sleeves don't ruck up the same as they did yesterday."

Charity gazed at her with dazzled eyes. "Oh, it's lovely," she said, and hastened away without listening to Ally's protest. She wanted her dress to be as pretty as the other girls'—wanted it, in fact, to outshine the rest, since she was to take part in the "exercises"—but she had no time just then to fix her mind on such matters.

She sped up the street to the library, of which she had the key about her neck. From the passage at the back she dragged forth a bicycle, and guided it to the edge of the street. She looked about to see if any of the girls were approaching; but they had drifted away together toward the Town Hall, and she sprang into the saddle and turned toward the Creston road. There was an almost continual descent to Creston, and with her feet against the pedals she floated through the still evening air like one of the hawks she had often watched slanting downward on motionless wings. Twenty minutes from the time when she had left Miss Hatchard's door she was turning up the wood-road on which Harney had overtaken her on the day of her flight; and a few minutes afterward she had jumped from her bicycle at the gate of the deserted house.

In the gold-powdered sunset it looked more than ever like some frail shell dried and washed by many seasons; but at the back, whither Charity advanced, drawing her bicycle after her, there were signs of recent habitation. A rough door made of boards hung in the kitchen doorway, and pushing it open she entered a room furnished in primitive camping fashion. In the window was a table, also made of boards, with an earthenware jar holding a big bunch of wild asters, two canvas chairs stood near by, and in one corner was a mattress with a Mexican blanket over it.

The room was empty, and leaning her bicycle against the house Charity clambered up the slope and sat down on a rock under an old apple-tree. The air was perfectly still, and from where she sat she would be able to hear the tinkle of a bicycle-bell a long way down the road. . . .

She was always glad when she got to the little house before Harney. She liked to have time to take in every detail of its secret sweetness—the shadows of the apple-trees swaying on the grass, the old walnuts rounding their domes below the road, the meadows sloping westward in the afternoon light—before his first kiss blotted it all out. Everything unrelated to the hours spent in that tranquil place was as faint as the remembrance of a dream. The only reality was the wondrous unfolding of her new self, the reaching out to the light of all her contracted tendrils. She had lived all her life among people whose sensibilities seemed to have withered for lack of use; and more wonderful, at first, than Harney's endearments were the words that were a part of them. She had always thought of love as something confused and furtive, and he made it as bright and open as the summer air.

On the morrow of the day when she had shown him the way to the deserted house he had packed up and left Creston River for Boston; but at the first station he had jumped off the train with a handbag and scrambled up into the hills. For two golden rainless August weeks he had camped in the house, getting eggs and milk from the solitary farm in the valley, where no one knew him, and doing his cooking over a spirit-lamp. He got up every day with the sun, took a plunge in a brown pool he knew of, and spent long hours lying in the scented hemlock-woods above the house, or wandering along the yoke of the Eagle River, far above the misty blue valleys that swept away east and west between the endless hills. And in the afternoon Charity came to him.

With part of what was left of her savings she had hired a bicycle for a month, and every day after dinner, as soon as her guardian started to his office, she hurried to the library, got out her bicycle, and flew down the Creston road. She knew that Mr. Royall, like everyone else in North Dormer, was perfectly aware of her acquisition: possibly he, as well as the rest of the village, knew what use she made of it. She did not care: she felt him to be so powerless that if he had questioned her she would probably have told him the truth. But they had never spoken to each other since the night on the wharf at Nettleton. He had returned to North Dormer only on the third day after that encounter, arriving just as Charity and Verena were sitting down to supper. He had drawn up his chair, taken his napkin from the sideboard drawer, pulled it out of its ring, and seated himself as unconcernedly as if he had come in from his usual afternoon session at Carrick Fry's; and the long habit of the household made it seem almost natural that Charity should not so much as raise her eyes when he entered. She had simply let him understand that her silence was not accidental by leaving the table while he was still eating, and going up without a word to shut herself into her room. After that he formed the habit of talking loudly and genially to Verena whenever Charity was in the room; but otherwise there was no apparent change in their relations.

She did not think connectedly of these things while she sat waiting for Harney, but they remained in her mind as a sullen background against which her short hours with him flamed out like forest fires. Nothing else mattered, neither the good nor the bad, or what might have seemed so before she knew him. He had caught her up and carried her away into a new world, from which, at stated hours, the ghost of her came back to perform certain customary acts, but all so thinly and insubstantially that she sometimes wondered that the people she went about among could see her. . . .

Behind the swarthy Mountain the sun had gone down in waveless gold. From a pasture up the slope a tinkle of cow-bells sounded; a puff of smoke hung over the farm in the valley, trailed on the pure air and was gone. For a few minutes, in the clear light that is all shadow, fields and woods were outlined with an unreal precision;

then the twilight blotted them out, and the little house turned gray and spectral under its wizened apple-branches.

Charity's heart contracted. The first fall of night after a day of radiance often gave her a sense of hidden menace: it was like looking out over the world as it would be when love had gone from it. She wondered if some day she would sit in that same place and watch in vain for her lover. . . .

His bicycle-bell sounded down the lane, and in a minute she was at the gate and his eyes were laughing in hers. They walked back through the long grass, and pushed open the door behind the house. The room at first seemed quite dark and they had to grope their way in hand in hand. Through the window-frame the sky looked light by contrast, and above the black mass of asters in the earthen jar one white star glimmered like a moth.

"There was such a lot to do at the last minute," Harney was explaining, "and I had to drive down to Creston to meet someone who has come to stay with my cousin for the show."

He had his arms about her, and his kisses were in her hair and on her lips. Under his touch things deep down in her struggled to the light and sprang up like flowers in sunshine. She twisted her fingers into his, and they sat down side by side on the improvised couch. She hardly heard his excuses for being late: in his absence a thousand doubts tormented her, but as soon as he appeared she ceased to wonder where he had come from, what had delayed him, who had kept him from her. It seemed as if the places he had been in, and the people he had been with, must cease to exist when he left them, just as her own life was suspended in his absence.

He continued, now, to talk to her volubly and gaily, deploring his lateness, grumbling at the demands on his time, and good-humouredly mimicking Miss Hatchard's benevolent agitation. "She hurried off Miles to ask Mr. Royall to speak at the Town Hall to-morrow: I didn't know till it was done." Charity was silent, and he added: "After all, perhaps it's just as well. No one else could have done it."

Charity made no answer: She did not care what part her guardian played in the morrow's ceremonies. Like all the other figures peopling her meagre world he had grown non-existent to her. She had even put off hating him.

"Tomorrow I shall only see you from far off," Harney continued. "But in the evening there'll be the dance in the Town Hall. Do you want me to promise not to dance with any other girl?"

Any other girl? Were there any others? She had forgotten even that peril, so enclosed did he and she seem in their secret world. Her heart gave a frightened jerk.

"Yes, promise."

He laughed and took her in his arms. "You goose—not even if they're hideous?"

He pushed the hair from her forehead, bending her face back, as his way was, and leaning over so that his head loomed black between her eyes and the paleness of the sky, in which the white star floated . . .

Side by side they sped back along the dark wood-road to the village. A late moon was rising, full orbed and fiery, turning the mountain ranges from fluid gray to a massive blackness, and making the upper sky so light that the stars looked as faint as their own reflections in water. At the edge of the wood, half a mile from North Dormer, Harney jumped from his bicycle, took Charity in his arms for a last kiss, and then waited while she went on alone.

They were later than usual, and instead of taking the bicycle to the library she propped it against the back of the wood-shed and entered the kitchen of the red house. Verena sat there alone; when Charity came in she looked at her with mild impenetrable eyes and then took a plate and a glass of milk from the shelf and set them silently on the table. Charity nodded her thanks, and sitting down, fell hungrily upon her piece of pie and emptied the glass. Her face burned with her quick flight through the night, and her eyes were dazzled by the twinkle of the kitchen lamp. She felt like a night-bird suddenly caught and caged.

"He ain't come back since supper," Verena said. "He's down to the Hall."

Charity took no notice. Her soul was still winging through the forest. She washed her plate and tumbler, and then felt her way up the dark stairs. When she opened her door a wonder arrested her. Before going out she had closed her shutters against the afternoon heat, but they had swung partly open, and a bar of moonlight, crossing the room, rested on her bed and showed a dress of China silk laid out on it in virgin whiteness. Charity had spent more than she could afford on the dress, which was to surpass those of all the other girls; she had wanted to let North Dormer see that she was worthy of Harney's admiration. Above the dress, folded on the pillow, was the white veil which the young women who took part in the exercises were to wear under a wreath of asters; and beside the veil a pair of slim white satin shoes that Ally had produced from an old trunk in which she stored mysterious treasures.

Charity stood gazing at all the outspread whiteness. It recalled a vision that had come to her in the night after her first meeting with Harney. She no longer had such visions . . . warmer splendours had displaced them . . . but it was stupid of Ally to have paraded all those white things on her bed, exactly as Hattie Targatt's wedding dress from Springfield had been spread out for the neighbours to see when she married Tom Fry. . . .

Charity took up the satin shoes and looked at them curiously. By day, no doubt, they would appear a little worn, but in the moonlight they seemed carved of ivory. She sat down on the floor to try them on, and they fitted her perfectly, though when she stood up she lurched a little on the high heels. She looked down at her feet, which the graceful mould of the slippers had marvellously arched and narrowed. She had never seen such shoes before, even in the shop-windows at Nettleton . . . never, except . . . yes, once, she had noticed a pair of the same shape on Annabel Balch.

A blush of mortification swept over her. Ally sometimes sewed for Miss Balch when that brilliant being descended on North Dormer, and no doubt she picked up presents of cast-off clothing: the treasures in the mysterious trunk all came from the people she worked for; there could be no doubt that the white slippers were Annabel Balch's. . . .

As she stood there, staring down moodily at her feet, she heard the triple click-click-click of a bicycle-bell under her window. It was Harney's secret signal as he passed on his way home. She stumbled to the window on her high heels, flung open the shutters and leaned out. He waved to her and sped by, his black shadow dancing merrily ahead of him down the empty moonlit road; and she leaned there watching him till he vanished under the Hatchard spruces.

XIII

The Town Hall was crowded and exceedingly hot. As Charity marched into it third in the white muslin file headed by Orma Fry, she was conscious mainly of the brilliant effect of the wreathed columns framing the green-carpeted stage toward which she was moving; and of the unfamiliar faces turning from the front rows to watch the advance of the procession.

But it was all a bewildering blur of eyes and colours till she found herself standing at the back of the stage, her great bunch of asters and goldenrod held well in front of her, and answering the nervous glance of Lambert Sollas, the organist from Mr. Miles's church, who had come up from Nettleton to play the harmonium and sat behind it, his conductor's eye running over the fluttered girls.

A moment later Mr. Miles, pink and twinkling, emerged from the background, as if buoyed up on his broad white gown, and briskly dominated the bowed heads in the front rows. He prayed energetically and briefly and then retired, and a fierce nod from Lambert Sollas warned the girls that they were to follow at once with "Home, Sweet Home." It was a joy to Charity to sing: it seemed as though, for the first time, her secret rapture might burst from her and flash its defiance at the world. All the glow in her blood, the breath of the summer earth, the rustle of the forest, the fresh call of birds at sunrise, and the brooding midday languors, seemed to pass into her untrained voice, lifted and led by the sustaining chorus.

And then suddenly the song was over, and after an uncertain pause, during which Miss Hatchard's pearl-grey gloves started a furtive signalling down the hall, Mr. Royall, emerging in turn, ascended the steps of the stage and appeared behind the flower-wreathed desk. He passed close to Charity, and she noticed that his gravely set face wore the look of majesty that used to awe and fascinate her childhood. His frock-coat had been carefully brushed and ironed, and the ends of his narrow black tie were so nearly even that the tying must have cost him a protracted struggle. His appearance struck her all the more because it was the first time she had looked him full in the face since the night at Nettleton, and nothing in his grave and impressive demeanour revealed a trace of the lamentable figure on the wharf.

He stood a moment behind the desk, resting his finger-tips against it, and bending slightly toward his audience; then he straightened himself and began.

At first she paid no heed to what he was saying: only fragments of sentences, sonorous quotations, allusions to illustrious men, including the obligatory tribute to Honorius Hatchard, drifted past her inattentive ears. She was trying to discover Harney among the notable people in the front row; but he was nowhere near Miss Hatchard, who, crowned by a pearl-grey hat that matched her gloves, sat just below the desk, supported by Mrs. Miles and an important-looking unknown lady. Charity was near one end of the stage, and from where she sat the other end of the first row of seats was cut off by the screen of foliage masking the harmonium. The effort to see Harney around the corner of the screen, or through its interstices, made her unconscious of everything else; but the effort was unsuccessful, and gradually she found her attention arrested by her guardian's discourse.

She had never heard him speak in public before, but she was familiar with the rolling music of his voice when he read aloud, or held forth to the selectmen above the stove at Carrick Fry's. Today his inflections were richer and graver than she had ever known them: he spoke slowly, with pauses that seemed to invite his hearers to silent participation in his thought; and Charity perceived a light of response in their faces.

He was nearing the end of his address . . . "Most of you," he said, "most of you who have returned here today, to take contact with this little place for a brief hour, have come only on a pious pilgrimage, and will go back presently to busy cities and lives full of larger duties. But that is not the only way of coming back to North Dormer. Some of us, who went out from here in our youth . . . went out, like you, to busy cities and larger duties . . . have come back in another way—come back for good. I am one of those, as many of you know. . . ." He paused, and there was a sense of suspense in the listening hall. "My history is without interest, but it has its lesson: not so much for those of you who have already made your lives in other places, as for the young men who are perhaps planning even now to leave these quiet hills and go down into the struggle. Things they cannot foresee may send some of those young men back some day to the little township and the old homestead: they may come back for good. . . ." He looked about him, and repeated gravely: "For *good.* There's the point I want to make . . . North Dormer is a poor little place, almost lost in a mighty landscape: perhaps, by this time, it might have been a bigger place, and more in scale with the landscape, if those who had to come back had come with that feeling in their minds—that they wanted to come back for *good* . . . and not for bad . . . or just for indifference. . . .

"Gentlemen, let us look at things as they are. Some of us have come back to our native town because we'd failed to get on elsewhere. One way or other, things had gone wrong with us . . . what we'd dreamed of hadn't come true. But the fact that we had failed elsewhere is no reason why we should fail here. Our very experiments in larger places, even if they were unsuccessful, ought to have helped us to make North Dormer a larger place . . . and you young men who are preparing even now to follow the call of ambition, and turn your back on the old homes—well, let me say this to you, that if ever you do come back to them it's worth while to come back to them for their good. . . . And to do that, you must keep on loving them while you're away from them; and even if you come back against your will—and thinking it's all a bitter mistake of Fate or Providence—you must try to make the best of it, and to make the best of your old town; and after a while—well, ladies and gentlemen, I give you my recipe for what it's worth; after a while, I believe you'll be able to say, as I can say today: 'I'm glad I'm here.' Believe me, all of you, the best way to help the places we live in is to be glad we live there."

He stopped, and a murmur of emotion and surprise ran through the audience. It was not in the least what they had expected, but it moved them more than what they had expected would have moved them. "Hear, hear!" a voice cried out in the middle of the hall. An outburst of cheers caught up the cry, and as they subsided Charity heard Mr. Miles saying to someone near him: "That was a *man* talking—" He wiped his spectacles.

Mr. Royall had stepped back from the desk, and taken his seat in the row of chairs in front of the harmonium. A dapper white-haired gentleman—a distant Hatchard—succeeded him behind the goldenrod, and began to say beautiful things about the old oaken bucket, patient white-haired mothers, and where the boys used to go nutting . . . and Charity began again to search for Harney. . . .

Suddenly Mr. Royall pushed back his seat, and one of the maple branches in front of the harmonium collapsed with a crash. It uncovered the end of the first row and in one of the seats Charity saw Harney, and in the next a lady whose face was turned toward him, and almost hidden by the brim of her dropping hat. Charity did not need to see the face. She knew at a glance the slim figure, the fair hair heaped up under the hat-brim, the long pale wrinkled gloves with bracelets slipping over them. At the fall of the branch Miss Balch turned her head toward the stage, and in her pretty thin-lipped smile there lingered the reflection of something her neighbour had been whispering to her. . . .

Someone came forward to replace the fallen branch, and Miss Balch and Harney were once more hidden. But to Charity the vision of their two faces had blotted out everything. In a flash they had shown her the bare reality of her situation. Behind the frail screen of her lover's caresses was the whole inscrutable mystery of his life: his relations with other people—with other women—his opinions, his prejudices, his principles, the net of influences and interests and ambitions in which every man's life is entangled. Of all these she knew nothing, except what he had told her of his architectural aspirations. She had always dimly guessed him to be in touch with important people, involved in complicated relations—but she felt it all to be so far beyond her understanding that the whole subject hung like a luminous mist on the farthest verge of her thoughts. In the foreground, hiding all else, there was the glow of his presence, the light and shadow of his face, the way his short-sighted eyes, at her approach, widened and deepened as if to draw her down into them; and, above all, the flush of youth and tenderness in which his words enclosed her.

Now she saw him detached from her, drawn back into the unknown, and whispering to another girl things that provoked the same smile of mischievous complicity he had so often called to her own lips. The feeling possessing her was not one of jealousy: she was too sure of his love. It was rather a terror of the unknown, of all the mysterious attractions that must even now be dragging him away from her, and of her own powerlessness to contend with them.

She had given him all she had—but what was it compared to the other gifts life held for him? She understood now the case of girls like herself to whom this kind of thing happened. They gave all they had, but their all was not enough: it could not buy more than a few moments. . . .

The heat had grown suffocating—she felt it descend on her in smothering waves, and the faces in the crowded hall began to dance like the pictures flashed on the screen at Nettleton. For an instant Mr. Royall's countenance detached itself from the general blur. He had resumed his place in front of the harmonium, and sat close to her, his eyes on her face; and his look seemed to pierce to the very centre of her confused sensations. . . . A feeling of physical sickness rushed over her—and then deadly apprehension. The light of the fiery hours in the little house swept back on her in a glare of fear. . . .

She forced herself to look away from her guardian, and became aware that the oratory of the Hatchard cousin had ceased, and that Mr. Miles was again flapping his wings. Fragments of his peroration floated through her bewildered brain . . . "A rich harvest of hallowed memories. . . . A sanctified hour to which, in moments of trial, your thoughts will prayerfully return. . . . And now, O Lord, let us humbly and fervently give thanks for this blessed day of reunion, here in the old home to which we have come back from so far. Preserve it to us, O Lord, in times to come, in all its homely sweetness—in the kindliness and wisdom of its old people, in the courage and industry of its young men, in the piety and purity of this group of innocent girls—" He flapped a white wing in their direction, and at the same moment Lambert Sollas, with his fierce nod, struck the opening bars of "Auld Lang Syne." . . . Charity stared straight ahead of her and then, dropping her flowers, fell face downward at Mr. Royall's feet.

III

A VISIT TO OLD NEW ENGLAND

10

Edward Bellamy, from *Six to One: A Nantucket Idyl*

(1878)

Edward Bellamy (1850–1898) is best known for his socialist utopian novel Looking Backward, *but the charming little novel excerpted here has quite another agenda. In* Six to One, *an educated, sophisticated New Yorker, much like Bellamy himself, finds himself in his doctor's office. Mr. Edgerton is not well. It is a case of "nervous exhaustion," a sort of illness common among the "brain workers" of the late nineteenth century. Bankers, journalists, college professors, and ministers were increasingly convinced that the strain of their work necessitated long vacations in places with clean air and cool breezes. Edgerton must leave his position as a journalist immediately, and take six months off somewhere "out of the reach of newspapers, telegraphs, and railroads." The doctor suggests Nantucket.*

Nantucket was only just beginning to attract summer visitors in the 1870s. One of its attractions was the very isolation that had created the "queer society and customs" the doctor thought would interest his patient. Visitors expected old buildings and quaint "old salts," telling tales of life at sea. The grass-grown streets and rotting wharves that testified to the collapse of the whaling business now had a new use: to provide vacationers with peace and quiet. And the title of the novel adds another, only half-joking description of Nantucket's charms. The island was so depopulated and depressed that its sex ratio was skewed; able-bodied men had left in search of work. Much like the idyllic "Surf City" imagined by the Beach Boys in the 1960s, where there were "two girls for every boy," Nantucket is a place where the ratio of women to men is "six to one."

SIX TO ONE: A NANTUCKET IDYL

Chapter I. The One

Opposite each other in the sanctum of Dr. Brainard, one of the most eminent of the younger physicians of New York City, sit the doctor himself, a man of thirty-five, and a younger man, of perhaps thirty. The doctor and Mr. Edgerton, his present caller, are close friends, whose intimacy dates from college days, and many is the hour of social relaxation they have passed together in each other's offices or at their common club. But the motive of this call is not social. Mr. Edgerton is consulting his friend professionally, concerning certain unpleasant symptoms that have been troubling him of late, symptoms the doctor has long since noticed but has shut his eyes to from a strong repugnance to regarding his friend in anything like a professional light. But now he reproaches himself with not having spoken long ago.

Mr. Edgerton as he sits, appears to be of medium height and is of that brown-haired, grey-eyed type, as common in the temperate zone as the red color among horses. The face indicates an intellectual temperament, perhaps rather more receptive than self-asserting, but without any suggestion of softness. He would be called fine looking if the nervous wrinkles could be smoothed out of his cheeks and eyebrows, and the harassed expression banished from his face. He is just now dispirited and gloomy. It is noticeable that his fingers have a way of nervously twitching, and that he is constantly changing his position in the easy chair he occupies. His eyes moreover belie their natural calm and candor of expression by unsteady and shifting glances, and a restless motion. He is saying to the doctor,

"I don't know what's the matter at all, but somehow I can't take any rest lately. I don't refer so much to sleeping, although I find that hard enough, as I've told you, but to the impossibility of lying off, of enjoying recreation and idleness, of taking a waking rest. Somehow my mind will not quit fretting over my work when I leave the office, as it used to. I find it next to impossible to relapse into a passive state, however tired I am, and I feel dreadfully tired all the while. But more excitement instead of less, is the only thing that rests me, and I know that must be wrong.

"And then the last half hour at the office is terribly long, terribly! longer than all the rest of the day. I have to use almost a literal spur to get through the last of my work. At times I come so squarely against a stump that it is a simple impossibility to write another line. My brain seems for the nonce as completely dead as a paralyzed arm, and I just have to go home, no matter what is pressing. That is one of the queerest sensations a man ever has, I fancy, and one of the most terrifying. The quality of my work too, falls off as the difficulty of it increases. I cudgel my brains in vain, and have pretty much made up my mind that I've overrated myself and been overrated, and that I ought to resign my position.

"About the only sign of vigor I have left, if that be one, is a constant fretfulness and crossness. The least thing puts me into an uncontrollable rage. I am often utterly ashamed of myself at the way I abuse my subs, but I can't help it. What on earth has come over me, Harry? Is there any name for it?"

There are few more trying experiences in a doctor's life than when he is called on to make a serious diagnosis for a sick friend. His sympathies would fain becloud the fatal clearness of his perceptions. After a pause the doctor replied, affecting a cheery tone.

"Old boy, your case is perfectly clear. You have overworked yourself and must stop short off and take a long rest."

"Drop my profession? Leave my place?" asked Edgerton with a scared, appealing look which cut the doctor to the heart.

"Even so, Frank," he answered in a brave tone. "Not for long, perhaps, but the sooner the better. No doubt a little real rest will soon build you up again."

But Edgerton understood perfectly what he meant—that he was a broken-down man. He had dimly anticipated something of the sort for a good while, but still the doctor's announcement fell on him with a crushing suddenness. At the very threshold of his best decade he was laid on the shelf. His work was done. He was dead among the living. He might indeed ultimately recover so as to be able to do some light work in easy hours, but this possibility was a mere mockery. There was something humiliating and wounding, at once to his vanity, his pride of intellect and position, his ambitions, both moral and material, in this intimation that he had become a mental invalid.

As these reflections successively came over him he fell into a sinking revery, in which he felt himself dropping, dropping, from one plane of depression to another, from one step to the one below, down, down, toward the bottom. He heard the doctor's voice a long way off, saying something like,

"Don't take it so hard, Frank; scores of men have come to me far worse off than you are, and some of them are as well to-day as any in the city. Cheer up, old fellow, your case is not a bad one."

"I thank God I'm not married," said Edgerton. "How could I bear to go home and tell my wife that I was a broken-down man?"

"Who said you were any such thing? I didn't," replied the doctor fiercely. "Your nerves are in a jangle, that's all, and you've got to let up on the demnition grind of your newspaper work long enough for a six months' summer vacation, beginning to-morrow; not a day later."

"To-morrow! It's impossible!" cried Edgerton, with a despairing sort of vehemence.

"Have I got to scare you some more!" asked the doctor. "Your case is not so bad but that I'm sure I can cure you, but every day you stick at work means a month longer to get well in and less chance of a cure at that. An immediate and long vacation is absolutely imperative. You must go away from the city to some place, if possible, out of reach of newspapers, telegraphs, and railroads. Climate doesn't much matter with you."

"There's no such place nowadays," said Edgerton. "I fancy you had better send me to an asylum for imbeciles and feeble-minded and have done with it."

"Time enough for that later," replied the doctor cheerily. "How would you like a few months at Nantucket to begin with? I was down there last summer and I don't believe there is a more out-of-the-way, switched off sort of place in the United States."

"What!" exclaimed the other, fairly shocked into a display of vivacity in spite of his depression. "That ridiculous little dead-alive down-east-sand-bank, where there are six women to one man!"

"Isn't that enough for you? because if not I can reassure you," said the doctor smiling." At this season the proportion is fifteen of the gentler to one of the sterner sex, a large part of the few men being now absent on the mainland at their winter occupations."

"I shouldn't think of objecting to an excess of ladies' society," Edgerton replied, "but these Nantucket women, I suppose, are mostly fishwives and ancient virgins pickled in the east wind."

"The more I think of it," pursued the doctor, reflectively, "the more the place strikes me as an admirable selection. It is now April and for three months there will be no summer visitors to disturb you there. You've no idea how much you will enjoy studying the queer society and customs of the place. That will give you just about enough occupation."

"Good God! Harry, you must be crazy! You can't think that a man who has lived for ten years in a newspaper office, transmitting the sensations of a world through his nerves every day, could stand being exiled to such a comatose community as Nantucket! I should go mad in a week!"

"Perhaps you will fret some at first, just as the drunkard does when he forswears vinous excitement for the monotony of a temperate life, but you have got to reconcile yourself to a diet of quiet or you will never do six months more work," replied the doctor. "I don't say that Nantucket is your only possible sanitarium, mind you. Perhaps you may think of others as good, but to me it seems about the thing."

The doctor did not press the matter, but leading the conversation upon the topics of hygiene in general and Edgerton's case in particular, finally succeeded in getting his patient into quite a cheerful frame.

"It doesn't seem to me really as if I could quite go Nantucket," said the latter, voluntarily returning to the subject some time later, "and yet in one way it would be quite convenient. I have some sort of an uncle or aunt, I don't quite remember which, living down there, to say nothing of a pretty cousin who once spent a summer at our homestead in Woodstock. They've asked me to make them a visit, but though it's scarcely polite to say so, I don't think anything but this would have ever led me to seriously consider their invitation."

The next day Edgerton went down to the evening newspaper office in which he held the position of managing editor, and had a long, and to him very trying, interview with the publishers. They were pained, surprised and entirely sympathetic when he told them the verdict of his doctor. Much against their will he insisted on making his resignation final, for thus alone, the doctor had advised him, could he secure himself the mental quiet and lack of preoccupation essential to his cure. Later he bade his colaborers and subordinates in the office good-bye, and what hurt him most was the look of pity which he saw in their faces. He appreciated how bitter a thing pity is until the spirit is wholly broken.

He came in again after all had gone, to take a last farewell of the familiar apartments that had known him so many years. He sat long in his old arm chair and leaned his head upon the ink-stained desk. Dusk fell and the office boy came in whistling to sweep out the room, but seeing the editor still there, hushed his piping and was about to retire. To his humble eye Edgerton had always been a sort of Jupiter Tonans, and little did he dream that the editor at that moment envied the office boy. But so it was. To Edgerton the lad seemed, by his connection with the working world, to stand above him, and he experienced a sense of moral inferiority in his presence. He said in a humble tone,

"You needn't go, Johnnie. Sweep away. Never mind me."

The day had been a bitter experience for him, but he already felt the better for it. He was much calmer, and that night, the first for many a week, he slept as soundly as a child. The next day he kept away from the office, wandering about the city and trying vainly to interest himself in doing nothing. Such a holiday would have been all too short had he been at work, but now the mere fact that he was no longer a worker made it insufferably long and wearisome. He somehow could not recall a single one of the hundred delightful recreations and excursions which, while still a slave to the desk, he had pictured to himself as charming uses of leisure. And at evening, as the newsboys began to cry his paper on the street, the sound made him so sick at heart and miserable, that he was fain to lock himself in his room and shut the windows close.

The next afternoon and the next, obeying a gravitation he could not resist, he began to haunt the newspaper offices again, and to wander about them after office hours, like an uneasy ghost revisiting the scenes of its passion, and such indeed he seemed to himself. He took pains to avoid meeting the men on these visits, but his habits became known to them, and it was the talk in the office that poor Edgerton had become a mere wreck.

The doctor got wind of the way matters were going, and meeting Edgerton one day, took him to task, and the big whiskered man confessed with weak tears in his eyes how wretched he was, and how hard he found it to tear himself away from his old life.

"I sympathize with ghosts," he said.

"This will never do in the world, never, sir. Do you want to spoil my credit as a doctor? If you do I don't propose to let you," cried the other, with great show of indignation. "You must leave the city this very day if I have to carry you out on my back."

And the energetic doctor took him to his lodgings, packed his trunks, settled with his landlady, locked up his closets, took him to the cars, got his ticket and saw him off for Woodstock, having exacted a solemn promise that in a week, at farthest he would go to Nantucket.

11

Sarah Orne Jewett, from *Deephaven*

(1877)

Sarah Orne Jewett (1849–1909) wrote the sketches that would be collected in Deephaven *when she was still in her twenties, but they show signs of the meticulous powers of observation and quiet intensity that would later distinguish her most highly regarded work,* The Country of the Pointed Firs. *In* Deephaven, *two young Boston women are vacationing in a place much like the town where Jewett actually lived: South Berwick, Maine. The town is, as the two women say, "utterly out of fashion," and they are drawn to it for some of the same reasons that brought visitors to Nantucket. The two are not ill, but they prefer the quiet and solitude of Deephaven to the bustle of a livelier resort. In this chapter, called "Deephaven Society," the narrator describes the pleasures of Deephaven: old women dressed in the styles of fifty years past; a church that has not yet replaced its old bass-viol with a new organ; and ladies of the old school, dignified and imposing.*

DEEPHAVEN SOCIETY

It was curious to notice, in this quaint little fishing-village by the sea, how clearly the gradations of society were defined. The place prided itself most upon having been long ago the residence of one Governor Chantrey, who was a rich ship-owner and East India merchant, and whose fame and magnificence were almost fabulous. It was a never-ceasing regret that his house should have burned down after he died, and there is no doubt that if it were still standing it would rival any ruin of the Old World.

The elderly people, though laying claim to no slight degree of present consequence, modestly ignored it, and spoke with pride of the grand way in which life was carried on by their ancestors, the Deephaven families of old times. I think Kate and I were assured at least a hundred times that Governor Chantrey kept a valet, and his wife, Lady Chantrey, kept a maid, and that the governor had an uncle in England who was a baronet; and I believe this must have been why our friends felt so deep an interest in the affairs of the English nobility: they no doubt felt themselves entitled to seats near the throne itself. There were formerly five families who kept their coaches in Deephaven; there were balls at the governor's, and regal entertainments at other of the grand mansions; there is not a really distinguished person in the country who will not prove to have been directly or indirectly connected with Deephaven. We were shown the cellar of the Chantrey house, and the terraces, and a few clumps of lilacs, and the grand rows of elms. There are still two of the governor's warehouses left, but his ruined wharves are fast disappearing, and are almost deserted, except by small barefooted boys who sit on the edges to fish for sea-perch when the tide comes in. There is an imposing monument in the burying-ground to the great man and his amiable consort. I am sure that if there were any surviving relatives of the governor they would receive in Deephaven far more deference than is consistent with the principles of a republican government; but the family became extinct long since, and I have heard, though it is not a subject that one may speak of lightly, that the sons were unworthy of their noble descent and came to inglorious ends.

There were still remaining a few representatives of the old families, who were treated with much reverence by the rest of the townspeople, although they were, like the conies of Scripture, a feeble folk.

Deephaven is utterly out of fashion. It never recovered from the effects of the embargo of 1807, and a sand-bar has been steadily filling in the mouth of the harbor. Though the fishing gives what occupation there is for the inhabitants of the place, it is by no means sufficient to draw recruits from abroad. But nobody in Deephaven cares for excitement, and if some one once in a while has the low taste to prefer a more active life, he is obliged to go elsewhere in search of it, and is spoken of afterward with kind pity. I well remember the Widow Moses said to me, in speaking of a certain misguided nephew of hers, "I never could see what could 'a' sot him out to leave so many privileges and go way off to Lynn, with all them children too. Why, they lived here no more than a cable's length from the meetin'-house!"

There were two schooners owned in town, and 'Bijah Mauley and Jo Sands owned a trawl. There were some schooners and a small brig slowly going to pieces by the wharves, and indeed all Deephaven looked more or less out of repair. All along shore one might see dories and wherries and whale-boats, which had been left to die a lingering death. There is something piteous to me in the sight of an old boat. If one I had used much and cared for were past its usefulness, I should say good by to it, and have it towed out to sea and sunk; it never should be left to fall to pieces above high-water mark.

Even the commonest fishermen felt a satisfaction, and seemed to realize their privilege, in being residents of Deephaven; but among the nobility and gentry there lingered a fierce pride in their family and town records, and a hardly concealed contempt and pity for people who were obliged to live in other parts of the world. There were acknowledged to be a few disadvantages,—such as living nearly a dozen miles from the railway,—but, as Miss Honora Carew said, the tone of Deephaven society had always been very high, and it was very nice that there had never been any manufacturing element introduced. She could not feel too grateful, herself, that there was no disagreeable foreign population.

"But," said Kate one day, "wouldn't you like to have some pleasant new people brought into town?"

"Certainly, my dear," said Miss Honora, rather doubtfully; "I have always been public-spirited; but then, we always have guests in summer, and I am growing old. I should not care to enlarge my acquaintance to any great extent." Miss Honora and Mrs. Dent had lived gay lives in their younger days, and were interested and connected with the outside world more than any of our Deephaven friends; but they were quite contented to stay in their own house, with their books and letters and knitting, and they carefully read Littell and "the new magazine," as they called the Atlantic.

The Carews were very intimate with the minister and his sister, and there were one or two others who belonged to this set. There was Mr. Joshua Dorsey, who wore his hair in a queue, was very deaf, and carried a ponderous cane which had belonged to his venerated father,—a much taller man than he. He was polite to Kate and me, but we never knew him much. He went to play whist with the Carews every Monday evening, and commonly went out fishing once a week. He had begun the practice of law, but he had lost his hearing, and at the same time his lady-love had inconsiderately fallen in love with somebody else; after which he retired from active business life. He had a fine library, which he invited us to examine. He had many new books, but they looked shockingly overdressed, in their fresher bindings, beside the old brown volumes of essays and sermons, and lighter works in many-volume editions.

A prominent link in society was Widow Tully, who had been the much-respected housekeeper of old Captain Manning for forty years. When he died he left her the use of his house and family pew, besides an annuity. The existence of Mr. Tully seemed to be a myth. During the first of his widow's residence in town she had been much affected when obliged to speak of him, and always represented herself as having seen better days and as being highly connected. But she was apt to be ungrammatical when excited, and there was a whispered tradition that she used to keep a toll-bridge in a town in Connecticut; though the mystery of her previous state of existence will probably never be solved. She wore mourning for the captain which would have befitted his widow, and patronized the townspeople conspicuously, while she herself was treated with much condescension by the Carews and Lorimers. She occupied, on the whole, much the same position that Mrs. Betty Barker did in Cranford. And, indeed, Kate and I were often reminded of that estimable town. We heard that Kate's aunt, Miss Brandon, had never been appreciative of Mrs. Tully's merits, and that since her death the others had received Mrs. Tully into their society rather more.

It seemed as if all the clocks in Deephaven, and all the people with them, had stopped years ago, and the people had been doing over and over what they had been busy about during the last week of their unambitious progress. Their clothes had lasted wonderfully well, and they had no need to earn money when there was so little chance to spend it; indeed, there were several families who seemed to have no more visible means of support than a balloon. There were no young people whom we knew, though a number used to come to church on Sunday from the inland farms, or "the country," as we learned to say. There were children among the fishermen's families at the shore, but a few years will see Deephaven possessed by two classes instead of the time-honored three.

As for our first Sunday at church, it must be in vain to ask you to imagine our delight when we heard the tuning of a bass-viol in the gallery just before service. We pressed each other's hands most tenderly, looked up at the singers' seats, and then trusted ourselves to look at each other. It was more than we had hoped for. There were also a violin and sometimes a flute, and a choir of men and women singers, though the congregation were expected to join in the psalm-singing. The first hymn was

"The Lord our God is full of might,
The winds obey his will,"

to the tune of St. Ann's. It was all so delightfully old-fashioned; our pew was a square pew, and was by an open window looking seaward. We also had a view of the entire congregation, and as we were somewhat early, we watched the people come in, with great interest. The Deephaven aristocracy came with stately step up the aisle; this was all the chance there was for displaying their unquestioned dignity in public.

Many of the people drove to church in wagons that were low and old and creaky, with worn buffalo-robes over the seat, and some hay tucked underneath for the sleepy, undecided old horse. Some of the younger farmers and their wives had high, shiny wagons, with tall horsewhips,—which they sometimes brought into church,—and they drove up to the steps with a consciousness of being conspicuous and enviable. They had a bashful look when they came in, and for a few minutes after they took their seats they evidently felt that all eyes were fixed upon them; but after a little while they were quite at their ease, and looked critically at the new arrivals.

The old folks interested us most. "Do you notice how many more old women there are than old men?" whispered Kate to me. And we wondered if the husbands and brothers had been drowned, and if it must not be sad to look at the blue, sunshiny sea beyond the marshes, if the far-away white sails reminded them of some ships that had never sailed home into Deephaven harbor, or of fishing-boats that had never come back to land.

The girls and young men adorned themselves in what they believed to be the latest fashion, but the elderly women were usually relics of old times in manner and dress. They wore to church thin, soft silk gowns that must have been brought from over the seas years upon years before, and wide collars fastened with mourning-pins holding a lock of hair. They had big black bonnets, some of them with stiff capes, such as Kate and I had not seen before since our childhood. They treasured large rusty lace veils of scraggly pattern, and wore sometimes, on pleasant Sundays, white China-crape shawls with attenuated fringes; and there were two or three of these shawls in the congregation which had been dyed black, and gave an aspect of meekness and general unworthiness to the aged wearer, they clung and drooped about the figure in such a hopeless way. We used to notice often the most interesting scarfs, without which no Deephaven woman considered herself in full dress. Sometimes there were red India scarfs in spite of its being hot weather; but our favorite ones were long strips of silk, embroidered along the edges and at the ends with dismal-colored floss in odd patterns. I think there must have been a fashion once, in Deephaven, of working these scarfs, and I should not be surprised to find that it was many years before the fashion of working samplers came about. Our friends always wore black mitts on warm Sundays, and many of them carried neat little bags of various designs on their arms, containing a precisely folded pocket-handkerchief, and a frugal lunch of caraway seeds or red and white peppermints. I should like you to see, with your own eyes, Widow Ware and Miss Exper'ence Hull, two old sisters whose personal appearance we delighted in, and whom we saw feebly approaching down the street this first Sunday morning under the shadow of the two last members of an otherwise extinct race of parasols.

There were two or three old men who sat near us. They were sailors,—there is something unmistakable about a sailor,—and they had a curiously ancient, uncanny look, as if they might have belonged to the crew of the Mayflower, or even have cruised about with the Northmen in the times of Harold Harfager and his comrades. They had been blown about by so many winter winds, so browned by summer suns, and wet by salt spray, that their hands and faces looked like leather, with a few deep folds instead of wrinkles. They had pale blue eyes, very keen and quick; their hair looked like the fine sea-weed which clings to the kelp-roots and mussel-shells in little locks. These friends of ours sat solemnly at the heads of their pews and looked unflinchingly at the minister, when they were not dozing, and they sang with voices like the howl of the wind, with an occasional deep note or two.

Have you never seen faces that seemed old-fashioned? Many of the people in Deephaven church looked as if they must be—if not supernaturally old—exact copies of their remote ancestors. I wonder if it is not possible that the features and expression may be almost perfectly reproduced. These faces were not modern American faces, but belonged rather to the days of the early settlement of the country, the old colonial times. We often heard quaint words and expressions which we never had known anywhere else but in old books. There was a great deal of sea-lingo in use; indeed, we learned a great deal ourselves, unconsciously, and used it afterward to the great amusement of our friends; but there were also many peculiar provincialisms, and among the people who lived on the lonely farms inland we often noticed words we had seen in Chaucer, and studied out at school in our English literature class. Everything in Deephaven was more or less influenced by the sea; the minister spoke oftenest of Peter and his fishermen companions, and prayed most earnestly every Sunday morning for those who go down to the sea in ships. He made frequent allusions and drew numberless illustrations of a similar kind for his sermons, and indeed I am in doubt whether, if the Bible had been written wholly in inland countries, it would have been much valued in Deephaven.

The singing was very droll, for there was a majority of old voices, which had seen their best days long before, and the bass-viol was excessively noticeable, and apt to be a little ahead of the time the singers kept, while the violin lingered after. Somewhere on the other side of the church we heard an acute voice which rose high above all the rest of the congregation, sharp as a needle, and slightly cracked, with a limitless supply of breath. It rose and fell gallantly, and clung long to the high notes of Dundee. It was like the wail of the banshee, which sounds clear to the fated hearer above all other noises. We afterward became acquainted with the owner of this voice, and were surprised to find her a meek widow, who was like a thin black beetle in her pathetic cypress veil and big black bonnet. She looked as if she had forgotten who she was, and spoke with an apologetic whine; but we heard she had a temper as high as her voice, and as much to be dreaded as the equinoctial gale.

Near the church was the parsonage, where Mr. Lorimer lived, and the old Lorimer house not far beyond was occupied by Miss Rebecca Lorimer. Some stranger might ask the question why the minister and his sister did not live together, but you would have understood it at once after you had lived for a little while in town. They were very fond of each other, and the minister dined with Miss Rebecca on Sundays, and she passed the day with him on Wednesdays, and they ruled their separate households with decision and dignity. I think Mr. Lorimer's house showed no signs of being without a mistress, any more than his sister's betrayed the want of a master's care and authority.

The Carews were very kind friends of ours, and had been Miss Brandon's best friends. We heard that there had always been a coolness between Miss Brandon and Miss Lorimer, and that, though they exchanged visits and were always polite, there was a chill in the politeness, and one would never have suspected them of admiring each other at all. We had the whole history of the trouble, which dated back scores of years, from Miss Honora Carew, but we always took pains to appear ignorant of the feud, and I think Miss Lorimer was satisfied that it was best not to refer to it, and to let bygones be bygones. It would not have been true Deephaven courtesy to prejudice Kate against her grand-aunt, and Miss Rebecca cherished her dislike in silence, which gave us a most grand respect for her, since we knew she thought herself in the right; though I think it never had come to an open quarrel between these majestic aristocrats.

Miss Honora Carew and Mr. Dick and their elder sister, Mrs. Dent, had a charmingly sedate and quiet home in the old Carew house. Mrs. Dent was ill a great deal while we were there, but she must have been a very brilliant woman and was not at all dull when we knew her. She had outlived her husband and her children, and she had, several years before our summer there, given up her own home, which was in the city, and had come back to Deephaven. Miss Honora—dear Miss Honora!—had been one of the brightest, happiest girls, and had lost none of her brightness and happiness by growing old. She had lost none of her fondness for society, though she was so contented in quiet Deephaven, and I think she enjoyed Kate's and my stories of our pleasures as much as we did hers of old times. We used to go to see her almost every day. "Mr. Dick," as they called their brother, had once been a merchant in the East Indies, and there were quantities of curiosities and most beautiful china which he had brought and sent home, which gave the house a character of its own. He had been very rich and had lost some of his money, and then he came home and was still considered to possess princely wealth by his neighbors. He had a great fondness for reading and study, which had not been lost sight of during his business life, and he spent most of his time in his library. He and Mr. Lorimer had their differences of opinion about certain points of theology, and this made them much fonder of each other's society, and gave them a great deal of pleasure; for after every series of arguments, each was sure that he had vanquished the other, or there were alternate victories and defeats which made life vastly interesting and important.

Miss Carew and Mrs. Dent had a great treasury of old brocades and laces and ornaments, which they showed us one day, and told us stories of the wearers, or, if they were their own, there were always some reminiscences which they liked to talk over with each other and with us. I never shall forget the first evening we took tea with them; it impressed us very much, and yet nothing wonderful happened. Tea was handed round by an old-fashioned maid, and afterward we sat talking in the twilight, looking out at the garden. It was such a delight to have tea served in this way. I wonder that the fashion has been almost forgotten. Kate and I took much pleasure in choosing our tea-poys; hers had a mandarin parading on the top, and mine a flight of birds and a pagoda; and we often used them afterward, for Miss Honora asked us to come to tea whenever we liked. "A stupid, common country town" some one dared to call Deephaven in a letter once, and how bitterly we resented it! That was a house where one might find the best society, and the most charming manners and good-breeding, and if I were asked to tell you what I mean by the word "lady," I should ask you to go, if it were possible, to call upon Miss Honora Carew.

After a while the elder sister said, "My dears, we always have prayers at nine, for I have to go up stairs early nowadays." And then the servants came in, and she read solemnly the King of glory Psalm, which I have always liked best, and then Mr. Dick read the church prayers, the form of prayer to be used in families. We stayed later to talk with Miss Honora after we had said good night to Mrs. Dent. And we told each other, as we went home in the moonlight down the quiet street, how much we had enjoyed the evening, for somehow the house and the people had nothing to do with the present, or the hurry of modern life. I have never heard that psalm since without its bringing back that summer night in Deephaven, the beautiful quaint old room, and Kate and I feeling so young and worldly, by contrast, the flickering, shaded light of the candles, the old book, and the voices that said Amen.

There were several other fine old houses in Deephaven beside this and the Brandon house, though that was rather the most imposing. There were two or three which had not been kept in repair, and were deserted, and of course they were said to be haunted, and we were told of their ghosts, and why they walked, and when. From some of the local superstitions Kate and I have vainly endeavored ever since to shake ourselves free. There was a most heathenish fear of doing certain things on Friday, and there were countless signs in which we still have confidence. When the moon is very bright and other people grow sentimental, we only remember that it is a fine night to catch hake.

12

Thomas Nelson Page, "Miss Godwin's Inheritance," *Scribner's Magazine*

(August 1904)

Thomas Nelson Page (1853–1922) was a southern local color writer, best known for stories that romanticized the "good old days" of slavery before the Civil War. In "Miss Godwin's Inheritance," he took a slightly different approach, setting the story in a village in southern Maine, not far from the actual town of York, where Page vacationed for over twenty years. Page based his story on the experience of his real-life friend Emily Tyson, who bought and restored the Hamilton House, an eighteenth-century mansion in South Berwick, Maine (not far from the house of Tyson's friend Sarah Orne Jewett). The fictional character, Mrs. Davison, suffers from a kind of malaise similar to that of Bellamy's Mr. Edgerton—she feels tired all the time, restless, and worn out—but the therapy she seeks here is different from Edgerton's. For Mrs. Davison the old house provides several opportunities unavailable to her in her city drawing room. Restoring and rearranging the place provides her with fulfilling, creative work. The house also helps to reestablish a link with her ancestors—a link that reminded her and everyone else of the gentility and social standing of her family. Perhaps most important, the house provides Mrs. Davison an opportunity to play the role of generous benefactor to the title character, Miss Godwin, the poverty-stricken Yankee woman who lives near by.

MISS GODWIN'S INHERITANCE

I

When my cousin Hortensia asked me one evening in the middle of winter to go with her the following week to look at a "summer place" for her on the Maine coast, it crossed my mind for a moment that she was slightly mad; but the glance that I gave her as she sat in her rocking-chair, just out of the tempered light of the reading-lamp, with her dainty gray skirts spread about her and the firelight flickering on her calm features and white hands as she plied her needlework, showed nothing to warrant my suspicion. Only the time was midwinter, the hour was nine o'clock in the evening, and even the tight windows and the heavy silken curtains drawn close could not shut out the sound of the driving sleet that had been falling all the evening.

I knew my cousin well; knew that notwithstanding her Quaker blood and quiet ways she was, as an old neighbor had long since aptly said of her, "a woman of her own head," and that she had during her married life enjoyed the full confidence of her husband, her senior by some years, and one of the strong members of the bar, and had always borne with notable success her full share of the exactions of a large establishment and a distinguished position. I knew further, that since her husband's death she had ably carried on his charitable work and maintained her position as one of the leaders, not of society, but of everything else that was good and lofty and dignified. So I put aside the thought that first sprang into my mind and declared my readiness to go with her anywhere and at any time that she might wish.

"But why on earth do you select that particular spot and this particular time to look at a country place?" I demanded.

The question evidently appeared apt to her, and she gave one of her little chuckles of pleasure which had just enough of the silvery sound to hall-mark it a laugh. Folding her hands for a moment in a way which she had either inherited from the portrait of her Quakeress grandmother, on her dining-room wall, or which she had learned by practice to make so perfect that it was the exact representation of that somewhat supercilious but elegant old dame’s easy attitude, she said:

“For the best reason in the world, my dear John! Simply—*because*.”

This ended it for the moment, but a little later, having, as I suppose, enjoyed my mystification sufficiently, she began to give her reasons. In the first place, she was “completely worn out” with the exactions of the social life which she had found gathering about her more and more closely.

“I feel so tired all the time—so dissatisfied,” she said, with a certain lassitude quite unusual with her. “I cannot stand the drain of this life any longer. My heart—”

“Your heart! Well, your heart is all right—that I will swear,” I interjected.

“Don’t be frivolous. My heart is my trouble at present.” She gave a nod of mock severity. “I consulted a doctor and he told me to go to some European watering place ending in ‘heim’; but I know better that that. It is ‘heim’ that I want, but it is an American ‘heim,’ and I am going to find it on this side the water. Like that Shunamitish woman, ‘I dwell among mine own people.’ ”

“She was ever one of my favorites,” I ventured; “but what is the matter with this ‘heim’?” I gazed about the luxurious apartment where Taste had been handmaid to Wealth in every appointment.

She shook her head wearily.

“I am so tired of this strenuous life that I feel that if I do not get out of it and go back to something that is calm and natural I shall die. It is all so hollow and unreal. Why, we are all trying to do the same thing and all trying to think the same thing, or, at least, say the same thing. We do not think at all. Scores of women come pouring into my house on my ‘days’ and pour out again, content only to say they have left cards on my table, and then if I do not leave cards on their tables they all think I am rude and put on airs because I live in a big house. Forty women called here to-day, and thirty-nine of them said precisely the same thing. I must get out of it."

"What was it?"

"*Nothing.*" Her face lit up with the smile which always made her look so charming, and of which some one had once said: "Mrs. Davison is not precisely a pretty woman, but her smile is an enchantment."

"And what did you say to them?"

"I gave them the exact equivalent—*nothing.* I must get out. My husband once said that the most dreadful thing on earth was a worldly old woman."

"You are neither worldly nor old," I protested.

She gazed at me calmly.

"I am getting to be both. I am past forty, and when a woman is past forty she is dependent on two things—her goodness and her intellect. I have lost the one and am in danger of losing the other. I want to go where I can preserve the few remnants I have left. And now," she added, with a sudden return of her vivacity, which was always like a flash of April sunlight even when the clouds were lowest, "I have sent for you this evening to show you the highest proof of my confidence. I wish to ask your advice, and I want you to give the best you have. But I do not want you to think I am going to take it, for I am not."

"Well, that is frank at any rate," I said. "We shall, at least, start fair and not be by the way of being deceived."

"Yes, I want it; it will help me to clarify my ideas—to arrive at my own conclusions. I shall know better what I do *not* want."

She gazed at me serenely from under her long eyelashes.

"Flattering, at least! How many houses do you suppose I build on those terms? And now one question before I agree. Why do you want to take a place which is, so to speak, nowhere—that is, as you tell me, several miles from anywhere?"

"Just for that reason—I want to get back to first principles, and I understand that the place I have in mind was one of the most beautiful old homes in all New England. It has trees on it that were celebrated a century ago, and a garden that is historical. Family-trees can be made easy enough; but only Omnipotence can make a great tree, and the first work of the Creator was to plant a garden."

"Oh! well, then, I give in. If there is a garden." For my cousin's love for flowers was a passion. Her name, Hortensia, was an inspiration or a prophecy. She could have made Aaron's rod bud.

"There is one other reason that I have not told you," she added, after a pause.

"There always is," I observed, half cynically; for I was not so pleased as I pretended with her flatly notifying me that my advice went for nothing.

She nodded.

"My grandfather and the owner of the old place used to be great friends, and my grandfather always said it was one of the loveliest spots on earth: 'A pleasant seat,' he called it. I think he had a little love affair there once with the daughter of the house. My grandmother was always rather scornful about it."

II

A week later we landed about mid-day at the little station just outside of the village where my cousin, with her usual prevision, had arranged to have a two-horse sleigh meet us. Unfortunately, the day before, a snow of two feet had added to the two feet which already lay on the ground and the tract outside of town had not been broken. The day, however, was one of those perfect winter days which come from time to time in northern latitudes when the atmosphere has been cleared; the winds, having done their work have been laid, and Nature, having arrayed herself in immaculate garb, seems well content to rest and survey her work. The sunshine was like a jewel. The white earth sparkled with a myriad myriads of diamonds.

The man to whom my cousin had written, Mr. Silas Freeman, was on the platform to meet us. A tall, lank person with a quiet face, a keen nose, and an indifferent manner. Bundled in a buffalo-robe coat he stood on the platform and gazed at us in a reposeful manner as we descended from the train. We passed him twice without his speaking to us, though his eyes were on us with mild and somewhat humorous curiosity. When, in response to my inquiries, the station agent had pointed him out, I walked up and asked if he were Mr. Freeman, he answered briefly: "I be. That's my name."

I introduced Mrs. Davison, and he extended his hand in its large fur glove indifferently, while a glance suddenly shot from his quiet eyes, keen, curious, and inspective. She instantly took up the running, and did so with such knowledge of the conditions, such clearness and resolution, and withal with such tact, that Mr. Freeman's calm face changed from granite to something rather softer, and his eyes began to light up with an expression quite like interest.

"No, he hadn't brought the sleigh, 's he didn't know's she'd come, seein' 's the weather w'z so unlikely."

"But didn't I write you I was coming?" demanded Mrs. Davison.

"Waal, yes. But you city folks sometimes writes more t'n you come."

Mrs. Davison cast her eye in my direction.

"You see there!—he knows them." She turned back to Freeman. "But I am not one of the 'city folks.' I was brought up in the country."

Mr. Freeman blinked with something between incredulity and mild interest.

"Well, you'll know better next time," continued my cousin. "Now remember, the next time I write, I am coming—if I do not, you look in the papers and see what I died of."

Whether it was the words or the laugh that went with them and changed them from a complaint to a jest, Mr. Freeman's solemnity relaxed, and he drawled, "All ri-ight."

"And now, can't we get the sleigh right away?" demanded Mrs. Davison.

"Guess so. But th' road beyond th' village ain't broken."

"Well, can't we break it?"

"Guess so."

"Well, let's try. I'm game for it."

"All ri-ight," with a little snap in his eye.

If, however, Mr. Silas Freeman did not show any curiosity as to our movements he was one of the few persons we saw who did not. The object of our coming was evidently known to the population at large, or to such portion of it as we saw. They peered at us from the porches of the white houses under the big elms, or from the stoops of the stores, where they stood bundled up in rough furs and comforters, and, turning as we passed, discussed us as if we were freaks of Nature.

As we drove along, plunging and creeping through the snow-drifts, Mr. Freeman began to unbend. "This road ain't broke, but somebody's been along here. Guess it's Miss Hewitt."

"Who is Miss Hewitt?"

"She's one o' Doct' Hewitt's girls—she's one of the good women—looks after them 's ain't got anybody else to look after 'em."

"I hope I shall know her some day," observed my cousin.

"She's a good one to know," remarked Mr. Silas Freeman.

We crept around the hill toward the river.

"Ah! 'twas Miss Hewitt," observed the driver to himself. "She's been to dig out F'lissy." He was gazing down across the white field at a small "shackelty" old cabin which lay half buried in snow, with a few scraggy apple trees about it.

When at length, after a somewhat strenuous struggle through snow-drifts up to our horses' backs, we stood on the portico of the old mansion, though the snow was four feet deep I could not but admit that the original owner knew a "pleasant seat" when he saw it. Colonel Hamilton, when he established himself on that point overlooking the winding river and facing the south, plainly knew his business.

The remains of a terraced lawn sloped in gracious curves around the hill in front, where still stood some of the grand elms which, even a century before, had awakened the enthusiasm of the owner's Southern visitor. Beyond, on one side, came down to the river's margin a forest of pines which some good fortune, in shape of a life-long litigation, had spared from the lumberman's axe, and which stood like an army guarding the old mansion and its demesnes, and screening them from the encroachments of modern, pushing life.

On the other side, the hill ran down again to the water's edge, the slope covered with apple trees which now stood waist deep in snow.

Behind, huddled close to the house, were a number of out-buildings in a state of advanced dilapidation, and yet behind these the hill rose nobly a straight slant of nearly half a mile, its crest, where once the avenue had wound, crowned with a fine row of elms and maples, a buttress and defence against the double storm of the north wind and the casual tourist.

Moreover, the original architect had known his business, or, at least, had known enough to give the owner excellent ideas, for the house was a perfect example of the Colonial architecture which seems to have blown across the country a century and a half ago like the breath of a classical spring, leaving in its path the traces of a classical genius which had its inspiration on the historic shores of the Ægean and the Mediterranean. From foundation to peaked roof with its balustrade, in form and proportion, through every detail of pillar and moulding and cornice, it was altogether charming and perfect.

I became suddenly aware that my cousin's eyes had been on my face for some time. She had been enjoying my surprise and delight.

"Well, what do you think of it?"

"It is charming—altogether charming."

"I thought you would like it."

"Like it! Why, it is a work of genius. That architect, whoever he was—"

"Helped to clarify the ideas of the owner."

"Helped to clarify! This is the work of a man of genius, I say."

"His name was Hamilton. He built it and owned it."

As we came out of the house and plunged around to the long-closed front door to take another look at the beautiful façade, my cousin gave an exclamation.

"Why, here is a rose, all wrapped up and protected." She was bending over it as if it had been a baby in its cradle, a new tone in her voice. "It is the only sign of care about the whole place. I wonder what kind it is?"

"I guess that's F'lissy God'in's rose-bush," said Mr. Freeman, who had followed us in our tour of inspection, now with an inscrutable look of reserve, now with one of humorous indulgence.

"Who is F'lissy Godwin?" asked Mrs. Davison, still bending over the twist of straw.

"She's one of 'em—she's the one as lives down the road a piece in that little old house under the hill you saw."

"Does anyone live in that house!"

"Waal, if you call it livin'. She stays there anyway. She wouldn't go to the New Home—preferred to stay right here, and comes up and potters around—I al'ays heard she had a rose-bush."

"Oh! She has a new home? Why on earth doesn't she go there?" questioned Mrs. Davison.

The driver's eyes blinked. "Guess she didn't like the comp'ny. That's what th' call the poorhouse." His eyes blinked again, this time with satisfaction at my cousin's ignorance. "They might's well ha' let her stay on up here. She wa'nt flighty enough to do any harm, and she'd ha' taken as good care of the house as anyone. But they wouldn't." His tone expressed such entire acquiescence that Mrs. Davison asked, "Who would not?"

"Oh, them others. They had the right, and they wouldn't; so she's lived down there ever since I knew her. All the others 're dead now—she's sort o' 'the last leaf on the tree.'"

The quotation seemed suddenly to lift him up to a new level.

My cousin's face had grown softer and softer while he was speaking.

"Poor old thing! Could I help her?"

"Waal, I guess you could if you wanted to."

"I do. Couldn't you give her something for me?"

"I guess I could, but you'd better get somebody else to do it. She'd want to know where it come from, and I d'n' know 's she'd take it if she knew it come from you as is buyin' the place."

"Oh! I see. But you need not tell her it came from me. You might give it to her as from yourself?"

It was the one mistake she made. His face hardened.

"Waal, no, I couldn't do that."

My cousin saw her error and apologized. He said nothing, but he softened.

"Miss Hewitt might do it. She's the one as hunts 'em up and helps 'em."

"Well, then I will get her to do it for me. She will know how."

"She knows how to do a good many things," observed Mr. Freeman quietly.

III

After this I knew that nothing would keep my cousin from buying the place if she could get it, and so in truth it turned out. After some negotiating, in which every edge was made to cut by the sellers, the deal was closed and the Hamilton place with all its "improvements, easements, appurtenances and hereditaments," became hers and her heirs' forever.

No child with a new toy was ever more delighted.

I received one evening an imperative message: "Pray come immediately," and on my arrival I knew at once that my cousin had gotten the place. Her eyes were dancing and all of her old spirit appeared to have come back. The flush of youth was on her cheeks. I found the big library table covered with photographs of the place and the house, inside and out, and if there was a spot on the table not covered by a photograph it held a book on gardening.

"Well, I have it."

"Or them," I observed quietly.

"Them?" with a puzzled look. "Never mind! I know it's an insult, though I do not know just how. Well, I have sent for you. I want—"

"My advice?"

"—You to carry out my ideas."

"How do you know I will?"

"Come, do not talk nonsense. Of course you will." She did not even take the trouble to smile. She began to sketch her views rapidly and clearly in a way that showed a complete comprehension of the case.

"The house is to be done just this way. And the grounds are to be restored as they were. All these old buildings are to be removed." She was speaking with a photograph in her hand showing the decrepit stables—"these—which are recent excrescences, pulled down; this moved back to its old site under the hill down there—and here is to be the garden just where it was—and as it was. See, here is the description."

She took from the table a small volume bound in red leather, and opened it.

"Here is an old letter written by my grandfather a hundred years ago, giving his impressions of the place when he visited it."

"'Here I am in the Province of Maine, where I arrived a few days ago, expecting to find myself in a foreign land. Imagine my surprise when I discovered that the place and the people are more like those among whom I was brought up in my youth than in any other part of New England which I have visited. Of course, I am speaking of its appearance in the summer, for this is July, and it might be early June. . . .'

"You don't want all this—he gives simply a description of the distinction in classes which he was surprised to find here—'many of the families having their coats of arms and other relics of the gentry-class.' Ah! here it is. Here is the description:

"'I was invited to Colonel H.'s and he sent down for me his barge manned by a half dozen sturdy fellows, just as might have been sent from Shirley or Rosewell or Brandon; and on my arrival I found the Colonel awaiting me on the great rock which dispenses with any need for a pier, except a float and a few wooden steps.

"'He has one of the pleasantest seats which I have found in all my travels—a house which, though not large, would have done justice to any place in Maryland or Virginia, and which possesses every mark of good taste and refinement. It fronts to the south and is bathed in sunlight the whole day long.

"'The garden immediately caught my attention, and I think I might say I never saw more beautiful flowers, which surprised me, for I had an idea that this region produced little besides rocks and Puritanical narrowness: of which more anon. The garden lies at the back of the house, beginning on a level, with formal borders and grass-walks where the turf is kept as beautiful as any that I ever saw in England, and where there is every variety of flower which Adam and Eve could have known in their garden. In the first place, roses—roses—roses! Then all the rest: Rush-leaved daffodils, the jonquilles—"narcissi," the Colonel's sister calls them; phlox of every hue; hollyhocks, peonies, gillies—almost all that you have. Then the shrubbery!—lilacs, syringas, meadowsweet, spiræa, and I do not know how many more. I could not get over the feeling that they had all been brought from home. Indeed, I saw a fat robin sitting in a lilac bush that I am sure I saw at home two months ago, and when I bowed to him he nodded to me, so I know he is the same. On the land-side the garden slopes away suddenly into an untilled stretch of field where the wild flowers grow in unrivalled profusion. This the Colonel's sister calls her "wild garden." A field of daisies looked as if it were covered with snow. An old fellow with a face wrinkled and very like a winter apple, told me that one "Sir William Pepperil brought them over, and that is the reason you don't find 'em anywhere else but here." I did not tell him of my friend the robin.

"'By the way, the Colonel's sister is a very charming young lady—dark hair, gray eyes with black lashes, a mouth which I think her best feature, and a demure air. She is so fond of her garden that I call her Hortensia."

"What's that?"

My cousin broke into a silvery laugh. "You know now where I got my name. But I don't think my grandmother ever quite forgave her."

She closed the book.

"Now, you see what I want—to restore it exactly as it was, and only to add what will carry out this idea."

"Are you going to have a gardener?"

"Of course—"

"A landscape gardener?"

"Yes, of course! And a man to furnish the house by contract—and another to select my pictures for me!" Her nose was turned up, and she was chopping out her words at me.

"Well, you need not be so insulted."

"I told you I wanted to *restore* it."

"I only wanted to know how much in earnest you are."

"Well, you put one new thing in that house, not in keeping with the idea I have, and you will know."

IV

With the first opening of Spring my cousin was at work on her "restoration." She had the good sense to select as her head workman—for she would have no contractor either in or out of the house—a local carpenter—an excellent man. But even with this foresight it must be said that her effort at restoration was not received with entire approbation by her new neighbors. The gossip that was brought to her—and there was no little of it—informed her that they considered her incoming as an intrusion, and regarded her with some suspicion and a little disdain. Some of them set out evidently to make it very clear to her that they did not propose to let her interfere in any way with their habits and customs. They were "as good as she was," and they meant her to know it.

In time, however, as she pushed on with her work, always good-natured and always determined, she began to make her way with them. Silas Freeman stood her in good stead, for he became her fast friend.

"She is rather citified," he agreed, "but she can't help that, and she ain't a bit airified."

I was present on an occasion when one of the first evidences of her gradual breaking into the charmed circle came. The work on the house was progressing rapidly. Rotted pediments, broken window frames, unsound cornices, lost spindles, being replaced by their exact counterparts; each bit that needed renewal or repair being restored with absolute fidelity under her keen eyes. And all the time she was rummaging around through the country picking up old furniture and articles that dated back and belonged to the time when her grandfather had visited the place. No child ever enjoyed fitting up a baby-house more keenly than she enjoyed fitting up this old mansion.

It was really beginning to show the effect of her tact and zeal. She had actually gotten two or three rooms finished and furnished, and had moved in, "'the better to see, my dear,'" she said to me. "Besides, I know very well that the only way to get workmen out of a house is to live them out. I mean to spend this summer here."

Outside, too, the work was progressing favorably, though the frost was scarcely out of the ground. The rickety buildings were all removed from her cherished ground "where once the garden smiled" and she was only awaiting a favorable season to lay out her garden and put in her seeds and slips, which were already being gotten ready.

It was one of those Sunday afternoons in April when Spring announces that she has come to pay you a visit, and leaves her visiting card in bluebirds and dandelions. The bluebirds had been glancing about the lawn all day, making dashes of vivid color against the spruces, and even a few robins had been flitting around, surveying the land and spying out choice places. Dandelions were beginning to gleam in favored spots, and a few green tufts were peeping up where jonquils had, through all discouragements, lived to shake their golden trumpets in sheltered places.

My cousin had enjoyed it all unspeakably. She had moved all day like one in a trance, with softened eyes and gentle voice. Before going to church she had, with her own hands, unwrapped the rosebush she had observed on her first visit, and I heard her bemoaning its poor, starved condition. "Poor thing—you are the only real old occupant," I heard her murmur. "You shall have new soil and I hope you will live."

V

The afternoon had been perfect and the sun had just stolen over toward the top of the western hill and was sending his light across the yard, tinging the twigs of the apple trees with a faint flush of pink, and we were watching the lengthening shadows when I became aware that there was someone standing in the old disused road just outside the yard. She was an old woman, and there was something so calm about her that she seemed herself almost like one of the shadows. She was dressed in the plainest way: an old black dress, now faded to a dim brown, a coat of antique design and appearance, in which a faint green under the arms alone showed that it, too, had once been black, a little old bonnet over her thin gray hair, which was smoothed down over her ears in a style of forty years before.

"There is someone," I said in a low tone. "Isn't she quaint?"

My cousin, seeing that she was a poor woman, moved down the slope toward her.

"Good afternoon," she said gently.

"Afternoon"—with a little shift of her position which reminded me of a courtesy. "Air you Miss Davison?"

"Yes, I am Mrs. Davison."

"The one 't bought the place?"

"Yes, I am that one. Can I do anything for you?" The tone of her voice was so kind that the old woman seemed to gain a little courage.

"Well, I thought I'd come up and see you a moment this Sabbath afternoon."

"Won't you come up and see the sunset?"

"Well, thank you—perhaps I will, if it will not discompose you."

My cousin smiled at her quaint speech. As the visitor came up the slope I saw her small, sunken eyes sweep the grounds before her and then rest on the rose-bush which my cousin had unwrapped that day.

"It is so beautiful from this terrace," pursued my cousin.

"Yes, it is," said the visitor. She stood and gazed at the sky a moment, then glanced half furtively at the house and about the grounds, and again her eyes rested on the rose-bush. Her faded weather-beaten face had grown soft.

"I have seen it very often from this spot. I used to live here."

"You did! Well, won't you walk into the house and take a cup of tea? I have just ordered tea for my cousin and myself."

The visitor gave me a somewhat searching look.

"Well, perhaps, I will, thank you." As she followed my cousin in, she crossed over to the side of the walk where the rose-bush was, and her wrinkled and knotted old hand casually touched it as she passed.

My cousin went off to see about the tea, and I was left with our visitor. She was pitifully shabby and worn-looking as she sat there, with shrunken shoulders and wrinkled face beaten by every storm of adversity, and yet there was something still in the gray eyes and thin, close-shut lips of the unconquerable courage with which she had faced defeat. She was too dazed to say much, but her eyes wandered in a vague way from one point to another, taking in every detail of the repair and restoration. The only thing she said was, "My!—My!" under her breath.

When my cousin returned and took her seat at the little tea-table with its silver service, the old lady simply sat passive and dazed, and to the polite questions of the former she answered rather at random.

Yes, she was a girl when she lived there. Her grandfather had left her the right to use one of the upstairs rooms, but "they" would not let her have it. "They did not like her to come on the place, so she didn't come much."

My! wasn't the tea good—"so sweet and warmin'?"

Every now and then she became *distraite* and vague. She appeared to have something on her mind or to be embarrassed by my presence, so I rose and strolled across to a window, and from there over toward the door. As I passed I heard her state timidly the object of her visit.

"I heard as you were a-goin' to dig up everything and set out fresh ones, so I came to ask you, if you had no particular use for it and were goin' to dig it up anyway, if you wouldn't let me have that old rose-bush by the walk. I'd like to take it up and carry it up to the graveyard—"

"Of course, you may have it."

"You see, that's the only thing I ever owned!" pursued the visitor.

I saw my cousin give a deep and sudden catching of her breath, and turn her head away, and after a grab at her skirt her hand went up to her face. The old woman continued quietly:

“I thought I’d write to you, and ask you about it; but then I didn’t. It wasn’t—just convenient.”

“Of course, you—m——” My cousin could not get out the words. There was a second of silence and then with shameless and futile mendacity she began to mutter something about having “such a bad cold.” She rose and dashed out of the room, saying to me with a wave of her hand as she passed:

“Tell her, Yes.”

When she returned to the room she had a fresh handkerchief in her hand and her eyes were still moist.

Before the old woman left, it was all arranged. The rose-bush was to be moved whenever Miss Godwin wished it; but meantime, as the best season for moving it had not come, my cousin was to take care of it for Miss Godwin, and Miss Godwin herself was to come up and look after it whenever she wished, and was certainly to come once a week.

“Well, I am sure I am very much obliged to you,” said the old woman, who suddenly appeared much inspirited. “I never would have ventured to do it if I hadn’t heard you were going to dig up everything anyhow, and I wouldn’t have asked *them* in any case, not if they had lived till Judgment Day.”

When Miss Godwin rose to go, my cousin suggested that she should walk down to her home with her, and as we started out she handed me several parcels and I saw that she herself had as many more.

At the door of her dark little habitation Miss Godwin showed some signs of nervousness. I think she was slightly alarmed lest we might insist on coming in. My cousin, however, relieved her.

“Here are a few little things—tea and coffee and sugar and—just a few little things. I thought they might taste a little better coming out of the old house, you know.” She was speaking at the rate of two hundred words a minute.

“Well—”

When we were out of earshot I waited for her to begin, but she walked on in silence with her handkerchief doubled in her hand.

“Your cold seems pretty bad!” I said.

“Oh, don’t!” she cried with a wail. “That poor little half-starved rose-bush!" she sobbed. "The only thing she ever owned! And she didn't even have a stamp to write and ask me not to throw it away! I wish I could give her the house."

"What would she do with it?"

"Make 'them' feel badly!" she cried with sudden vehemence.

VI

All that spring and summer my duties in the way of helping my cousin to "clarify her ideas" took me from time to time to Hamilton Place, and every week Miss Godwin used to come to look after her "estate," as the rose-bush was now dubbed. Under the careful treatment of my cousin's gardener, and watched over by my cousin's hawk eyes, the rose-bush appeared to have gotten a new lease of life, as under the belated sunshine of my cousin's friendliness and sympathy the faded mistress also quite blossomed out.

Every week she came in to tea, and my cousin, with her tact, drew her on to sit at the tea-table and pour tea.

The crowning event of her life was the house-warming that my cousin gave to the neighbors. They were all there, and possibly among them were some whom, as my cousin had said, she would have liked to make feel badly. Whatever the motive, my cousin invited Miss Godwin to pour tea, and to her mind, not Solomon in all his glory was arrayed like her, in her new black dress with "a real breast-pin."

For some time she had been coming every day to help about things, but much of her time was spent in pothering about the rose-bush, watching two buds that were really beginning to give promise of becoming roses.

"They all knew now" that the rose-bush was hers, and she wanted "them to see that it had roses on it." They had said "it weren't of no account."

The day of the event she came early. The summer night had been kind. The buds were real roses. She spent much of the day looking at them. No matter what she was doing she went out every few minutes to gaze at them, and each time my cousin watched her secretly with delight.

Suddenly, toward afternoon, just when the guests were expected, I heard my cousin give a cry of anguish: "She is crazy! She is cutting them!" She rushed to the door to stop her. On the threshold she met Miss Godwin. She was pale, but firm and a trifle triumphant.

"Oh! What have you done?" cried my cousin.

Miss Godwin became a little shy.

"They are the only things I have, and I would have liked you to wear them if you had not been in black; so I thought I would put them in a vase for you."

"I will wear one and you shall wear the other," said my cousin, "and then I will press mine and keep it."

I shall never forget the expression on Miss Godwin's face.

"Me?—My!—" with a deep intaking of her breath. "Why I haven't worn a rose in fif—forty years!"

I have reason to think she understated it.

My cousin took one of the roses—the prettier of the two—and without a word pinned it on her.

When the guests arrived it was interesting to watch Miss Godwin. At first she was all a-flutter. Her face was pale even through the weather-beaten tint of her faded cheek, and her eyes followed Mrs. Davison with mute appeal. But in a little space she recovered her self-possession; her head rose; her pallor gave way to something that was almost color, and she helped my cousin with what was quite an air.

My cousin could not have done a cleverer thing than place her at the tea-table.

Silas Freeman expressed the general judgment. When he was bidding her good-by he said, with a kindly light in his eyes, "Weäll, I guess you was about right in that thing you said that time."

"What was that?"

"That you wa'n't altogether city folks."

13

William Dean Howells, from *The Vacation of the Kelwyns*

(1920)

William Dean Howells (1837–1920) published The Vacation of the Kelwyns *in the last year of his life, but it is based on Howells's own experience many years earlier, in 1876. That summer, Howells and his family had been forced to flee their summer home in Shirley, Massachusetts, unable to deal with the increasingly hostile and violent couple who were providing their board. In this novel, the Kelwyns believe they have found a good vacation spot for themselves and their children, but they soon find out otherwise. The central conflict between the Kelwyns and their rural hosts is thoroughly typical: the urban family wants fresh cream, fresh butter, fresh fruit and vegetables—luxuries not usually to be found in the New England countryside. The husband and wife who work for them do not share their views on food, and bristle at the suggestion that their tastes are inferior. These chapters explore not only the culinary differences between country and city folk, but some of the cultural differences, too. Like Wharton's* Summer, The Vacation of the Kelwyns *suggests that fantasies about the purity and decency of rural New England life rest on a profound misunderstanding.*

IV

They had no right to complain, but it certainly did not comport with their prepossessions that the farmer, when he came, should arrive in the proportions of a raw-boned giant, with an effect of hard-woodedness, as if he were hewn out of hickory, with the shag-bark left on in places; his ready-made clothes looked as hard as he. He had on his best behavior as well as his best clothes, but the corners of his straight wide mouth dropped sourly at moments, and Kelwyn fancied both contempt and suspicion in his bony face, which was tagged with a harsh black beard. Those unpleasant corners of his mouth were accented by tobacco stain, for he had a form of the tobacco habit uncommon in New England; his jaw worked unceasingly with a slow, bovine grind; but when the moment came, after a first glance at Kelwyn's neat fireplace, he rose and spat out of the window; after Mrs. Kelwyn joined them in her husband's study, he made errands to the front door for the purpose of spitting.

Kelwyn expected that she would give him a sign of her instant rejection of the whole scheme at sight of the man, who had inspired him with a deep disgust; but to his surprise she did nothing of the kind; she even placated the man, by a special civility, as if she divined in him an instinctive resentment of her husband's feeling. She made him sit down in a better place than Kelwyn had let him take, and she inspired him to volunteer an explanation of his coming alone, in the statement he had already made to Kelwyn, that he guessed the Woman would have come with him, but the Boy had got a pretty hard cold on him, and she was staying at home to fix him up.

Kelwyn said, to put a stop to the flow of sympathy which followed from his wife, that he had been trying to ask Mr. Kite something about the cooking, but he thought he had better leave her to make the inquiries.

"Oh yes," she said, brightly. "You can give us light bread, I suppose?"

The man smiled scornfully, and looked round as if taking an invisible spectator into the joke, and said, "I guess the Woman can make it for you; I never touch it myself. We have hot biscuit."

"*We* should like hot bread too, now and then," Mrs. Kelwyn said.

"You can have it every meal, same's we do," the man said.

"We shouldn't wish to give Mrs. Kite so much trouble," Mrs. Kelwyn remarked, without apparent surprise at the luxury proposed. "I suppose she is used to broiling steak, and—"

"Always *fry* our'n," the man said, "but I guess she can broil it for you."

"I merely thought I would speak of it. We don't care much for pies; but we should like a simple pudding now and then; though, really, with berries of all kinds, and the different fruits as they come, we shall scarcely need any other desserts. We should expect plenty of good sweet milk, and we don't like to stint ourselves with the cream. I am sure Mrs. Kite will know how to cook vegetables nicely."

"Well," the farmer said, turning away from the Kelwyns to his invisible familiar for sympathy in his scorn, "what my wife don't know about cookin', I guess ain't wo'th knowin'."

"Because," Mrs. Kelwyn continued, "we shall almost *live* upon vegetables."

"I mean to put in a garden of 'em—pease, beans, and squash, and sweet-corn, and all the rest of 'em. You sh'an't want for vegetables. You've tasted the Shaker cookin'."

"My husband dined with them the day he was up there."

"Then he knows what Shaker cookin' is. So do we. And I guess my wife ain't goin' to fall *much* below it, if any."

He looked round once more to his familiar in boastful contempt, and even laughed. Kelwyn's mouth watered at the recollection of the Shaker table, so simple, so wholesome, and yet so varied and appetizing, at a season when in the absence of fresh garden supplies art had to assist nature so much.

"Oh, I am sure we shall be very well off," said Mrs. Kelwyn. "We shall bring our own tea—English breakfast tea."

"Never heard of it," Kite interrupted. "We always have Japan tea. But you can bring whatever you want to. Guess we sha'n't steal it." This seemed to be a joke, and he laughed at it.

"Oh no," said Mrs. Kelwyn, in deprecation of the possibility that she might have given the ground for such a pleasantry. "Well, I think I have spoken of everything, and now I will leave you two to arrange terms."

"No, no! Don't go!" her husband entreated. "We'd better all talk it over together so that I can be sure that I am right."

"That's the way *I* do with *my* wife," Kite said, with a laugh of approval.

The Kelwyns, with each other's help, unfolded to him what they had proposed doing. As they did so, it seemed to them both a very handsome proposal, and they were aware of having considered themselves much less in it than they had feared. As it appeared now, they had thought so much more of their tenants than they had imagined that if it had not been too late they might have wished they had thought less. Afterward they felt that they had not kept many of the advantages they might very well have kept, though again they decided that this was an effect from their failure to stipulate them, and that they remained in their hands nevertheless.

Kite sat listening with silent intensity. He winked his hard eyes from time to time, but he gave no other sign of being dazzled by their proposal.

"You understand?" Kelwyn asked, to break the silence which the farmer let ensue when he ended.

"I guess so," Kite answered, dryly. "I'll have to talk to the woman about it. You must set it down, so I can show it to her the way you said."

"Certainly," Kelwyn said, and he hastily jotted down the points and handed the paper to Kite; it did not enter into Kite's scheme of civility to rise and take it. He sat holding the paper in his hand and staring at it.

"I believe that's right?" Kelwyn suggested.

"I guess so," said Kite.

"I don't believe," Mrs. Kelwyn interposed, "that Mr. Kite can make it out in your handwriting, my dear. You do write such a hand!"

"Well, I guess I will have to get you to read it," Kite said, reaching the paper to Kelwyn, without rising, but letting him rise to get it.

Kelwyn read it carefully over, dwelling on each point. Kite kept a wooden immobility; but when Kelwyn had finished he reared his length from the lounge where it had been half folded, and put his hat on. "Well, I'll show this to the woman when I get back, and we'll let you know how we feel about it. Well, good-morning." He got himself out of the house with no further ceremony, and the Kelwyns remained staring at each other in a spell which they found it difficult to break.

"Don't you suppose he could read it?" she asked, in a kind of a gasp.

"I have my doubts," said Kelwyn.

"He didn't seem to like the terms, did you think?"

"I don't know. I feel as if *we* had been proposing to become *his* tenants, and had been acting rather greedily in the matter."

"Yes, that was certainly the effect. Do you believe we offended him in some way? I don't think *I* did, for I was most guarded in everything I said; and unless you went against the grain with him before I came down—"

"I was butter in a lordly dish to him, before you came down, my dear!"

"I don't know. You were letting him sit in a very uncomfortable chair, and I had to think to put him on your lounge. And now, we're not sure that he will accept the terms."

"Not till he has talked it over with the 'woman.' I almost wish that the woman would refuse us."

"It gives us a chance to draw back, too. He was certainly very disagreeable, though I don't believe he meant it. He may have been merely uncouth. And, after all, it doesn't matter about *him*. We shall never see him or have anything to do with him, indoors. He will have to hitch up the horse for us, and bring it to the door, and that will be the end of it. I wish we knew something about *her*, though."

"He seemed to think his own knowing was enough," Kelwyn mused. "She is evidently perfection—in his eyes."

"Yes, his pride in her was touching," said Mrs. Kelwyn. "That was the great thing about him. As soon as that came out, it atoned for everything. You can see that she twists him round her finger."

"I don't know whether that's a merit or not."

"It's a great merit in such a man. She is probably his superior in every way. You can see how he looks up to her."

"Yes," Kelwyn admitted, rather absently. "Did you have a feeling that he didn't exactly look up to us?"

"He despised us," said Mrs. Kelwyn, very promptly. "But that doesn't mean that he won't use us well. I have often noticed that in country people, even when they are much smoother than he was, and I have noticed it in working-people of all kinds. They do despise us, and I don't believe they respect anybody but working-people, really, though they're so glad to get out of working when they can. They think we're a kind of children; or fools, because we don't know how to do things with our hands, and all the culture in us won't change them. I could see that man's eye taking in your books and manuscripts, and scorning them."

"I don't know but you're right, Carry, and it is very curious. It's a thing that hasn't been taken into account in our studies of the conditions. We always suppose that the superiors despise the inferiors, but perhaps it is really the inferiors that despise the superiors, and it's that which embitters the classes against one another."

"Well," said Mrs. Kelwyn, "what I hope is that the wife may have education enough to tolerate us, if we're to be at their mercy."

"I hope she can read writing, anyway," Kelwyn said. "And it's droll, but you've hit it in what you say; it's been growing on me, too, that they will have us at their mercy. I had fancied that we were to have them at ours."

The scheme looked more and more doubtful to the Kelwyns. There were times when they woke together in the night, and confessed the same horror of it, and vowed each other to break it off. Yet when daylight came it always looked very simple, and it had so many alluring aspects that they smiled at their nightly terrors.

It was true, after all, that they could command the situation, and whether they cared to turn the Kites out of the farm or not, they could certainly turn them out of the house if they proved unfit or unfaithful. They would have, for the first time, a whole house to themselves, for they should allow the Kites only servants' quarters in it, and they would have the whole vast range and space for very little more money than they had ordinarily paid for farm board. They could undoubtedly control the table, and if the things were not good they could demand better. But a theory of Mrs. Kite grew upon Mrs. Kelwyn the more she thought of Kite's faith in his wife, which comforted her in her misgivings. This was the theory of her comparative superiority, which Mrs. Kelwyn based upon the probability that she could not possibly be so ignorant and uncouth as her husband. It was, no doubt, her ambition to better their lot which was urging him to take the farm, and she would do everything she could to please. In this view of her, Mrs. Kelwyn resolved to meet her half-way; to be patient of any little failures at first, and to teach the countrywoman town ways by sympathy rather than by criticism. That was a duty she owed her, and Mrs. Kelwyn meant to shirk none of her duties, while eventually claiming all her rights. She said this to herself in her reveries, and she said it to her husband in their conferences during the days that followed one another after Kite's visit. So many days followed before he made any further sign that Mrs. Kelwyn had time to work completely round from her reluctance to close the engagement with him, or his wife, rather, and to have wrought herself into an eagerness amounting to anxiety and bordering upon despair lest the Kites should not wish to close it. With difficulty she kept herself from making Kelwyn write and offer them better terms; she prevailed with herself so far, indeed, as to keep from making him write and ask for their decision. When it came unurged, however, she felt that she had made such a narrow escape that she must not risk further misgivings even. She argued the best from the quite mannerly and shapely letter (for a poor country person) which Mrs. Kite wrote in accepting the terms they offered. She did not express any opinion or feeling in regard to them, but she probably knew that they were very good; and Mrs. Kelwyn began to be proud of them again.

V

It was the afternoon of such a spring day as comes nowhere but in New England that the Kelwyns arrived at their summer home. There was a little edge of cold in it, at four o'clock, which the bright high sun did not soften, and which gave a pleasant thrill to the nerves. The blue sky bent over the earth a perfect dome without the faintest cloud. The trees, full foliaged, whistled in the gale that swept the land, and billowed the long grass, and tossed the blades of the low corn. All was sweet and clean, as if the spirit of New England housekeeping had entered into Nature, and she had set her house in order for company.

Mrs. Kelwyn kept feeling like a guest during the drive over from the station, and she had an obscure resentment of the feeling as a foreshadowed effect from an attempt on Mrs. Kite's part to play the hostess. She must be the mistress from the first, and, though Mrs. Kite was not to be quite her servant, she must be made to realize distinctly that the house was Mrs. Kelwyn's, and that she was in it by Mrs. Kelwyn's favor; this realization could not begin too soon.

But it had apparently begun already, and when the caravan of the Kelwyns drew up under the elms at the gable of old Shaker Family house, nothing could have been more to Mrs. Kelwyn's mind than the whole keeping of the place, unless it was the behavior of Mrs. Kite. She did not come officiously forward in welcome, as Mrs. Kelwyn had feared she might; she stood waiting in the doorway for the Kelwyns to alight and introduce themselves; but Mrs. Kelwyn decided that this was from respect and not pride, for the woman seemed a humble creature enough when she spoke to her: not embarrassed, but not forth-putting.

She had the effect of having on the best dress she had compatible with household duties, and she looked neat and agreeable in it. She was rather graceful, and she was of a sort of blameless middlingness in looks. A boy, somewhat younger than the elder Kelwyn boy, stood beside her and stared at the two young Kelwyns with strange eyes of impersonal guile.

It was a relief for the moment, and then for another moment a surprise, not to see Kite himself about; but Mrs. Kelwyn had scarcely drawn an indignant breath when the man came hulking round the corner of the house, where he stopped to swear over his shoulder at the team he must have left somewhere, and then advanced to the wagon piled high with the Kelwyns' trunks, and called out to them rather than to the Kelwyns, "Well, *how* are you!"

The house was everything Kelwyn had painted it. Mrs. Kelwyn explored it with him to give him the pleasure of her approval before she settled down to the minute examination of their quarters; and together, with their children, they ranged up and down stairs and through the long passages, feeling like a bath the delight of its cool cleanliness. Mrs. Kite, who met them on their return from their wanderings, said the Shaker ladies had been up the day before, putting on the last touches before they should come. It was pleasant to know that they had been expected and prepared for, but Mrs. Kelwyn fancied that, though the housekeeping had been instituted by the Shaker ladies, it must have been the Shaker gentlemen who had looked after the house furnishing. She had expected that there might be a Shaker stiffness in the appointments, but that there would also be a Shaker quaintness; and she had imagined her rooms dressed in the Shaker gear, which the house must once have worn, and which would have been restored from the garrets and basements of the other community dwellings. But the Shakers had not imagined anything of that kind. Whichever of them it had been left to had laid one kind of ingrain carpet in all the rooms, and furnished the chambers in a uniformity of painted pine sets. There was a parlor set of black walnut, and there were painted shades at the windows. All was new, and smelled fresh and wholesome, but the things had no more character than they had in the furniture warerooms where they were bought. Apparently the greatest good-will had been used, and Mrs. Kelwyn could well believe that the Shakers supposed they had dealt much more acceptably by them than if they had given them the rag carpets and the hooked rugs, the high-post bedsteads and splint chairs which she would have so much rather had.

The Kelwyns were a long time getting settled into temporary form; the robins were shouting their good-nights around them, and a thrush was shrilling from the woods that covered the hill slope behind the house, when the tinkle of a far-off bell called them to supper. Then they found themselves suddenly hungry, and they sat down in the old Shaker refectory with minds framed to eager appreciation of what good things might be set before them. Mrs. Kite gave a glance at the table before she left it to them; and said that she would be right there in the kitchen if they wanted anything. She really went down-stairs beyond the kitchen to the ground floor, where she had four or five rooms with her family.

The Kelwyns had a four o'clock dinner at home, and now it was a quarter past seven as they sat down with their orderly little boys at the supper which Mrs. Kite had imagined for them. There were two kinds of cake on the table: three slices of pound-cake, translucent but solid, at one end of the table, and thicker slices of marble-cake, with veins of *verde antique* varying its surface of Siena yellow, at the other. A dish of stewed fruit stood in the centre, which proved to be dried apples; at Mrs. Kelwyn's right elbow was the teapot; on one hand of Kelwyn was a plate of butter, and on the other a plate of bread cut from a loaf of which the half remained beside the pieces. In the bewilderment of realizing the facts he lifted successively the butter and the bread to his nose, which involuntarily curled from them, in the silence broken by Mrs. Kelwyn's lifting the teapot lid an instant, and then clapping it to with a quick "Ugh!"

"Isn't it our tea?" he asked, quietly.

"It's *all* of it, I should think," said his wife. "She doesn't know how to make English breakfast tea, evidently. She's steeped it like green tea, and it's as strong as lye. What's the matter with the butter?"

"I don't know what to liken its strength to."

"And the bread?"

"It seems like what they used to call salt-rising bread. I haven't smelt any since I was a boy."

He stretched the plate toward her, and when she brought it within range of her nose she averted her face with a wild "Phew!"

and an imploring cry of "Elmer!" while she made play with her hands as if fighting away mosquitoes.

"I remember that when it was hot you could eat it if you hurried; but when it was cold!"

He said no more, and his wife could not speak. The elder of the two well-behaved little boys made a preliminary noise in his throat, and then, not being quelled, ventured to ask, "Mamma, may I say something?"

"What is it, dear?" his mother returned, tenderly, as from the sense of a common sorrow.

"Oh, nothing," the boy said, politely. "But is this all, or do they begin with the dessert in the country?"

Kelwyn laughed harshly, and his wife looked at him with reproach. She had been about to bid the child eat what was set before him and not make remarks, but in despair of setting him the example she felt that she must forbear the precept. "I'm afraid it isn't the dessert, dear," she answered, gently. "I'm afraid it's—all."

"All?" the boy echoed, in a husky tone, and at the melancholy sound his younger brother, who took his cue from him in everything, silently put up his lip.

"Elmer!" their mother demanded. "What are you going to do?"

"I'm going to get something to eat." Kelwyn pushed back his chair and launched himself forward as in act to start for the kitchen door.

His wife intercepted him with the appeal: "No! Wait, Elmer! We must begin as we can carry out."

This saying has always an implication of reserved wisdom, and besides Kelwyn was willing to be intercepted; he sank back into his chair.

"*I* must talk with her, and I must think what to say, what to do. We mustn't be harsh, but we must be firm. I'm afraid she's done her best on mistaken lines. She's tried to realize our ideals, but if she had been left to her own it might have been different. We are bound to suppose so."

"And in the mean time we are starving," Kelwyn argued.

"I know all that, my dear," his wife retorted. "But we must begin as we can carry out; and in the first place there must be no going to them: they must come to us. Will you bring the bell off the bureau in mamma's room?" she bade the eldest boy, and the youngest ran with him; they returned in better spirits, and climbed back to their places in eager expectation.

"May I ring it?" the eldest brother asked.

"*I* want to ring it," the youngest entreated.

"No, darlings, mamma must ring," said the mother, with a tenderness meant for them and a stateliness meant for Mrs. Kite. She rang almost majestically at first; then indignantly; then angrily.

Mrs. Kite put her head in from the kitchen. "Oh! I thought I heard a bell ringin' somewhere," she concluded, in apology for her intrusion.

"Yes," said Mrs. Kelwyn, with a sternness from which she gave herself time to relax before she added: "Could you give us some eggs, Mrs. Kite? Soft boiled?"

"Oh, *fried*, mamma!" the eldest boy, who was Francis, entreated.

"*I* want fried," his younger brother whispered, with the lack of originality innate in younger brothers.

"'Sh!" said their mother. "Francy, I'm astonished. Carl! Won't you come in, Mrs. Kite?"

Mrs. Kite came in and sat down.

"And could you," Mrs. Kelwyn pursued, in the petition which she tried to keep from making itself a command, "give us some of your hot biscuit?"

The children could not keep from noiselessly clapping their hands; arrested in the act by their mother's frown, they held their hands joined and appeared to be saying a grace.

"Why, yes," Mrs. Kite assented. "But I guess they ain't very hot any more. The fire's gone down—"

"I suppose you could make it up again," Mrs. Kite assented.

Kelwyn was taking involuntary notes of her, and he could not have said whether she was assenting willingly or unwillingly. She might have been meek or she might have been sly; she could have been pretty or plain, as you thought; her pale sandy hair might have been golden; her gray eyes blue. A neutrality which seemed the potentiality of better or worse things pervaded her.

"Well, we should like some soft-boiled eggs—or fried," Mrs. Kelwyn said, in concession to her children, "if it's just as easy. We have a late dinner at home, and we're rather hungry."

"Why," said Mrs. Kite, "if you'd 'a' sent word I'd 'a' had a warm supper for you—milk toast and some kind of meat."

"Oh, this is very nice," said Mrs. Kelwyn, absently, from her apparent absorption with the milk which she was inspecting in its pitcher. "There seems to be something in the milk—"

"Is that *so*?" Mrs. Kite inquired, interestedly. "It *does* look kind of speckled." She examined it, and then sat down again with the jug in her lap. "Must 'a' got in from the rafters in the cellar. But I can get you some warm from the cow as soon as Alvin comes in from milkin'. I guess that will be clean enough."

"And could you get us a little fresher butter?" Mrs. Kelwyn pursued, passing the plate to Mrs. Kite, who took it passively.

"Why, ain't the butter all right?" she asked.

"It's rather strong," Mrs. Kelwyn admitted.

"Well, I guess I can fix that." Mrs. Kite put it in her lap with the milk-pitcher, and sat contentedly expectant.

"And I am afraid that the tea has stood rather long," Mrs. Kelwyn said. "You know that with this kind, you merely pour on the hot water and bring it to the table."

"My! We keep ours on the stove all day! I guess Alvin wouldn't think he was drinking tea unless he could taste the bitter. Well," Mrs. Kite rose in saying, "I'll get you the things as soon as I can, but, as I *said*, the fire's out, and—"

She left the rest to their imagination as she let herself into the kitchen, with the milk-pitcher in one hand, the teapot in the other, and the butter-plate in the hollow of her arm.

Kelwyn rose and put the bread beyond smelling-distance on the side-table.

"Now, don't you say one word, please," said his wife, "till we see what she can do."

"Oh, I'm not disposed to be critical. I'm rather sorry for her, though she didn't seem put to shame, much. I suppose I ought to have opened the door for her."

"She managed," said Mrs. Kelwyn, coldly.

In the kitchen presently they heard heavy clumping steps as of a man coming in, and after a moment what seemed a kind of hushed swearing. But a rattling of the stove-lids presently followed, and then the pungent odor of wood smoke stole encouragingly through the kitchen door. There was now and then the sound of steps, but there were spaces of silence in which the Kelwyn family drowsed in their chairs.

The door flew open at last, and Mrs. Kite came in with a pitcher. "Thought I'd bring in some milk for the little boys while it was warm. The things will be ready right away now." She went out, cutting short with the shutting door the steady hiss of frying.

Mrs. Kelwyn put the pitcher to her face mechanically, and then set it down at arm's-length. Her husband silently looked [a] question, and she audibly explained, "Cowy." They were helpless against a lack of neatness which gave the odor of the cow's udder to the milk, and Kelwyn thought how promptly they had once dismissed their milkman at home for cowy milk. The children were eagerly intent on the frying eggs, which then ceased to fry, leaving a long silence to ensue, till Mrs. Kite pushed open the door with one of her elbows and one of her feet, and reappeared with the fried eggs on a platter, and the teapot; Kite hulked in after her with a plate of biscuit and butter, and set them down with a glower at his guests and hulked out.

"I don't believe but what you'll find everything all right now," she said, "though I presume, I *did* let the tea stand a little mite long, to your taste."

Mrs. Kelwyn said, "Oh, I dare say it will be nice," and Mrs. Kite, after a look at the table, flapped out, not cheerfully, but self-contentedly, on her heel-less shoes. Then the Kelwyns examined the food put before them.

The eggs, with their discolored edges limp from standing in the pork fat, stared up dimly, sadly; the biscuits, when broken open, emitted an alkaline steam from their greenish-yellow crumb; the tea was black again. Kelwyn remained scrutinizing the butter.

"What is it?" his wife asked.

"It looks like—sugar."

"What?"

He pushed it to her, and she scrutinized it in her turn. "It is—it actually is! She's tried to sweeten it by working sugar into it!" She fell back into her chair, and tears came into her eyes. "What are we going to do, Elmer?"

"Here, Carl," said his father, recklessly, "have an egg. Have an egg, Francy."

"And a biscuit, papa?" Francy asked; and Carl parroted after him. "And a biscuit, papa?"

"Yes, all you can eat."

"Do you want to kill them, Elmer?" their mother palpitated.

"It's filth, but it isn't poison," said Kelwyn, and he spread each of the boys a biscuit with the sugared butter, and set them the example of eating the things put before them. "Give me some of that bitter black tea, Carry, with plenty of cowy milk in it."

"*I* want some cowy milk, papa," Francy whispered; and Carl whispered, too, "*I* want some cowy milk, papa."

"You shall have all the cowy milk you can drink," said their father, and he commanded their mother, who was keeping one hand on the teapot and the other on the milk-pitcher: "Pass me the cowy milk, Carry; give me some bitter black tea. Eat your blear-eyed eggs, boys, and have some more. Take another bilious biscuit, with plenty of sugar-butter on it. My dear, you're not eating anything!"

"Are you crazy, Elmer?" his wife demanded. "You won't sleep a wink. You'll be dead before morning."

"I shall not be dead unless that brute murders me in my bed, and if I don't sleep a wink I shall be awake to prevent him," Kelwyn said, not fearlessly, but recklessly.

The boys, rapt in their supper, did not hear him. His wife shuddered out: "What in the world shall we do?"

14

Sinclair Lewis, from *Babbitt*

(1922)

George Babbitt is not looking for a colonial vacation: his own city provides up-to-date "colonial revival" bungalows in the latest style. Babbitt is not looking for a return to the farm or an "Old Home Week" experience, either. In these two passages, Sinclair Lewis (1885–1951) explores the wilderness vacation and what it offers to a man like Babbitt, struggling to escape from the stultifying conformity of his life as a real estate agent in the imaginary Midwestern town of Zenith.

The first time Babbitt goes to Maine, he travels with his old college friend, Paul. Babbitt's wife Myra and his son Ted and daughter Veronica join them later. On that first trip, the "wilderness cure" seems to be working; Babbitt and Paul relax, become more natural, reminisce about their youthful idealism. Like Bellamy's Mr. Edgerton, they feel the tension of the modern world receding into the background. Babbitt's second trip to Maine is different. This time, he goes alone; Paul has been sent to prison for shooting his wife, and Babbitt is increasingly dissatisfied with his own life. The second trip fails, just as all his illusions are failing: this time, even the wilderness does not offer Babbitt peace. His fantasies about an escape to the wilderness are punctuated by the local guide, who has his own fantasies—about escaping to the city.

II

Though he exulted, and made sage speculations about locomotive horse-power, as their train climbed the Maine mountain-ridge and from the summit he looked down the shining way among the pines; though he remarked, "Well, by golly!" when he discovered that the station at Katadumcook, the end of the line, was an aged freight-car; Babbitt's moment of impassioned release came when they sat on a tiny wharf on Lake Sunasquam, awaiting the launch from the hotel. A raft had floated down the lake; between the logs and the shore, the water was translucent, thin-looking, flashing with minnows. A guide in black felt hat with trout-flies in the band, and flannel shirt of a peculiarly daring blue, sat on a log and whittled and was silent. A dog, a good country dog, black and woolly gray, a dog rich in leisure and in meditation, scratched and grunted and slept. The thick sunlight was lavish on the bright water, on the rim of gold-green balsam boughs, the silver birches and tropic ferns, and across the lake it burned on the sturdy shoulders of the mountains. Over everything was a holy peace.

Silent, they loafed on the edge of the wharf, swinging their legs above the water. The immense tenderness of the place sank into Babbitt, and he murmured, "I'd just like to sit here—the rest of my life—and whittle—and sit. And never hear a typewriter. Or Stan Graff fussing in the 'phone. Or Rone and Ted scrapping. Just sit. Gosh!"

He patted Paul's shoulder. "How does it strike you, old snoozer?"

"Oh, it's darn good, Georgie. There's something sort of eternal about it."

For once, Babbitt understood him.

III

Their launch rounded the bend; at the head of the lake, under a mountain slope, they saw the little central dining-shack of their hotel and the crescent of squat log cottages which served as bedrooms. They landed, and endured the critical examination of the habitués who had been at the hotel for a whole week. In their cottage, with its high stone fireplace, they hastened, as Babbitt expressed it, to "get into some regular he-togs." They came out; Paul in an old gray suit and soft white shirt; Babbitt in khaki shirt and vast and flapping khaki trousers. It was excessively new khaki; his rimless spectacles belonged to a city office; and his face was not tanned but a city pink. He made a discordant noise in the place. But with infinite satisfaction he slapped his legs and crowed, "Say, this is getting back home, eh?"

They stood on the wharf before the hotel. He winked at Paul and drew from his back pocket a plug of chewing-tobacco, a vulgarism forbidden in the Babbitt home. He took a chew, beaming and wagging his head as he tugged at it. "Um! Um! Maybe I haven't been hungry for a wad of eating-tobacco! Have some?"

They looked at each other in a grin of understanding. Paul took the plug, gnawed at it. They stood quiet, their jaws working. They solemnly spat, one after the other, into the placid water. They stretched voluptuously, with lifted arms and arched backs. From beyond the mountains came the shuffling sound of a far-off train. A trout leaped, and fell back in a silver circle. They sighed together.

IV

They had a week before their families came. Each evening they planned to get up early and fish before breakfast. Each morning they lay abed till the breakfast-bell, pleasantly conscious that there were no efficient wives to rouse them. The mornings were cold; the fire was kindly as they dressed.

Paul was distressingly clean, but Babbitt reveled in a good sound dirtiness, in not having to shave till his spirit was moved to it. He treasured every grease spot and fish-scale on his new khaki trousers.

All morning they fished unenergetically, or tramped the dim and aqueous-lighted trails among rank ferns and moss sprinkled with crimson bells. They slept all afternoon, and till midnight played stud-poker with the guides. Poker was a serious business to the guides. They did not gossip; they shuffled the thick greasy cards with a deft ferocity menacing to the "sports;" and Joe Paradise, king of guides, was sarcastic to loiterers who halted the game even to scratch.

At midnight, as Paul and he blundered to their cottage over the pungent wet grass, and pine-roots confusing in the darkness, Babbitt rejoiced that he did not have to explain to his wife where he had been all evening.

They did not talk much. The nervous loquacity and opinionation of the Zenith Athletic Club dropped from them. But when they did talk they slipped into the naïve intimacy of college days. Once they drew their canoe up to the bank of Sunasquam Water, a stream walled in by the dense green of the hardhack. The sun roared on the green jungle but in the shade was sleepy peace, and the water was golden and rippling. Babbitt drew his hand through the cool flood, and mused:

"We never thought we'd come to Maine together!"

"No. We've never done anything the way we thought we would. I expected to live in Germany with my granddad's people, and study the fiddle."

"That's so. And remember how I wanted to be a lawyer and go into politics? I still think I might have made a go of it. I've kind of got the gift of the gab—anyway, I can think on my feet, and make some king of a spiel on most anything, and of course that's the thing you need in politics. By golly, Ted's going to law-school, even if I didn't! Well—I guess it's worked out all right. Myra's been a fine wife. And Zilla means well, Paulibus."

"Yes. Up here, I figure out all sorts of plans to keep her amused. I kind of feel life is going to be different, now that we're getting a good rest and can go back and start over again."

"I hope so, old boy." Shyly: "Say, gosh, it's been awful nice to sit around and loaf and gamble and act regular, with you along, you old horse-thief!"

"Well, you know what it means to me, Georgie. Saved my life."

The shame of emotion overpowered them; they cursed a little, to prove they were good rough fellows; and in a mellow silence, Babbitt whistling while Paul hummed, they paddled back to the hotel.

V

Though it was Paul who had seemed overwrought, Babbitt who had been the protecting big brother, Paul became clear-eyed and merry, while Babbitt sank into irritability. He uncovered layer on layer of hidden weariness. At first he had played nimble jester to Paul and for him sought amusements; by the end of the week Paul was nurse, and Babbitt accepted favors with the condescension one always shows a patient nurse.

The day before their families arrived, the women guests at the hotel bubbled, "Oh, isn't it nice! You must be so excited;" and the proprieties compelled Babbitt and Paul to look excited. But they went to bed early and grumpy.

When Myra appeared she said at once, "Now, we want you boys to go on playing around just as if weren't here."

The first evening, he stayed out for poker with the guides and she said in placid merriment, "My! You're a regular bad one!" The second evening, she groaned sleepily, "Good heavens, are you going to be out every single night?" The third evening, he didn't play poker.

He was tired now in every cell. "Funny! Vacation doesn't seem to have done me a bit of good," he lamented. "Paul's frisky as a colt, but I swear, I'm crankier and nervouser than when I came up here."

He had three weeks of Maine. At the end of the second week he began to feel calm, and interested in life. He planned an expedition to climb Sachem Mountain, and wanted to camp overnight at Box Car Pond. He was curiously weak, yet cheerful as though he had cleansed his veins of poisonous energy and was filling them with wholesome blood.

He ceased to be irritated by Ted's infatuation with a waitress (his seventh tragic affair this year); he played catch with Ted, and with pride taught him to cast a fly in the pine-shadowed silence of Skowtuit Pond.

At the end he sighed, "Hang it, I'm just beginning to enjoy my vacation. But, well, I feel a lot better. And it's going to be one great year! Maybe the Real Estate Board will elect me president, instead of some fuzzy old-fashioned faker like Chan Mott."

On the way home, whenever he went into the smoking compartment he felt guilty at deserting his wife and angry at being expected to feel guilty, but each time he triumphed. "Oh, this is going to be a great year, a great old year!"

III

There was about the house an unofficial theory that he was to take his vacation alone, to spend a week or ten days in Catawba, but he was nagged by the memory that a year ago he had been with Paul in Maine. He saw himself returning, finding peace there, and the presence of Paul, in a life primitive and heroic. Like a shock came the thought that he actually could go. Only, he couldn't, really; he couldn't leave his business, and "Myra would think it sort of funny, his going way off there alone. Course he'd decided to do what ever he darned pleased, from now on, but still—to go way off to Maine!"

He went, after lengthy meditations.

With his wife, since it was inconceivable to explain that he was going to seek Paul's spirit in the wilderness, he frugally employed the lie prepared over a year ago and scarcely used at all. He said that he had to see a man in New York on business. He could not have explained even to himself why he drew from the bank several hundred dollars more than he needed, nor why he kissed Tinka so tenderly, and cried, "God bless you, baby!" From the train he waved to her till she was but a scarlet spot beside the brown bulkier presence of Mrs. Babbitt, at the end of a steel and cement aisle ending in vast barred gates. With melancholy he looked back at the last suburb of Zenith.

All the way north he pictured the Maine guides: simple and strong and daring, jolly as they played stud-poker in their unceiled shack, wise in woodcraft as they tramped the forest and shot the rapids. He particularly remembered Joe Paradise, half Yankee, half Indian. If he could but take up a backwoods claim with a man like Joe, work hard with his hands, be free and noisy in a flannel shirt, and never come back to this dull decency!

Or, like a trapper in a Northern Canada movie, plunge through the forest, make camp in the Rockies, a grim and wordless caveman! Why not? He *could* do it! There'd be enough money at home for the family to live on till Verona was married and Ted self-supporting. Old Henry T. would look out for them. Honestly! Why *not*? Really *live*— He longed for it, admitted that he longed for it, then almost believed that he was going to do it. Whenever common sense snorted, "Nonsense! Folks don't run away from decent families and partners; just simply don't do it, that's all!" Then Babbitt answered pleadingly, "Well, it wouldn't take any more nerve than for Paul to go to jail and—Lord, how I'd like to do it! Moccasins—six-gun—frontier town—gamblers—sleep under the stars—be a regular man, with he-men like Joe Paradise—gosh!"

So he came to Maine, again stood on the wharf before the camp-hotel, again spat heroically into the delicate and shivering water, while the pines rustled, the mountains glowed, and a trout leaped and fell in a sliding circle. He hurried to the guides' shack as to his real home, his real friends, long missed. They would be glad to see him. They would stand up and shout, "Why, here's Mr. Babbitt! He ain't one of these ordinary sports! He's a real guy!"

In their boarded and rather littered cabin the guides sat about the greasy table playing stud-poker with greasy cards: half a dozen wrinkled men in old trousers and easy old felt hats. They glanced up and nodded. Joe Paradise, the swart aging man with the big mustache, grunted, "How do. Back again?"

Silence, except for the clatter of chips.

Babbitt stood beside them, very lonely. He hinted, after a period of highly concentrated playing, "Guess I might take a hand, Joe."

"Sure. Sit in. How many chips you want? Let's see, you were here with your wife, last year, wa'n't you?" said Joe Paradise.

That was all of Babbitt's welcome to the old home.

He played for half an hour before he spoke again. His head was reeking with the smoke of pipes and cheap cigars and he was weary of pairs and four-flushes, resentful of the way in which they ignored him. He flung at Joe:

"Working now?"

"Nope."

"Like to guide me for a few days?"

"Well, jus' soon. I ain't engaged till next week."

Only thus did Joe recognize the friendship Babbitt was offering him. Babbitt paid up his losses and left the shack rather childishly. Joe raised his head from the coils of smoke like a seal rising from surf, grunted, "I'll come 'round t'morrow," and dived down to his three aces.

Neither in his voiceless cabin, fragrant with planks of new-cut pine, nor along the lake, nor in the sunset clouds which presently eddied behind the lavender-misted mountains, could Babbitt find the spirit of Paul as a reassuring presence. He was so lonely that after supper he stopped to talk with an ancient old lady, a gasping and steadily discoursing old lady, by the stove in the hotel-office. He told her of Ted's presumable future triumphs in the State University and of Tinka's remarkable vocabulary till he was homesick for the home he had left forever.

Through the darkness, through that Northern pine-walled silence, he blundered down to the lake-front and found a canoe. There were no paddles in it but with a board, sitting awkwardly, amidships and poking at the water rather than paddling, he made his way far out on the lake. The lights of the hotel and the cottages became yellow dots, a cluster of glow-worms at the base of Sachem Mountain. Larger and ever more imperturbable was the mountain in the star-filtered darkness, and the lake a limitless pavement of black marble. He was dwarfed and dumb and a little awed, but that insignificance freed him from the pomposities of being Mr. George

F. Babbitt of Zenith; saddened and freed his heart. Now he was conscious of the presence of Paul, fancied him (rescued from prison, from Zilla and the brisk exactitudes of the tar-roofing business) playing his violin at the end of the canoe. He vowed, "I will go on! I'll never go back! Now that Paul's out of it, I don't want to see any of those damn people again! I was a fool to get sore because Joe Paradise didn't jump up and hug me. He's one of these woodsmen; too wise to go yelping and talking your arm off like a cityman. But get him back in the mountains, out on the trail—! That's real living!"

IV

Joe reported at Babbitt's cabin at nine the next morning. Babbitt greeted him as a fellow caveman:

"Well, Joe, how d' you feel about hitting the trail, and getting away from these darn soft summerites and these women and all?"

"All right, Mr. Babbitt."

"What do you say we go over to Box Car Pond—they tell me the shack there isn't being used—and camp out?"

"Well, all right, Mr. Babbitt, but it's nearer to Skowtuit Pond, and you can get just about as good fishing there."

"No, I want to get into the real wilds."

"Well, all right."

"We'll put the old packs on our backs and get into the woods and really hike."

"I think maybe it would be easier to go by water, through Lake Chogue. We can go all the way by motor boat—flat-bottom boat with an Evinrude."

"No, sir! Bust up the quiet with a chugging motor? Not on your life! You just throw a pair of socks in the old pack and tell 'em what you want for eats. I'll be ready soon as you are."

"Most of the sports go by boat, Mr. Babbitt. It's a long walk."

"Look here, Joe: are you objecting to walking?"

"Oh, no, I guess I can do it. But I haven't tramped that far for sixteen years. Most of the sports go by boat. But I can do it if you say so—I guess." Joe walked away in sadness.

Babbitt had recovered from his touchy wrath before Joe returned. He pictured him as warming up and telling the most entertaining stories. But Joe had not yet warmed up when they took the trail. He persistently kept behind Babbitt, and however much his shoulders ached from the pack, however sorely he panted, Babbitt could hear his guide panting equally. But the trail was satisfying: a path brown with pine-needles and rough with roots, among the balsams, the ferns, the sudden groves of white birch. He became credulous again, and rejoiced in sweating. When he stopped to rest he chuckled, "Guess we're hitting it up pretty good for a couple o' old birds, eh?"

"Uh-huh," admitted Joe.

"This is a mighty pretty place. Look, you can see the lake down through the trees. I tell you, Joe, you don't appreciate how lucky you are to live in woods like this, instead of a city with trolleys grinding and typewriters clacking and people bothering the life out of you all the time! I wish I knew the woods like you do. Say, what's the name of that little red flower?"

Rubbing his back, Joe regarded the flower resentfully. "Well, some folks call it one thing and some calls it another. I always just call it Pink Flower."

Babbitt blessedly ceased thinking as tramping turned into blind plodding. He was submerged in weariness. His plump legs seemed to go on by themselves, without guidance, and he mechanically wiped away the sweat which stung his eyes. He was too tired to be consciously glad as, after a sun-scourged mile of corduroy tote-road through a swamp where flies hovered over a hot waste of brush, they reached the cool shore of Box Car Pond. When he lifted the pack from his back he staggered from the change in balance, and for a moment could not stand erect. He lay beneath an ample-bosomed maple tree near the guest-shack, and joyously felt sleep running through his veins.

He awoke toward dusk, to find Joe efficiently cooking bacon and eggs and flapjacks for supper, and his admiration of the woodsman returned. He sat on a stump and felt virile.

"Joe, what would you do if you had a lot of money? Would you stick to guiding, or would you take a claim 'way back in the woods and be independent of people?"

For the first time Joe brightened. He chewed his cud a second, and bubbled, "I've often thought of that! If I had the money, I'd go down to Tinker's Falls and open a swell shoe store."

After supper Joe proposed a game of stud-poker but Babbitt refused with brevity, and Joe contentedly went to bed at eight. Babbitt sat on the stump, facing the dark pond, slapping mosquitos. Save the snoring guide, there was no other human being within ten miles. He was lonelier than he had ever been in his life. Then he was in Zenith.

He was worrying as to whether Miss McGoun wasn't paying too much for carbon paper. He was at once resenting and missing the persistent teasing at the Roughnecks' Table. He was wondering what Zilla Riesling was doing now. He was wondering whether, after the summer's maturity of being a garageman, Ted would "get busy" in the university. He was thinking of his wife. "If she would only—if she wouldn't be so darn satisfied with just settling down—No! I won't! I won't go back! I'll be fifty in three years. Sixty in thirteen years. I'm going to have some fun before it's too late. I don't care. I will!"

He thought of Ida Putiak, of Louetta Swanson, of that nice widow—what was her name?—Tanis Judique?—the one for whom he'd found the flat. He was enmeshed in imaginary conversations. Then:

"Gee, I can't seem to get away from thinking about folks!"

Thus it came to him merely to run away was folly, because he could never run away from himself.

That moment he started for Zenith. In his journey there was no appearance of flight, but he was fleeing, and four days afterward he was on the Zenith train. He knew that he was slinking back not because it was what he longed to do but because it was all he could do. He scanned again his discovery that he could never run away from Zenith and family and office, because in his own brain he bore the office and the family and every street and disquiet and illusion of Zenith.

"But I'm going to—oh, I'm going to start something!" he vowed, and he tried to make it valiant.